CONTRACEPTION

"Our World, Reimagined"

Degen Hill

E-book
ISBN-13: 978-1-7321364-0-3
Print
ISBN-13: 978-1-7321364-1-0

This book is dedicated to those who think outside the box

ACKNOWLEDGEMENTS

First, I'd like to thank the countless people I ran this idea by. Without our discussions to sort through all the details, this couldn't have been possible.

I'd also like to personally thank Sudeshna Sarkar and Jarrod Williams for their tremendous help in editing this novel. Their patience and commitment to the project was a crucial part of getting it to where it is now.

Finally, I'd like to thank my mother, Quincy Davenport, for her continued support and belief in me throughout my life.

1. BEFORE

Earth – Year 2060

> *Due to the stress of overpopulation, the world was feeling the effects of an overrun planet. The global population had reached catastrophic proportions. Water, land, and air pollution ran rampant, while clean food and water were luxuries. The planet could no longer sustain its growing number of inhabitants, and deep inside, everyone knew it.*

■ Shots rang out in the darkness. Those desperate to survive broke into people's homes and shops, taking whatever they could get their hands on. Food was scarce these days, as were most necessities. With the world's population reaching upwards of 12 billion people, there just wasn't enough anymore. Everyone had been warned, but no one listened.

Every day, more dire warnings of catastrophe continued to pour in and the radio and TV continued to spit them out with a kind of grim satisfaction: "The conflict between France and Germany continues as both have now declared war over control of Sardinia with the fall of Italy less than a week ago; both states desperate to supply their citizens with new land in order to reduce their congested cities. In other news, due to the climate imbalance caused by factories and nuclear energy production, mega-storms continue to wreak havoc over many large cities. If you are in a major city, we recommend getting to high ground, as the torrential downpour continues to mix with the city sewage, which can have detrimental effects if you come in contact with it. Food shortages continue..."

It was the same news every day, or some variant of it. The world was overpopulated, but somehow still refused to admit that it was ill-equipped to deal with mankind's greatest problem – man himself.

Physical space, food, clean water, jobs, real estate, and resources – everything was now in short supply. Technology had done its best to curb the effects of overpopulation, but people kept reproducing despite countless initiatives. The world in the mid-2050s was in a state that many researchers and scientists had actually predicted, but their warnings had ultimately been ignored.

Nations fought wars over resources, land, and for the mere sake of survival, while at home, cities were filthy and rife with crime as the population continued to surge and governments not only struggled to feed their people, but could also no longer manage them. Jails were full, and the diminishing number of police was no match for an overflowing population and the crime that came with it.

Cities were full of people crammed together like chickens in a coop. The price of real estate had shot through the roof all over the world, so people set up shanty houses amongst the towering apartment buildings. The times were tough and everyone knew it, but despite efforts by governments, outreach groups, NGOs, and activists, nothing could be done.

Over the years, several population control policies had been implemented, many taking a page from China's one-child policy; however, similar to China's struggles, it was not enough to curb the growth, and many countries didn't have an adequate way to deal with those who had a second child illegally. Home births in the cities and countryside were still a common occurrence around the world, with families believing more children meant increased labor, and would lead to a higher production of crops. Many other policies were myopic, lacking the necessary measures to deal with the issue effectively.

For some time, there were rumors that a solution had been discovered, but it wasn't until the year 2060 our worst nightmares were finally realized.

Starting in 2059, world leaders, population specialists, researchers, sociologists, and analysts had been holding closed-door meetings to figure out a solution to an overpopulated planet. For months, these specialists and world leaders had been meeting in secret locations all over the world, but none of their suggestions seemed viable. The only thing they agreed on was that something needed to be done. In pursuit of this goal, solutions were put forth. Some seemed to defy logic while others made further attempts to repopulate the failed colonies on Mars.

Finally, the German Chancellor took the floor, eyeing the room, and with strong determination said, "We can no longer continue living this way. Germany itself is overrun, and we no longer have the money or resources to care for our citizens, let alone refugees and foreigners."

Many other leaders around the table nodded, having experienced the same struggle in their own countries; however, it wasn't until a young Russian analyst proposed a radical idea that things were set in motion.

"So much depends on the population," he started. "Not just environmental impacts, but also social well-being, economic vitality, infrastructure, and a sense of community, to name a few. Fundamentally, the way we shape our world is a manifestation of the kind of humanity we bring to bear. At the primary level, the problem is ourselves. More than half of the world's population already live in cities, and another four billion people are projected to move to urban areas by 2075. The way we build our society will be at the heart of so much that matters, from climate change and economic vitality to our well-being and a sense of a globalized world. The only choice is to reduce the population."

Voices began to buzz around the table.

"And how do you propose we do that?" asked one of the diplomats.

"We've already started doing that," said the Filipino President. "We've stepped up efforts to kill criminals, with even the most basic of crimes such as drug use being an offense punishable by death. But even then, it's simply not enough."

The Austrian President looked around the table before saying, "In our country, we've worked to promote a number of things to decrease life expectancy, but the population continues to rise. Why is the onus of the situation on us as leaders? We need to provide a system in which our citizens actively take part in managing themselves, without the government being the bad guy. How do we possibly do that?"

"It's simple," an analyst said. "You legalize murder, but establish guidelines. Our governments can't and shouldn't be involved; it must be done by the people and for the people, as objectively as possible. The easiest way to remove our governments from the situation is to create an artificially and universally imposed selection process for candidates hoping to have a child. This will give rise to natural selection, wherein only the most cunning, tactical and strong will end up spreading their genes, while at the same time decreasing the population."

The protests round the table was almost deafening. Many world leaders looked horrified at the thought of murdering innocent people while others were convinced that this might be the only solution they had.

"This is preposterous," yelled Alfonso Bellami, the exiled Italian Prime Minister. "Violence has decreased massively over time due to civilizational achievements, such as literacy, contributions to science, and communication that promotes empathy. And now you're asking us to consider increasing violence through some sort of murderous selection process?"

The newly established Dictator of Mexico nodded his head, "Prime Minister, I understand your concerns as I think we can all agree that what this analyst is proposing is radical, to say the least. For a long time, we have believed that people are more valuable alive than dead. But look around you, look at your cities. Is the current population trajectory sustainable? What are people actually contributing? Famine? Pollution? Crime? Perhaps now is the time for something radical to be done."

"We'll be no better than cavemen living in prehistoric times," responded the Australian Minister of War. "Children are a symbol of the continuation of a species, and if we intend to regulate that through the slaughter of humans, our species will die."

"Our planet is deteriorating," said a scientist from the back. "Climate change has reached unparalleled levels, our ozone layer is disintegrating, and our supply of water, food and clean air can no longer meet the demand. All our advancements in science and technology and our knowledge of the world will be lost if we do not do something immediately. We must think of the greater good, for if we do not act now, there will be nothing left."

The room was quiet as they all worked to put aside their morals and personal beliefs in an attempt to view the situation with the greater good in mind.

The Chinese President finally spoke up from his seat where he had remained silent. "We all want the same thing, and we have to be the ones to make the tough choices. That's why we are in this room today, because we were chosen to do the best for our countries. Every great city, country, or state was built not on diplomacy, they were built on tough decisions and blood. If we are to uphold our values not only as people but as leaders of our countries, then we all know what needs to be done."

The American President nodded and added, "History will not judge us on the challenges we faced, but on the vision we showed. That time is now. We can't undo the past, all we can do is face what's ahead. As long as we recognize that we share one future, we will survive. This policy might bring out the worst in people, but in doing so, we'll succeed in bringing about a better world."

The room sat in silence, realizing the choices they made at this meeting would impact humanity in ways that the world had never seen. However, not everyone was so eager to jump at the analyst's proposal.

"With the untold billions of people now dominating this earth, is there an optimal global number of humans for each passing generation we're planning for here?" inquired the King of Spain.

The analyst responded, "I don't think we should establish a precise number. Let nature take its course, the natural ebb and flow of the policy will serve our purpose. If the policy is too aggressive, it can be refined until it suits our needs as a planet."

"So, how exactly do you propose that we start killing off people?"

"That's what we're here to figure out," said the analyst.

"Whatever we do," remarked the representative of Peru, "We'd better figure something out soon. Our world won't last much longer."

In that moment, facing the world's extinction, it became clear that no single nation could solve the issue alone. Over the next few months, policy experts from around the world came together to construct what would be known as the Contraception Initiative. The debates were heated, with world leaders quick to give their opinion, focusing more on the bigger picture rather than showing concern for the immediate population.

"What about those who choose not to have children?" asked a lawmaker.

"What about them?" retorted Tom Griffiths, the English Prime Minister.

"Do you think they should be compensated in any way? One could argue that they are making the ultimate sacrifice by not burdening the world with a child."

"Should we reward people for graduating university? No, they get to enjoy a higher pay and a better standing in society. I suppose you'd argue that people who drive fusion-powered cars should also be compensated. Again, no. They save hundreds of dollars a year by not having to purchase fuel. For those who don't apply to Contraception, they get to live without a target on their back. That's their reward."

Discussions like this took place on every topic and every scenario related to having a child. The policy needed to cover a broad spectrum of cultures, religions, and societies.

The world's leaders came together as one, working not as representatives of their nations, but of humanity. The group of international policymakers labored for months until they had figured out every nuance, covered every loophole, and implemented ways to make the policy universally applicable.

Once they had what was deemed a "sound" policy, those who drafted it opened it up to the public for criticism and challenges, continuing to refine it. University students, scholars, morality experts, murderers – a wide variety of people were allowed to testify before the Contraception board, sharing their thoughts on the policy. Small changes were made and then, it finally happened. The Contraception Initiative came into being, but not without a reaction from the public.

Many people supported the policy, understanding that drastic steps needed to be taken to combat the effects of an overpopulated planet; however, many human rights and religious groups posed loud and frequent opposition. They took the moral high ground, claiming the Contraception Initiative violated the morality of most religions and infringed upon people's natural right to life. The governments of the world pushed forward anyway, establishing a protocol, creating marketing campaigns, building application centers, and finally implementing the policy in every corner of the world.

Protests still occurred, but the benefits of the system soon showed and the initial resistance to the Contraception Initiative became nothing more than a murmur in the street. People initially struggled with the idea of murdering their fellow man, but with everyone doing it, Contraception soon became the new normal.

The world finally had a solution; not the most humane, but better than letting ourselves descend into even more chaos.

2. VICTOR

Shanghai, China – Year 2070

Contraception was the first policy that all countries, even those not in the United Nations, ever agreed on. It was the first universal policy implemented that affected every single person on the planet.

• Victor glanced at his Rolex; it was a few minutes to 19:30; almost showtime. From the pocket of his black tailored suit, he took out a glass tablet with his long, black-gloved fingers. It held the name, age, sex, current occupation, address, body metrics, and picture of his next target: Lisa Hua, a 29-year-old nurse.

He stared up at the apartment building as the sky turned a blood-red color; the sun was setting. China's summer heat didn't bother Victor; he had grown accustomed to it while tracking targets in the Middle East. He reached into his inner breast pocket and took out a cigarette, placed it between his lips, quickly struck a match, and lit it. He took a puff and stared down the street. Taxis blared their horns, people on bicycles whizzed by, the holograms of advertisements all competing for airspace seemed to melt and twist into a Picassoesque array of light.

He continued to smoke until he saw a blue car approach and turn left into the underground garage of the apartment complex. Hello Lisa, he thought.

Some people lived minimal lives, enjoying the simple pleasures that life offered. For Victor, killing was where he derived pleasure, and it had soon become one of his favorite pastimes. He flicked the still smoking cigarette out onto the street, repositioned the silenced Sig Sauer in his left inner suit pocket, and proceeded up the stairs to the front door of the building. He scanned the electronic list of tenants on the display panel and rang a random number.

"Hello?" came a female voice from the metal box on the wall.

"Hi there, I hate to be a burden, but I seem to have left my keys at work this morning and was hoping you might do me a favor and buzz me in. My wife will return home soon, and I need to get these flowers into some water."

"Go fuck yourself," the old woman yelled as the intercom clicked off. Victor had expected as much. Trust in strangers had virtually vanished since Contraception. With most people either a potential target or killer, tenants no longer allowed strangers to enter their buildings without verifiable proof of who they were.

He shrugged at the woman's response and reached into his jacket pocket. He pulled out a black canister and, after looking around, positioned himself in front of the door to the building.

Aiming the canister at the door handle, he pressed the top of it, causing a black liquid to shoot out, covering the handle. He stepped back and slid his sleeve up to check his watch. When he glanced back at the handle again, it had melted, the hot metal dripping to the ground. The entire part where the locking mechanism used to be now lay in a puddle on the ground. Victor smiled. With one hand, he pushed open the door, stepped over the pool of melted steel on the ground and walked inside. A security guard came from around the corner.

He looked at Victor and said, "You're not a resident here, how did you get inside?" His eyes flashed towards the door and on seeing the silver metal on the ground, he reached for the can of pepper spray on his hip. But before the old man could grab the can, Victor's gun was firmly pressed against his brow.

"You're going to do exactly as I say," Victor said, walking towards the man.

As the guard cowered against the wall, Victor blinked twice. Something in his eye lit up for a moment before returning to normal.

His eyes looking right into the guard's, Victor smiled and said, "Repeat after me: 'Mrs. Hua, it's Chao, the security guard from downstairs. A package arrived for you this afternoon. Just need a signature confirming you've received it.'"

The guard hesitated, but with a gun so close to him he could smell the gunpowder of a freshly shot round, he reluctantly repeated what Victor had told him. Victor blinked again, then used the stock of his gun to knock the man unconscious, watching as his body crumpled to the ground. He straightened his suit, holstered the gun, and approached the elevator. Once inside, he pressed 65.

Lisa had been working at the hospital for five years and always came home with blood on her scrubs. Contraception had changed how hospitals operated, and the number of patients had increased hundredfold. Insurance companies no longer covered any damage caused either to a person or their belongings, if someone was authorized by Contraception to kill them. They claimed those who applied to have a child understood the consequences – with one insurance company even claiming, "Your baby, your problem."

One of the most significant issues facing hospitals was the fact that many people who had never killed someone before had a big problem following through. Lisa believed that during a Contraception kill, fear and panic set in in many people and they soon abandoned the attempt, leaving hundreds of victims headed for the nearest hospital. Hospitals had opened wards exclusively for victims of Contraception-related injuries, which were divided into gunshots, blunt object attacks, poison or injection, and lacerations and stab wounds. Lisa worked with laceration and stab wound patients, seeing firsthand just how far applicants were willing to go to have a child.

Today, her pink scrubs were sprayed with multiple people's blood, the worst case being a young man who had been the target of someone wielding a rusty machete. His entire left hand had been cut off while he was on his motorcycle at a red light. A pedestrian lingering on the crosswalk had suddenly pulled out the weapon and swung it across the waiting bike, taking the young man's left hand with it.

Fortunately for the victim, a garbage truck had run the red light and struck the attacker, killing him instantly. As soon as Lisa had removed the plastic bag covering the young man's wound, her scrubs were painted with a splattering of crimson blood, and her ears filled with the screams of the young man in agony.

"I just wanted to have a child," he had screamed, writhing in pain. "I thought I'd have time before my name was selected!"

For Lisa, it had been just another day. She sighed thinking of the scene as she put her eyes against the scanner installed on her door. The lock clicked open and let her inside. Her husband wasn't home yet as he worked late nights as a lawyer for a non-profit fighting against Contraception. But regardless of their beliefs, they had to play by the rules if they wanted to have a child. They had applied four months ago and so far, had killed only one out of the three on their list.

Almost immediately, Victor appeared outside the door. He took off one of his gloves and put two fingers in his eye, removing the contact lens that had lit up earlier. Carefully, he placed it over the peephole of Lisa's door. Immediately, the perimeter of the lens lit up, signaling it was now on.

As she placed her coat on the coat rack and was about to take off her shoes, Lisa heard a knock at the door.

Puzzled, as she wasn't expecting anyone, she went to the door and asked, "Who is it?" before looking out the peephole.

As Victor stood outside, the electronic contact digitally replaced his face with the face of the guard. The recording he had made just moments ago started to play. The contact pieced together a video of the guard, creating a life-like impression that he was outside her door. It seemed as if Chao was telling Lisa about a package that had arrived. She relaxed. Chao was a familiar face. Every day she met him when she left for work and he wished her a good morning.

"One second, Mr. Chao," she called out. She placed her thumb on a panel, unlocking the first set of locks, then slid a hefty bolt out of its socket to open the large metal door. To her shock, it was not Chao but a tall, strong-jawed stranger outside who moved with lightning speed to shove the silenced barrel of his gun flush against her temple. With his other hand, he took the contact off the door and put it in his pocket. She stared at the man before her. He had dark black hair, chiseled features, and his piercing blue eyes seemed to stare into her soul.

"Hello Lisa, so nice of you to let me in," he said, pushing her back with the gun against her forehead. Before she could scream, he put his gloved finger against her lips and said, "Ah, ah, ah, we wouldn't want that, now would we?"

He removed his finger and closed the door as they crossed the threshold.

"But, where's…" her voice trailed off as Victor interrupted her.

"Now Lisa, I'm sure you can understand what's about to happen; you're going to die." Lisa's mouth twitched but before she could scream, Victor put an admonishing finger against her lips once again to silence her.

"It's come to my attention that you've already killed one person on your Contraception list. Congratulations! I remember my first kill, it was a thrilling experience."

Lisa stood paralyzed in shock with the cold steel metal pressed against her skin.

She whispered, "So you're the applicant who received my name as a target?"

Victor chuckled. "Not exactly. Children are such a bore," he said, rolling his eyes.

"On a somewhat unrelated subject, you've been sneaking medical supplies to patients who were deemed untreatable. Now, there's an ethical dilemma, eh? But fortunately for me, you've applied to have a baby and submitted your name with the application, which means when I kill you, your death won't appear to be a murder, but rather a sanctioned Contraception kill that someone forgot to scan."

Lisa looked at him, not comprehending what was going on.

"What? I haven't been…"

"Lisa," he said, stressing the first part of her name, "The time for prevarication is over. Your name was on 'the list' long before you applied to Contraception. By the way, it was a bold move choosing to submit your name instead of your husband's. You don't see a lot of women stepping up these days."

Victor took his gun away from her head. Gesturing with it, he said, "The fact of the matter is, Contraception was designed to reduce the population. As a nurse, you save lives. That's official.

However, you've also been using finite resources to save people not worth saving. I know you were doing what you thought was right, but that's not how the world works anymore. You understand that. I'm sorry you won't be able to continue with your Contraception list. But that's life. Goodbye, Lisa."

As Lisa's eyes widened in panic, Victor pulled the trigger. There was a sound like the patter of raindrops as the interior of her skull painted the wall, resembling the blood on her scrubs. Victor found the matching pattern on her scrubs and the mess on the wall suiting. He approached her body and pulling the small glass tablet out of his pocket and deftly scanned her wrist with it.

Immediately a message flashed on the screen. "Lisa Hua – kill confirmed." Then a second message flashed on the device, confirming that 150,000 yuan ($20,000) had been deposited into his account. A third notification on the top of the screen indicated that Lisa Hua's name had been removed from 'the list.'

Victor was in the business of killing and these days, the world couldn't get enough of it.

3. NOW

Beijing, China – Year 2070

In a survey taken of successful Contraception applicants, 93% said having a baby was worth killing three people. However, 72% of couples said they would not apply to have a second child.

▪ Li Hu's interest in man and human behavior had developed long before he became an associate professor of ethics at Peking University in Beijing, even before he opened his first textbook at university. Throughout childhood, his curiosity often led him into unique situations – not all of which were pleasant.

Once he had stuck his hand inside a beehive to see what was inside. It resulted in a trip to the hospital and weeks of recovery. But that didn't seem to diminish his curiosity, as he was soon back looking for new things to understand, usually through trial and error.

With the setting sun illuminating his home office, Li leaned back in his aged leather chair and thought about how the world had ended up where it was now. "*Bù pò bù lì,*"[1] he thought regretfully.

---

[1] Without destruction there can be no construction (You can't make an omelet without breaking eggs)

It was fascinating to him how such simple expressions could be applied to some of the world's largest issues.

He stared at the glass wall in front of him. The official website of Contraception with its unique logo reflected back at him, almost seducing him into applying. For weeks, he had been vacillating about applying, unsure whether he could take someone else's life. Above all, he felt angry for living in a society that was forcing him to choose between being a good person and having a child. He supposed that in every civilization, there were unhappy people living within the established structure and order of their time. For Li, in 2070, it was no different.

Life was not the same as it had once been, and his only option was to adapt to how things were, or cease to exist. The weight of the decision he was pondering was something he thought no man should ever have to bear. He sighed as he gazed at the triangular logo, knowing that in order to have a child, there was no other alternative.

His glance drifted to the books on his shelf, some of which were written by him, including "China's Shifting Morality," "Understanding Chinese Characteristics," and "The Way of the Serpent: An Examination of China's Social Policies." He had always thought that through writing, he would be able to make an impact; to change the way people understood or perceived something. However, his hopes for a better future remained just words on a page, as a decade ago, those in power had chosen a different route for humanity. His thoughts on the way life should be lived, despite his extensive research and proposed alternatives, were now just manuscripts left to collect dust in his home.

Although this wasn't the life he had intended to live, it was the reality in which he found himself. There was no right or wrong. Not anymore. The world had changed, and so had people's beliefs about morality.

The three triangles that comprised the Contraception logo stared back at Li, taunting him, "Could you do it? Do you have it in you? What is a life worth?"

He looked away. Li had never thought of himself as a murderer. Another expression popped into his mind, "There's a first time for everything." He waved his wrist and the screen went blank. He could not contemplate this decision any longer; he knew what was required of him.

With a resolve he had felt many times before when making a decision, he got up from his chair and walked out of the room, no longer able to sit and reflect on his verdict. Now was the time for action. He had made up his mind and now, he had to go through with it.

***

Over the past four years, Li and his wife, Mei, had been talking, and at times arguing, over having a child. Ten years ago, it was a simple process. Once pregnant, you went to the hospital, had your baby, and returned home. That was it. There were no restrictions, guidelines, or consequences except those that a baby naturally brings to one's life.

However, things were different now. The previous decade of violence had forced those in power to make tough choices. One of them was Contraception, one of the few policies that the entire world agreed on.

Li thought back on his role as a commentator on the Contraception Initiative. He was part of an international university team that had published a paper on the ethicality of the proposal. Times were tense, with the whole world watching and demanding a solution for the growing population, and his thoughts as a sociologist and researcher were listened to, but not heeded.

"Killing people is not a solution," his professor, a sociology expert, had said before a panel of policy experts, world leaders and population analysts. "What we have is a situation that calls for extreme measures, but murder should never be a part of the plan."

Li's words were used to help write the speech his teacher gave, but they knew that since this policy had been so heavily researched and planned, it would be carried out regardless of who proposed a counterargument.

After listening to the arguments against the initiative for months, the team of analysts, researchers and diplomats had made a decision. In 2060, the world finally implemented the Contraception Initiative, referred to as Contraception or simply Contra, as a means to suppress the swelling population. It did not take long for the plan to become a normal part of everyone's lives, as man's inner animal desire to procreate took over. Despite the risks that Contraception presented to applicants, people still wanted to have babies.

Li thought of the first days of the initiative, how it had changed the lives of those on earth forever and continued to do so.

Today, to have a child, an individual or a couple needed to apply through Contraception, submitting either the man or woman's name during the formal in-person application process. Once the application was approved, the applicant received three glass tablets, each eventually providing the picture and profile of a target selected at random from a database of other applicants.

Only one profile was given at a time. Only once the first target was confirmed dead, would the second tablet download another profile chosen at random from the database; the same would happen with the third tablet until all three targets were eliminated. These three targets had to be confirmed dead before the applicant could proceed to have a child.

The catch was, once a person's application had been submitted, his or her name was added to the database, which meant he or she could be selected as a target and sent to a new applicant. The only way a person's name could be removed from the database of potential targets was is if they died, or rescinded their application, or successfully killed three people and had their baby.

Unfortunately, until the baby was born, the applicant's name remained in the database with the risk of being given to another applicant.

But morality aside, the initiative had worked. Li thought how the world had changed in the ten years since Contraception had become an integrated part of everyday life. The population had started to drop, and the fear of being added to the hitlist had curbed thousands of couples' desire to have a child.

As with most things in life, there was a price to pay. A decreased global population brought about a reduction in things like crime, theft and burglary, but violence and murder soon became society's biggest commodity. The three names from Contraception became the sole focus of those wanting to have a kid. Mercenaries willing to do the dirty work for money and guns and ammunitions shops started popping up almost overnight. With no regard for life, killing became an easy way for some people to make a quick buck.

Although the population continued to decline, Li couldn't help but speculate about the way in which Contraception was impacting human civilization as a whole. Society was evolving into something so much more sinister than just a deadly number game.

No matter through whatever means someone eliminated their three targets, that person was regarded as the *winner*. If a person successfully killed three people, the outcome could be labeled as "favorable," no matter if they achieved it through cleverness, luck, strength, or any other recourse.

Successful applicants who had a child had not only disposed of a "weaker" candidate but had also created a next generation with the genes of someone who had "prevailed." Life was all about weeding out the weak, forming a smaller, but more developed, if ruthless, civilization. Society might have been growing smaller, but it was also becoming stronger and smarter. Humans had attempted to create a mechanism to expedite natural selection, but few believed Darwin would have been proud.

However, despite the ability of these individuals on the quest to reproduce, it had no impact on whether they would be good parents. In a morally degenerate society, there were even some couples who applied to Contraception just for the adrenaline rush of legally killing people, or to feel the thrill of being hunted. Once their three targets were eliminated, they simply rescinded their application, claiming that now wasn't the best time to have a child. The system itself wasn't flawed, but at times, the people who used it were.

Regardless of all the risks and dangers, the world still wanted to have kids. Li recalled a recent argument he had had with Mei, with her asserting that the creation of life was worth potentially dying for.

He looked at the books on the shelf once again, wondering if any of them still had meaning – morality, values, and the concept of good versus evil. The way the world now behaved had caused Li to challenge the ideals he had cherished for so long.

"Drastic times call for drastic measures," he thought, again thinking how a phrase could so easily be applied to justify murdering someone to have a child.

As Li pondered over how life had changed so abruptly, a voice rang out, interrupting his thoughts, "Hey, dinner!"

He had forgotten that Mei was at home, cooking. He went into the kitchen, kissed her and helped carry the dishes out to the dining room.

As they sat down at the table, he said, "I know I'd been so against this, but I think now is the time for us to embrace the next step."

"I recognize the risks, I know I could die, but I can't stop thinking about the life we would be creating. I love you and I want to have a baby with you."

He sat down as he waited for her reaction.

For months, he had argued against having a child, concluding that it wouldn't be worth it. However, his views had changed. It wasn't a singular moment but the life he had been living that drove him to change his mind. He wanted something more, he wanted a purpose, someone to carry out his legacy long after he was gone. There was an almost animalistic desire to have a child since he turned twenty-nine last year. The arguments with Mei had been a frequent occurrence ever since Contraception had been implemented and altered the decisions that millions of people once thought to be a humanistic right.

Mei didn't speak immediately. She sat quiet at the other side of the table, looking at him with warmth in her eyes.

"I love you too," she said finally. "And I want nothing more than to have a baby, but we have to be prepared for some tough choices."

They both knew there were several things to deal with. First, was it worth the risk of being someone's target, clinging to the hope that that person might rescind their application? Li knew that once he himself was in, he would either complete the application or die trying.

Second, could he and Mei kill someone? Could he morally accept murdering someone to have a child?

"Could you do it?" he asked her, looking up from his plate of grilled fish and rice. He continued to move the rice around on his plate with his chopsticks as Mei made eye contact with him and answered, "I think if we were careful about it, then it could be done."

She took a sip of beer while maintaining eye contact with him. "How would you do it?" he asked. "Let's say we're given an old man, a young man, and a middle-aged woman. What's the plan?"

Talking about murdering people had replaced the subject of how one would spend their money if they won the lottery. People fantasized about it all the time, and more often than not, practiced what they preached.

"I'd want to pace it out," she said. "It's risky doing them all at one time, and definitely not without a plan. One, two and three, all should be dead within a month, two at most."

Li nodded in agreement. Mei continued, "Because we are allowed to kill only the person we are assigned, it pretty much rules out explosives or anything like that. Besides, that would be too messy to confirm the kill."

Li nodded again.

When a person received a target, they were technically allowed to kill that person, but if anyone else died during the process, accidentally or not, that would be considered murder. The issue of self-defense during a Contraception kill had been raised before the board of the initiative, as well as the United Nations.

After much deliberation, it was ruled that a death resulting from self-defense would be handled in the same manner as it was under the current legal system. Evidence needed to be presented and the police, along with a judge, ruled on a case-to-case basis whether the death was self-defense or not.

For applicants, the rule of thumb was to keep the kill clean and not to let anyone get in the way. The rule was to confirm the kill, the murdered person's wrist or fingerprints had to be scanned into the glass tab with the authorized applicant's fingerprints. Bombs tended to complicate that.

"What about poison?" said Li, thinking it would be a smooth and relatively non-violent way to finish the job.

"That's always a possibility, but I like the idea of some form of violence being involved. I mean, if I am going to take a life, I want to be the one doing it, up close and personal."

While she said this, there was something in Mei's expression that showed a fire within her. Mei was a passionate woman, from the way she cooked and spoke to the manner in which she lived her life. She loved to try new things and be right in the thick of things.

Her eyes glittered as she said, "Just imagine being able to watch life slip away from them as you slowly wring..."

"Alright, alright," Li said hastily. He realized Mei hadn't changed her mind about having a kid; he was also certain she would have no problem with the process. The incessant arguments had finally come down to them agreeing to apply to have a child.

"And you? How would you kill them?" she asked him.

"Easy, the old man gets pushed down the stairs. The young man would require an object of some sort, a crowbar or steel pipe, and as soon as you land that first blow, it would be over. And the woman? Perhaps we could poison her, but it would also be interesting to throw a toaster into the bathtub while she's in there for a soak."

"What if she doesn't take baths?"

"Well, let's imagine she's a bather in this scenario. I'd like to try out electrocuting someone with a toaster, like in the movies."

"Fair, but how many people actually take baths these days?" Mei enjoyed a healthy debate.

"Ok, well, if she's not taking a bath, maybe I could hit her over the head with the toaster, and that would be that. Satisfied?"

Mei smiled and nodded. Her teeth shone dazzlingly white against her tanned skin and pink lips. She loved Li with a passion that at times frightened her. The thing she loved most about him was the way he saw the world. He understood how people worked, what made them tick, and she loved his curiosity about life.

Li held Mei's gaze as he chose his words carefully, "My name will be on the application. Our child will need his mother."

In his mind, there was never any question about this. Losing Mei was too great a risk. Mei started to speak, but Li interrupted her, "I love you. This is how it's going to be."

"I was going to say 'I know.'"

"You know what?"

"That we would submit your name. There's no way you'd put me in harm's way." She continued to eat her fish with a hint of a smile.

"Somehow, I feel you're using my love for you against me." They both laughed. However, another issue needed to be addressed before they could consider applying.

"How do we ensure your safety?" asked Mei. She knew that this discussion and the choice following it would alter their lives forever. With what was basically "acceptable murder," safety had become people's number one priority. Once Contraception was implemented, new services sprang up all over the place. Fortified walls, reinforced glass, retina-scan security locks, bulletproof clothing, and bodyguards. It was normal these days to see corporate businessmen and their rich wives escorted through the streets by beefy bodyguards to ensure their safety during the Contraception process.

The heavy sun set over the Hu apartment while the smog and humidity clung to the summer Beijing air.

Li finished the last of his fish, rested the chopsticks on his plate and said, "I guess now we have to plan and prepare."

Night began to fall and darkness crept over the city. The sound of metal grates being pulled down over windows and heavy-duty locks being set in place was everywhere. Nights had become even more dangerous, considered prime time for people to make their Contraception list a little shorter. Although guns were officially banned by the Chinese government in 1949, the warm night air continuously carried the loud crack of gunshots as someone met their fateful end on the other side of the barrel.

One could no longer take a late-night stroll in the park; at least not someone eager to have a child. The night now belonged to those committed to having a baby – busy hunting down their targets in a frenzied attempt to fulfill their dream of conceiving. Only those who had chosen to live without a child in their life could walk around late at night with no fear. All the deaths that Contraception was responsible for had reduced the population, and the reduced population had also caused regular crime to drop significantly. These days, the only ways of life were enjoying life without a child, killing those on one's list to ensure a successful application, or enjoying life with one's newborn.

Life had become a sharper version of survival of the fittest.

4. THE APPLICATION

Beijing, China

After applying, 21% of applicants withdraw their applications for "personal" reasons.

▪ The following morning found Mei in the kitchen, cooking eggs, and bacon. Her fondness for American-style breakfast could be traced to the years she had spent studying for her Masters of Engineering at MIT.

As a little girl growing up in China, she had always known that she didn't fall in line with what one would consider a "traditional" Chinese girl. She questioned authority, challenged her teachers, and spoke of revolution and change. She was consistently struck down, both figuratively and literally as her parents and superiors reminded her that little girls in China should not think like that.

At twenty-two, having received her architecture degree from Hong Kong University, she left for the United States in search of a place where her ideals would be met with open arms. She found that place at MIT where she also discovered how much she loved American food.

Mei always had a fire inside her. At a young age, this manifested itself as her perpetual need to run. She thought of her long runs as a teenager past Tian'anmen Square and through the university district in Wudaokou. Despite the turmoil from an overcrowded and at times, warring, capital city, Wudaokou had been well-preserved. Later, as a college student, she was at the top of her class as she discovered that she had a natural aptitude for designing architecture. She had always been studious and found that she could absorb materials quicker than her peers. It was her attitude and eagerness to share her ideas in a country that didn't value individuality that had got her into a lot of trouble.

As Mei waited for the bacon to turn crisp, the front door opened and Li walked in, his black shirt wet with sweat. He smiled at her and took out one of his headphones. She thought he looked sexy, with the drenched shirt clinging to his lean body and his black hair tossed from the wind. It was a look that gave her a frisson of desire every time she saw him like this. Even inside, he couldn't seem to stand still. He bent down and grasped his right ankle, pulling it up to stretch his leg. Li was a fitness fanatic who ran and worked out every morning. He found it to be a good way to clear his head before he went to teach university students who still struggled to understand the social implications of Contraception, a favorite topic these days.

Mei thought he would make a great father. This was one of the determining factors she used to justify ending the lives of three other people who probably had never crossed their lives before or done them any harm. She had spent her childhood watching her mother become a shadow of herself, living the life her in-laws, parents and husband wanted her to live, and a rebellious Mei had decided long ago that her life was the most important thing to her in this world. She would do whatever was in her power to make her dreams come true.

"How was your run?" she asked tenderly.

A shadow fell over his face. "Saw four bodies along the river and three more lying in the street," he said somberly. His wife glanced over at him as he shook his head in disgust. "They stank, like really stank, as if they'd been there for a while." He sighed heavily, "I don't think things are getting any better out there. Contraception preaches a better society, but those bodies, they were just lying there, lifeless and bloody. Dispo has its hands full lately."

Dispo was the slang for the Contraception Disposal Unit, which the Contraception Board had created to deal with the influx of dead bodies due to their initiative. They operated like sanitation workers, hauling off bodies, identifying them, and then contacting the families for the latter to claim them for a proper send-off.

Once a kill had been authorized and the target confirmed dead, Dispo would automatically be notified of the location and a team would be dispatched to retrieve the corpse. The emergency contact for the dead, whose information was pre-programmed into a person's pass, would be notified within 24 hours to claim the body for an official funeral. If no contact could be made and no one came to claim the body, the dead target would be cremated by Dispo. The world had no more space for burials as land had become a precious commodity.

Mei checked the toast, prepared two plates and set them on the table. Li removed his shoes, sat down and took a sip of his orange juice.

"Today's the day then? The day everything changes?"

Mei also sat down, took his hand into both of hers, and nodded. "After your class, I'll meet you outside of the university and we'll do this together."

It was the biggest decision both of them had ever made. Though once it was done, they would be plunged into tension and danger, for now it was a comforting feeling knowing that they were not on anyone's list, at least for the time being.

After breakfast, Li kissed Mei goodbye, took his single-speed bicycle and rode through the early morning streets to Peking University. Driverless cars had replaced many of the taxis in the city, making it safe to ride a bike in Beijing again. Years ago, overcrowding and man's inherent carelessness had caused biking to dwindle in what used to be known as the bicycle capital of the world. Thanks to advancements in technology, hopping into a car and needing only to program the destination had increased the flow of traffic and efficiency of one of Beijing's oldest problems –traffic congestion. No longer did cars randomly stop on the side of the road, or buses clog up multiple traffic lanes. Automation had streamlined the whole process.

Li flew through the streets, absentmindedly noting how much life had changed over his lifetime. The wind whipped his face and his hair streamed behind. There were many other single bicyclists like him. These days, it was rare to see couples out together. As one of them most likely had a potential target on their back, it was too risky to be out in public.

Li realized he would have to rethink his day-to-day mode of transportation as this afternoon was about to change more than just how he got to work. Still, as the rising sun brought a warm glow with it, he felt relaxed. Also, he was convinced that the decision he was about to make in a few hours was the right one, and with exactly the right person. As soon as he had met Mei, he knew she was the one for him; the woman he would make a new life with.

While studying ethics at Boston University, he had met Mei at a bar on a winter night. He walked in and saw her at his favorite dive bar, a place he frequently visited when trying to escape from the monotony of university life. As he walked in, he noticed her sitting at the bar, sketching something intently in a worn leather journal. Her hair was up in a bun, and she was casually dressed in a black sweater. A pint of beer stood before her. She had something about her that drew Li to her, an aura that made him catch his breath as he pulled out the old bar stool next to her. She seemed focused, but relaxed, beautiful, yet down to earth.

Mei didn't acknowledge his presence as he took a seat; she continued sketching complex diagrams, letting the pencil fly across the paper while occasionally taking a sip of her beer. Her taut jawline, sharp cheekbones, and long, supple legs suggested she was into fitness. Li ordered a beer and took a sip.

Just as he was about to say something, Mei, without looking up from her book, said bluntly, "Don't do it. I'm not interested."

Li was taken aback, so he simply replied, "*Qiān zǎi nán féng.*"[2] It made Mei look up and she was surprised by what she saw. He didn't look like a bar hopper out to pick up women for causal flings. He looked to be about twenty-four, with an open face, warm brown eyes and dark hair that fell above his eyebrows. He looked lean and fit, his broad shoulders were outlined underneath his black pea coat. He smiled in a friendly, and she was intrigued by his expression. His eyes seemed to know something that she didn't.

"I'm Li Hu, I study ethics, and from the looks of it," he said, peering down at her sketchbook, "you are an aspiring cartoonist."

Mei held back a smile and retorted, "For your information, this cartoon, as you so eloquently put it, happens to be a design I'm working on as an engineering student at MIT."

"MIT? Ah, yes, I've heard of that. Small school, lots of nerds, robots and stuff, right?" He raised his finger, ordering another pint of beer.

Li and Mei spent the next couple of hours talking as the fire inside the bar kept the place warm against the snowy winter weather

---

[2] Hard to meet in a thousand years (idiom); extremely rare opportunity

that raged outside. This was the start of what would become a romance that traveled across continents for the young lovers to stay together.

Li finally arrived at the university, the big buildings of the school huddled together like giant metallic beasts against the rising sun. The pergolas in the background served as a reminder of how great this country had once been. As Li walked up the giant steps leading to the lecture hall, he wondered how these institutions had failed society. As a place where students were educated and prepared to be the leaders of tomorrow, society had somehow ended up with a means to murder people, completely disregarding the humaneness that separated humans from animals.

Li entered the building and began to walk through the halls to go to his classroom. So many young faces rushed by him, enjoying life with no real concern about the tough choice that would soon face them. He knew they had thought about it, even discussed it, but now that he had chosen to apply, he knew that intellectually discussing Contraception was a lot different than actually taking part in it. In a couple of years, these students would need to make the same decision that Li had made just a day ago.

Whether they wanted it or not, Contraception was on everyone's mind, including Li's. Choosing to have a child or not was no longer a simple choice. Dying in consequence now weighed in on the equation. The ultimate question was, "Is it worth it?"

As Li entered his lecture hall, he placed his brown leather messenger bag on the table and took out his lecture notes. His class today focused on the morality of man, a challenging topic to deal with in today's desensitized world. As students flooded into the classroom, Li took a piece of chalk and wrote the word "Man" on the board.

When everyone was settled in, he asked, "What defines man? What separates us from animals?"

One student raised his hand and said, "Divorce."

The room chuckled and Li smiled too as he clarified his question, "What intrinsically makes man, man? What is that thing we share that can be recognized across borders, races, religions, or sexual orientations?"

Another student submitted an idea, "The right to life, education and clean water."

"Yes," said Li, "But what is behind that? What is the underlying factor that makes us believe all humans deserve these rights?"

"Morals and values?" A student from the back chimed in.

"Precisely," Li said, as he turned back to the board and wrote the words the student had said next to "Man."

Then turning back to his class, he asked, "And where do these morals and values come from?"

"From our environment and experiences."

"Correct," said Li. His students were particularly on the ball that morning.

A girl from the back had a question. "So, as we constantly form our morals and values, what makes them so flexible? I mean, like I understand the necessity for something like Contraception, but isn't it morally wrong to kill people?"

Li would often reach this point in class. No matter what subject he taught, someone would always bring it back to Contraception.

"This system, if you will, was designed by men with flexible morals. But perhaps it's for the best because we wouldn't have got to see our true colors as a human race unless our back was up against a wall. We can understand the limits of what makes us 'good' when confronted with a challenging situation. Survival and ensuring the continuity of our species is more important than being a decent human. Contraception is living proof of the lack of morality in our modern society but remember, this is not, and certainly won't be the last time we question society's morals."

"We have had war, genocide, crime, violence and deceit throughout our thousands of years of history. As a believer in the enlightenment of man over time, my faith in mankind was let down as Contraception was not only passed, but was also embraced. We sacrificed a better society for the mere sake of a continued society."

"But professor," came a small voice, "How can we develop a system of morals and values against the pre-determined standard of what society deems to be 'normal'? What about the people who grow up experiencing only what society is like with Contraception? It will no longer be about whether killing people is good or bad, but simply a requirement for having children."

"Great thinkers," replied Li, "have always been the ones to change the course of history. Society and men's minds have always been malleable, and it is with that hope that I encourage all of you to think beyond yourselves and ask questions that impact your community, and ultimately, the world. Perhaps above all, is this the world you want to live in? Because if it isn't, then do something about it."

The bell rang as Li finished. He glanced at his thin glass band, it was almost time to meet Mei to proceed with their application.

"Thank you everyone, and I'll see you next week!"

The class was full of soft buzz as Li packed up his satchel and made his way once again through the bustling halls and out into the warm Beijing air.

He glanced down at his wrist; a message flashed on the band: "One minute."

As he waited, he thought about where this decision was about to take him and his family. He was unwavering in his resolve to have a child, but he couldn't also help pondering if this decision were to be one of his last.

A black and yellow taxi pulled up along the sidewalk, the window rolled down, and Mei said: "Let's go, professor."

He hopped into the taxi as Mei programmed the coordinates to the Contra Center. People around the world had shortened the official title of the Contraception Initiative to just Contra, and in China, people had come up with a parody, Center of Non-Traditional Regulations Administration, making fun of the Chinese government's fondness for acronyms.

Contra, as a universal system, had been established as a policy with universal rules and requirements. Each country was required to establish multiple Contra locations for its citizens to formally apply. Most were in major cities, with a few smaller locations in less populated areas. The design and location of the building was up to each individual country, but the system, means of operation, function and regulations had been unanimously agreed upon by the world's leaders.

The Contra Centers were much like embassies, but belonged to the world, and facilitated the murder of individuals instead of working to promote peace. Contraception was a requirement for anyone eager to have a child. Under Contra, both the president of a country and a farmer were required to apply and both expected to meet the same requirements.

Money, however, made things easier. Hitmen could be contracted; however, an applicant was still required to scan his or her thumb on the tablet before scanning the victim as a hitman was not authorized to kill applicants' targets. Like all systems on earth, people usually circumnavigated the official process, and Contra was no exception.

As they pulled up to the building of glass and metal, the Hus were reminded of how non-traditional the city had become after China had transitioned from a developing country into what the rest of the world and it itself finally deemed "developed." Traditional architecture, though still around, had not been used in any of Beijing's buildings since 2035 and its Contra Center was a good example of Beijing showcasing its modern, developed architectural style to the rest of the world.

Spanning 50 stories and one of the biggest Contra centers in the world, this was the place which dealt with all the applications and was responsible for hundreds of thousands of deaths in China. It was, so to speak, the purveyor of death.

Li swiped the center console of the taxi with his glass band. By 2040, the world had completely phased out cash and coins. Besides the obvious reasons, such as the hassle and wear and tear, the development of crypto-currency in the early 2000s had led to the globalized use of "credits," a universal digital currency which had made its way into the mainstream and eventually become standard. Now, data linking one's account could be embedded into one's wrist, with the glass band acting as the facilitator between the account and the receiver. A simple swipe was all it took to complete a transaction.

Under Contraception, each newborn was assigned a 30-digit string of letters and numbers that would serve as their global ID number, which was officially entered into a system at the hospital – a number that was linked with you until death, detailing every aspect of your life. This became what was known as one's "pass," which once passed through scanners allowed people to purchase a house, enroll in school, travel outside the country, buy insurance, get admitted into a hospital, and make purchases larger than $1,000. This "pass" was embedded in the DNA around the bones of one's wrist, so that the swiping could be done quickly and efficiently.

Li remembered when he got his implant. These days, babies legally born under Contraception had them implanted at the hospital, but for those already born, the process was one he would never forget.

It was announced that within one year of Contraception, every single individual in the world was required to have an injection in the wrist. The injection contained a plasma-like substance containing electronic sub-atomic particles linked to the recipient's DNA. The plasma would cool, forming a band that was permanently attached to the tissue and bone of the wrist. Combined with the external glass band, these electronic particles contained the entire life of a person. They served as a person's bank account, means of application for a job, and as they contained every piece of information that made up the person, they also served as the only thing that would work in the scanners that were now a part of everyday life.

Following the implementation of Contraception, these "passes" would also identify those who were legally born. The few who didn't abide by Contraception and had babies secretively could not get the passes for their progeny. Someone who did not have a pass was automatically rejected by society.

As technology advanced, purchases made online, including air tickets or anything else that required authorization, required a person's pass. To avoid moving the wrist continuously, technology was adapted to fit around the embedded 'pass,' thus making the glass band a universally ubiquitous piece of tech. The impact of Contraception on the world was one of the most significant and impactful to ever take place. It changed the way humans thought, lived, forced technology to adapt, and it altered how people thought about life itself.

After paying the fare, Li slowly exited the vehicle with Mei behind him. They both stared at the glass monstrosity that stood before them and with a determined, yet wary look in their eyes, headed into the building that held their fate.

High above them gleamed the Contraception logo. Reflected onto the side of the building, the digital logo comprised three hollow triangles, each with a different color outlining the shape, with the inside left blank. Light blue, purple, and dark purple, colors which traditionally represented peace and royalty, but were chosen for the sake of political correctness as they were not used together in any country's national flag. The triangles were arranged so that all three were interlocked, with two sharing the same horizontal plane and the third centered a bit lower than the other two.

Hand in hand, Li and Mei walked in through the big glass door, their footsteps echoing on the seemingly endless white marble floor. A huge chandelier hung from the ceiling. Li looked up and upon closer inspection, saw it was made of weapons, including guns, sabers, swords, knives, grenades and other metal weapon-like objects he could not name.

"Modern art?" he asked.

"More like some kind of sick joke," Mei snorted.

Men in black suits walked around the main lobby. The Hus went towards a large circular kiosk marked "Reception."

"Good afternoon and welcome to Beijing's Contra Center," said a beautiful young Chinese girl, wearing a black World War II pilot hat and a black uniform. The contrast the black made in the otherwise all white interior, along with her red lipstick, was stark.

"We're looking to apply to have a child," Mei said.

"Please take the elevator to the thirty-second floor, you can apply there," the smiling attendant said.

While waiting for the elevator, Mei looked at Li, gripped his hand and said, "Are you sure about this?"

He squeezed her hand back and said, "With you, I'm always sure."

The large glass elevator opened, and the Hus stepped in.

The thirty-second floor was a buzz of noise and with more people in all black suits milling around. As the elevator opened, Li and Mei were escorted by a young man, also in a black suit, to an office at the back of the floor. Gesturing them to sit, he went out of the room.

Sitting behind a large mahogany desk across from the Hus was a middle-aged man with short hair. He had perfect white teeth and a narrow face. The glint in his eye seemed to convey the excitement he felt for his job.

Behind him was a painting of China's Cultural Revolution in a large frame. The painting depicted four soldiers in worn military garb shackling a beaten man to a wooden post in a public square as the Red Guards fired their guns into the crowd to keep them from interfering. The man's glasses were broken, and his tattered clothes showed that he was an academic that had been deemed a revolutionary, and thus, subjected to be humiliated in the public square. Splotches of blood could be seen coming from many of the onlooker's clothes as the fierce look in the guard's eyes conveyed their conviction in their belief.

"Simpler times, eh?" remarked the man, noticing the couple staring at the painting.

"My name is Xi, and I will be your point of contact throughout the Contra process. Questions, advice, updates, I'm your guy."

There was nothing on the desk except for a large tablet of glass, which the man swiped to turn it on.

"Hello and let me extend an official warm welcome to Contra! If you're here, that must mean you've decided to have a baby, always an exciting next chapter in a young couple's life. Let's hope that both of you are around to enjoy it," he said, winking. "Sorry, sorry, crude humor. But seriously, you never know. Please place your fingers on the glass, both of you, and we can begin the application."

Li and Mei both did so and immediately, both their profiles appeared on the glass in front of Mr. Xi, containing every bit of information that defined them as people.

"Ah, a professor and an architect, a clever couple indeed! Alright, I'm going to run through a list of questions, all standard procedure of course, and then we can get you on your way. Sounds good?"

"Sure," replied Li, sitting in one of the two black chairs facing Mr. Xi.

"You understand that to have a child, or as Contra defines it, to physically give birth, the three names you will be given must be confirmed dead before that baby pops out. You must confirm the kills on each glass tablet I'll give you, one for each target. The names, as they are for every application, are assigned at random from the database of other applicants. It's important to remember that only one profile will be uploaded at a time. Once that kill is confirmed, the next profile will be selected at random and uploaded, and so on."

"The cost of applying is that one of your names will be added to that pool. And have we decided who that lucky person will be between the two of you?"

Li took a deep breath and replied, "Me. I will add my name."

"Excellent choice," said Mr. Xi, "Very noble of you to not sacrifice your wife. We've had a lot of couples lately submit the wife's name, not very chivalrous if you ask me."

He then pressed a button on the glass in front of him and a contract appeared.

"This is all very standard Mr. Hu. It says that you agree to have your name added to the database and that you understand the potential to, well, be legally murdered. Consider it a sacrifice for having a child. Your name will be removed from the database only if you are confirmed dead, either from a Contra contract or natural causes, or you rescind your application, or you complete your three kills and have a child."

"This is the important part: your name will still be in the database until your lovely wife has the child. If the latter occurs, first, congratulations, because that is no easy feat. At that point in time, whoever received your profile will be issued a new name from the database and you will be free to live your life with a child."

Mr. Xi looked at them. Then leaning a little over the table, he said, "Speed is the name of the game. I've been working here since Contraception was first implemented and everyone who dies does so because they take too long. Get your kills, have your baby, and get off the list."

He sat back in his chair, folded his hands in front of him, and in a more formal tone said, "This agreement also states that both you and your wife, Mrs. Mei, are legally allowed to kill ONLY the three names you will be given; by any means you see fit. Anyone else found to have been murdered by your doing and not legally approved by Contra will see you prosecuted to the full extent of the law. I can see what you're about to ask and yes, the use of explosive devices is allowed, but not for mass murder. Once the three kills are confirmed, the hospital will allow you to give birth. Remember, you must have your baby before you are considered a free man. If at the time of birth, you have not confirmed your three kills, the baby will immediately be terminated, and you will be banned from applying through Contra again. So, I suggest you either make sure those kills are confirmed before that baby comes out or wait to conceive until after you've handled your business. Is this all understood?"

Li and Mei both nodded. Mr. Xi gestured at the glass tablet. They obediently placed their fingers on it, confirming their agreement, and as soon as they had done so, Mr. Xi clapped his hands, reached into his pocket to pull out a small piece of glass, roughly the size of the antiquated iPhone 6, and laid it on top of the desk.

After a few seconds, he exclaimed, "Remarkable! A very exciting day for you both, I'm sure. Mr. Hu, you will have 48 hours before your name is officially 'available' to be given to another applicant. As a precautionary measure, I suggest you get your affairs in order. Ah, and I almost forgot, your targets!"

Mr. Xi stood up, walked over to the Cultural Revolution painting, slid it left with his hands and placed his palm over a digital scanner. The wall moved, revealing a glass panel. Mr. Xi took the smaller glass tablet he had lifted from the desk and inserted it into a slot in the wall. The panel sucked the tablet in while three more panels suddenly shot out. Mr. Xi withdrew three blank tablets from the panels, then folded the panels together and slid the painting back over the entire contraption. He placed the three blank tablets on the desk in front of Li and Mei.

"Here we are, Mr. Executioner," he said, giggling. "Just a little joke, but look at you, so fit, so strapping. I bet between the two of you, you'll have these names taken care of in no time." He picked up one of the blank tablets and gestured to Li. "Once you do your business and place the target's fingerprints or wrist against this device, along with yours, it will automatically confirm the kill, flashing green to signify that the person is dead. Believe me Mr. Hu, this is 2070, so please don't try to trick the technology."

"One last thing, the names won't expire, so please feel free to take all the time you need. Any questions?"

"I have a question," said Li. "What if, for example, my target finds out I have been assigned to kill him? Could he then kill me in self-defense without any consequences?"

"A common question," Mr. Xi nodded. "Every dead person must be scanned within 15 minutes of being killed. Each tablet is programmed for a specific target and authorized only to be scanned by either you or your wife. Sure, your target might kill you, but without the proper authorization, the police would be alerted as it would be classified as a 'normal murder' compared to one sanctioned by us. Any wrongful scan will immediately alert the authorities. And, if by chance, someone were to kill you and you weren't scanned by the proper individual within 15 minutes, then your death would be investigated as a regular murder, which rarely occurs these days. He would be prosecuted in accordance with the laws of this great nation. You are legally safe from everyone except the person who receives your profile and has the authorization to kill you."

Li and Mei had known most of this before this meeting, as friends, neighbors and students had discussed every possible way of how to fool the system. From all these discussions, none of the ways seemed plausible.

"We understand," Li replied in a solemn voice.

Mei looked across the table and asked, "What if something happens to our target? Like, what if she gets hit by a car?"

"That happens from time to time. Don't worry, if anything happens to your target, a new one will be selected, again at random, and I will call to notify you of the change."

The way in which Mr. Xi spoke seemed off-putting, considering the subject matter. It was almost as if it made him cheerful that he was facilitating death.

"Furthermore," began Mr. Xi, "Mr. Hu, if you are killed before you both kill your three targets, then Mrs. Hu, unfortunately, cannot have a child as your prerequisites for having a child will not have been met. It's like a race, kill or be killed. Don't you find it exciting!?"

"Oh, and if for some reason, Mrs. Hu is fortunate enough to have twins, that is what we here at Contra call a 'two for three.' You kill three, but nature blesses you with two. We most certainly would not punish you for a natural occurrence."

"However, on the opposite end of the spectrum, Contra allows you to have only one child. So if you have just one and the kid has perhaps one arm or a brain problem, well, that's not on us. If you so wish, you may try again. You'll be required to start the process all over again."

"Conversely, if the baby dies during birth, you may conceive again with no additional murder necessary. Contra is for the betterment of humanity and I wish you both the best as you begin this exciting chapter of your lives!"

However, he had not finished.

"On the other hand," he said, smiling in anticipation of their question, "if the person who receives your profile dies, then your name will simply be given to someone else. The system requires you to kill three people, but each applicant can have only one open target at a time."

"Believe me, the initial plan was a mess. Initially, we disclosed all three profiles at the same time but then realized we had created a sort of Ponzi scheme, which came crashing down when someone died. So, we decided that having each applicant focus on one target at a time was more effective."

With that, Mr. Xi picked up the three glass plates and handed them across the table to Li, who placed them inside his jacket pocket as Mei watched in silence.

"When will the first profile be selected and uploaded?" Li asked.

"Within an hour or so. Good luck out there and I hope you both succeed in having a child. Society is so much stronger now that the weak have died off. A good day to both of you!"

He stood up and gestured to the door. The Hus were silent, digesting what they had just experienced.

The door to the room slid open and they stood up Li looked back at the painting on the back wall and felt a mix of anger and disappointment for the society he was now part of. The 'new normal' was nothing that anyone could have anticipated. Here he was, an ethics professor who had just signed a contract to kill three people.

As Li and Mei made their way through the ornate marble lobby, the young lady who had directed them to the elevator caught their eyes and said "Happy hunting." Her bright red lips smiled and there was an almost maniacal look in her eyes. Li and Mei hurried out of the glass door, back in the bustling street. It was noon and the sun had risen. The heat mixed with the smog, adding to the discomfort that the Hus felt.

"I'll take a taxi back to school and finish up my work and then meet you at home. We have a lot to prepare for in the next 48 hours," Li said.

Mei nodded and kissed him fervently.

"We'll get through this," she whispered.

"I know," he said, grabbing her hand and squeezing it before he hailed another automated taxi to take him back to the university.

Before he got inside, Mei said sardonically, "I suppose that Contra has at least made catching a taxi easier."

"Right, because in an overpopulated world, that's my biggest concern," he said in the same tone.

As the taxi sped away, the giant glass and metal facade of the imposing Contra Center receded. Li hurtled down Beijing's busy roads towards a future that neither he nor Mei had ever anticipated.

5. THE PLAN

Beijing, China

When Contraception first introduced its logo, it was said that each triangle represented one of the three people a person had to kill while the inner triangle stood for the child one was allowed to have once fulfilling the requirements. The symbolism was not only explicitly explained to the public, but people were reminded of the policy every time the logo was flashed on the news, seen on a Contra building, displayed in marketing campaigns, and branded on all the white Dispo vehicles and uniforms.

▪ When Li finally arrived home, he found Mei sitting at the dining room table, fidgeting with her cup of green tea. In her other hand, she was holding a tablet and scrolling through it with her thumb.

Li set his bag down and walked over to her. He bent to kiss her and put his hand over her restless fingers to calm her nerves.

"What's up with you?"

"I downloaded the Contraception contract and it's absurd. I know they have to cover their bases, but I can't imagine these things happening to us. Listen: If we were to get a divorce, we have to divide up the kills, which will transfer over to our next marriage in addition to the kills of our new partners. Here's another good clause: If either spouse dies after the child is born, and the remaining parent remarries, that new couple will need to apply to have another child."

Li shook his head, "These are horrible to imagine."

"Or this: Although Contraception was designed for married couples, allowing both spouses to legally kill one of their targets, individuals are also allowed to apply. However, Contra highly recommends not doing so as killing your targets can have a physical and emotional toll on you, and a spouse is much more likely to make the situation bearable."

"Well, at least they're concerned about our well-being, though in a grotesque and deranged sort of way," Li said drily.

"I can't look at this anymore," Mei said, looking up at him. "Let's just focus on what we need to do."

He placed his hand on her slim shoulder and said: "So, shall we see whose life is now in our hands?"

He sat in the chair across from her, took the three glass tablets out from his jacket pocket and laid them on the table. Two remained blank, but one now had a picture and bio displayed on it. Li pushed the two blank tablets to the side and focused his attention on the holographic face that now stared back at him. The tablet showed the digital picture of a middle-aged woman named Sophie Xu, who worked as an elementary schoolteacher.

Li shook his head in disbelief. "Well, this is a great start. We've got to kill a teacher."

Mei glanced at her husband and said, "No one said it would be easy, but it can be done, we will get it done. If this is who we have to start with, then so be it."

Li nodded, thinking that in 48 hours, someone else could be having this same conversation while holding a glass tablet with his name and bio on it. He went to the fridge and opened a beer, taking a long sip from the brown bottle.

"In the meantime," he said, "We've got to get this apartment ready, and I need to make sure that work is taken care of before summer vacation starts."

They spent the rest of the evening detailing the fortifications that needed to be made to their apartment. Metal sheeting over the windows in case of a sniper attack, reinforced doors, an iris-scanner built into the front door, and above all, they needed to arm themselves.

These days, most attacks took place in public, as people, just like what the Hus were doing, were in defense mode, which started with securing the home. In most cases, it was near impossible to kill someone once they had entered their reinforced fortress of a home, especially in China, where acquiring weapons was a greater challenge. Li thought about what the best defense could be, and finally decided a gun would be the best choice – quick, efficient and easy to carry; however, it was hard to obtain one.

The next morning, he woke up and as usual, biked to work, reveling in the feeling of security that the next 24 hours provided him. The worst part, he thought, would be not knowing if his name had been given out or not. Sometimes, it took months before a person's bio was selected from the database, while others had been chosen as soon as the 48 hours were up.

Li had called and made an appointment with someone in the psychology department, Professor Wang, an old friend who had grown up with him. Wang had served in the People's Liberation Army before choosing to teach at Peking University.

After entering the psychology department on that early and cool morning, Li headed straight to Wang's office. He knocked and opened the door, to be greeted by a tall man of around forty, with a rosy face, wearing thin black-framed glasses and a red sweater with the sleeves rolled up.

"Li, so wonderful of you to drop by! How are things?" Wang asked as he ushered Li into his office.

Li took a seat, choosing his words with care, "Good, but I'm afraid I need to get straight to business as time is of the essence. Mei and I applied at Contra yesterday to have a baby, which explains why I'm here."

"I'm not sure if congratulations are appropriate for such an occasion. Personally, I couldn't do it," replied Wang. He was meticulous in his approach to decision making, and had devoted the past year trying to establish an equation that showed that Contra was not worth the risks or moral sacrifice.

Li looked around the office, taking in the chalkboards filled with words such as "values," "integrity," and "mankind" crammed in between mathematical equations.

His reply was somber. "It was quite an experience. Can you believe they give you only 48 hours before someone can potentially end your life?"

"It's an extraordinary system that they've established, and to think that it works. Whatever happened to revolution or the defense of our society?" said Wang, shaking his head in disbelief. "So, what can I do for you, my friend? Need me to take care of someone on your list?" he said darkly.

Li relaxed. "No, not quite. I'm sure you'd make an excellent hitman. I need protection, and you know exactly what I'm talking about."

Wang nodded. This was not the first time he had used his connections in the army to get things not available to the public.

"Anything in particular you're looking for?" he asked.

Li shook his head, "Something portable and light. Anything more will be wonderful."

Wang stood up and walked around his desk.

"I'll have something for you by tomorrow, and I'll go to your place, wouldn't want you risking it out here after your 24-hour cushion expires."

Li heaved a sigh of relief. He knew he could count on Wang.

"I owe you."

"Yes, you do," said Wang, "You think Chinese military weaponry is cheap?" They both laughed.

"Until tomorrow then."

The two men shook hands and Li stood up and walked out of the office. He felt relieved to have the business of the weapon taken care of. The next step would be even more of a challenge.

As Li walked down the hallway, he thought of what he would say to the dean. He walked into the office and was met by a young, cute secretary.

"Mr. Hu, how are you today?"

"Fine, thank you," he said. "I was hoping to chat with Dean Fu if he's in at the moment."

The secretary nodded and led him into the dean's office.

"Li, how are you these days?" said Dean Fu, standing up as Li entered. "Still leading the good fight against oppression and evil?" he chuckled.

Li smiled as he sat down, "Dean, for some time, I've been contemplating having a child. Yesterday, Mei and I finally went ahead with it. At Contra, my name was submitted along with our application. I know that I usually teach summer classes, and although I find them stimulating, for the safety of my life and the school, I would like to take a break this summer to get my affairs in order."

Li knew the dean respected a direct approach in communication but still wasn't sure what to expect in response.

The dean nodded. "Li, you are one of our best teachers, albeit at times you cross the line of what may or may not be deemed sensitive by the Party. I won't ask you any questions about your business, and I'll let you have the summer off. I expect you to finish the rest of your classes before summer vacation starts and I absolutely expect you back here for the start of the fall semester. Do I make myself clear?"

"Yes sir," replied Li. "Thank you again, you have my word."

The two men shook hands with an air of admiration and understanding between them. As Li left the room, he glanced down at his band. Time was ticking by since he had left Contra. Of his 48-hour shield, less than 24 hours remained.

Li called Mei before he stepped into his classroom. At this time, she was usually at home, drafting blueprints, designing sketches for organizations looking for a more modern touch. Mei preferred to work for herself, not having the temperament or patience to deal with the rigmarole of an office setting. She had a small office in their apartment where she sketched and drew designs for architects, engineers, or anyone else requiring her skills.

She picked up the phone immediately. "So, how'd things go?" she asked.

"Smoothly, and on your end?" Mei glanced up from the glass template she had been drawing on and looked towards the front door. The serviceman was tightening the last screw and he waved at her to signal the completion of his work. "The iris scanner has been installed, and a reinforced door put in. Our home will be about as safe as it can be."

Li felt better. Nothing could be as reassuring for his sense of safety as twelve inches of reinforced steel separating him and a potential attacker.

"I'll be home soon. We've got to get started on how to approach our list."

"See you soon. Love you," said Mei.

"I love you too," said Li. He double-tapped his band to end the call and stepped into the auditorium for his lecture on humanity in the modern world. Once he set down his satchel and folded his jacket over the desk, he took out a piece of chalk and wrote "Motives" on the board.

He looked at his class and asked, "Why do people do the things they do? What motivates them? Today, we'll once again use Contraception as a framework for these questions. So, let's start with the most basic, why does Contraception work? What motivates people to have a baby so much that they're willing to kill three people to do it?"

"This isn't a very academic answer," said one student, "But maybe some people just want a baby. Perhaps they've always dreamed of being a mother and a father."

"Sure, that's a reason. Any others?"

"Maybe it's just who we are."

"Can you expand on that?" said Li, addressing the young man who had spoken.

"Biologically, survival has always meant breeding. Humans do not differ from animals in that respect. So, despite the challenges or today's 'requirements' to have a baby, people can't fight their biology. Despite every logical thing telling them it's risky and morally wrong, they still do the same thing that animals in nature do."

"That's a strong motivator for sure. One might even argue that many of our choices are based on unconscious motivators; things that drive us to do things without us directly understanding the reason. Our biology would be a good example of that."

"Let's see where you all stand. If you believe you will apply to Contraception in the next ten years, raise your hands."

About two-thirds of the class raised their hand, including Li.

One student asked, "So you'd apply too?"

"Well, as a matter of fact, I already have."

Some students applauded while others whispered with their neighbors.

"But Professor Li," said a Chinese student, "Weren't you part of an organization that argued against Contraception 10 years ago or something?"

"I was," he said. "But things change."

"What changed?" another student asked.

Li sat on his desk and looked around his classroom. "Life changed. It sounds like a silly answer, but it's true. I met a girl, we built a life together, and we got married. Having a child was something I've always wanted to do. I wanted to share my knowledge of the world with someone I brought into this world. I don't know, maybe it goes back to biology. I understand the logic, especially that against having a child. I risk my life; I have to kill people, and let's face it, babies are expensive."

There was an uproar and one student yelled, "So, you're going to murder innocent people?"

Li had asked himself the same question and hadn't arrived at a solid enough reason to justify it. So, he said, "That's the law, and that's how society works these days. We exchange money for food, we date before we marry, and now, we kill three people before we have a baby."

"Aren't you worried about dying?"

"Yes, very much so." Li remained calm while continuing to answer the question. "But again, that's one more risk I take, among a thousand other risks present in my everyday life. I could be killed through Contraception, but I could very well be killed right here by one of you. Is it likely? Probably not. But it could happen."

He stood up from the desk and faced his class. "Today is the last day of class, and as soon as the last person is out of that door, your grades will be uploaded to the mainframe where you'll be able to see how much you actually learned or just memorized from this semester. Anyway, I wish you all a fun and educational summer, and I'll see you back here in the fall!"

"Maybe!" shouted a student from the back.

Li smiled and said, "Not funny!"

The students stood up and some of them approached Li, thanking him for the semester. He wiped away the writing on the board although the word 'Motives' remained imprinted on his mind. He took another look at the empty classroom and then headed for the door. Like his students, Li was also free for the summer, although that was not a word he would use to describe his present situation.

As he left the university, he felt a sense of readiness for life. He was nervous for what was yet to come, but also felt prepared. The choices that he had set in motion 24 hours ago seemed so much more significant than any he had made in the twenty-nine years of his life. Going to college, marrying Mei, buying an apartment together, everything seemed to fall in place now, including murdering three people to have a baby. It was too late not to be on board.

When Li arrived home, Mei opened the door, which was heavier than the previous one. He stood at the open door, admiring the craftsmanship, touching it from top to bottom.

"It's solid," said Mei, smiling. She motioned for him to approach the front of the door and helped him register his retina. Afterwards, he put his satchel down and plopped onto the gray couch in the center of the room, Mei joined him, and he placed an arm around her.

"We've got to get started soon. That woman, the teacher, what was her name again?" he asked.

Without looking at him, Mei said, "Sophie Xu, also in Beijing."

"Right. Professor Wang is coming over tomorrow with some equipment that I've asked him for. We can discuss strategy then. Tonight is my last night as an unmarked man. So what should we do?"

"Let's go out. We should take advantage of the time we have before…" she paused and before she could finish, Li interjected.

"My thoughts exactly," he said, leaning in to kiss her as she smiled.

As night fell on Beijing, the bleeding sun sank behind the horizon and the moon rose high in the sky, illuminating the sprawling city below. The Hus could be seen leaving their building and heading off into the cool night to enjoy one last night of freedom. The city came alive at night, as street noodle vendors turned on the red lanterns attached to their carts and made their way to their nightly posts. Neon signs lit up the street as the night began to divide into two distinct groups.

Half the night belonged to those reveling in the freedom of not being a target uploaded to a glass tablet in an applicant's pocket. There was no fear of death, nor the apprehension that at any moment everything they believed in and loved could end.

The other half of the night belonged to those out for a purpose. For those with three glass tablets, the night symbolized an opportunity to be one step closer to the goal of bringing life into this world. Even as the first group enjoyed merrymaking and peace of mind, gunshots and screams could be heard and palpable signs of fear could be noticed throughout the once great city of Beijing.

For the Hus, tonight was a chance to enjoy normalcy one last time for the unforeseeable future. Li and Mei weren't sure how things would play out, but they were committed to having this baby or die trying. Once many people used to say, "I would die for my kid" but now, the question that each person had to ask themselves was, "Would I die to have a kid?"

The next evening, Li sat at home, reliving the night he had spent with Mei the day before. They had gone out for street food and drinks, talking about love and laughing about incidents from their past.

Today, conversely, had a restlessness to it that hadn't seemed to be there yesterday. Li was in the living room, twirling a pen between his fingers as the faint noise of a TV program played in the background. He was expecting a visit from his friend Professor Wang, which had weighed on his mind all day. Getting weapons from the military was challenging enough, let alone the consequences that would arise if Wang was caught distributing them to non-military personnel.

His reverie was broken by a quiet knock on the door. Li swiped the air with his wrist, and the TV turned off as he headed to the door. He tapped his glass band to the door, and the sound of bolts sliding could be heard as he pulled the door open.

"Some heavy-duty stuff you've got here my friend!" Professor Wang stood outside the door, wearing a navy-blue suit and carry a bulky looking briefcase, the kind one might see in the possession of a demolition expert.

"Please come in," Li ushered him in. Professor Wang entered the apartment and placed the heavy case on the coffee table. He used both his hands to lift it. Then he swiped his wrist across the front of the case, opened it and flipped it around with a smile so that Li could see the contents.

It was an amazing sight. Wang pressed a button and the first layer popped open to reveal a second layer underneath. The case contained a variety of weapons and instruments, some of which Li had never seen before.

"You've got a friend, I've got a friend, everyone's got a friend. It just so happens that my friends can get their hands on some of the best military weaponry that China, or the world, has ever seen."

Wang grabbed a small black gun, a Sig Sauer 15200, from the top shelf, cocked it back revealing it was empty, and put it down in front of Li.

"This, my friend, is like your bread and butter of guns. Tech has changed, but this baby has pretty much stayed the same, minus some small enhancements. It's classic, reliable, and always there when you need it." He continued as Li looked on with curiosity, "This beauty has gone through significant design changes, with this one here being from 2054. One of my favorite features is its precision-sensors that adjust the firing pin's strength depending on the type of bullet it's firing."

He gestured towards the rest of the top shelf, "Included is a variety of different bullet types to suit a variety of needs. You've got your standard hollow point, and poison-tipped, electrifying, paralyzer, and shrapnel blast, in case you've got several fellas after you."

Li picked up the gun carefully. "But how can a paralyzer bullet not kill someone compared to a hollow point shot from the same gun?"

Wang nodded as if he had been expecting this question.

"The built-in sensors that identify the bullet in the chamber and then adjusts the recoil and force with which that bullet is shot. For example, a stun bullet will be shot at a slower velocity, while an electrifying bullet will be discharged at a faster speed, but with a lower amount of pressure to not damage the electrical components inside the bullet. Tech, it's a beautiful thing."

Li put the gun back into the foam cutout of the top shelf and fixed his attention on the gadgets below.

He picked up a wiry, thin piece of metal that weighed almost nothing, and had the flexibility of a piece of rope. In total length, it was about 40 centimeters.

Professor Wang watched Li play with the piece of metal and said, "Besides prototype 501, this doesn't have an official name yet. But don't be fooled, this thing is deadly. Once programed to your fingerprint, you double-tap it and throw it at the nearest attacker or object. Once this little guy gets hold of something, it will cut through whatever is around until both sides touch again. Let me show you."

Wang took it out of Li's hand and walked over to the kitchen to grab a banana from the fruit bowl. He held the banana in one hand, while with the other, double tapped the metallic string and whipped it around the banana. The string-like material began to tighten and in a matter of seconds, sliced the banana as both its sides came together as one. Li double-tapped the rope again and it became limp. He put it back into the box.

"Useful for more 'intimate' contact. Believe me, it can cut through anything."

"So, this is where all the taxpayers' dollars are going, eh?" commented Li.

"What do you want? A new road? Or something that might save your life?" Wang challenged him. "This last one is my favorite," he continued.

This time, he picked up a series of different sized blades. Li inspected them and said: "Knives, what's so special about these?"

Wang looked at him. "For years, inaccurate knife throwing has been a waste of time, until now. These knives have been programed to seek out the human heart once thrown. I'm not exactly sure how it works, something about identifying the heartbeat of someone. Throw this thing like a regular knife and it will self-direct towards the heart of your intended target. Everything else in here is basic stuff, some small flash-bangs, and lock incinerators in case you need to break in. I know what lies ahead of you, and I wish I could do more."

Li closed the lid of the arsenal before him and extended his hand to Professor Wang.

The two men shook hands as Li said with emotion, "You've done more than enough for me over the years, and I can't thank you enough for this."

Wang looked at him. He looked grave as he said quietly, "I hope this is enough to do what you need to do. Now, it's all up to you."

6. SOPHIE XU

Beijing, China

According to data from Contra Centers, 75% of couples apply in the husband's name, which means the majority of the targets are male. As a result, the world population is now in a skewed 65-35 female-to-male ratio.

■ At 4:00 on a Tuesday morning, Li woke up, got out of bed, and laced up his shoes. Mei had pleaded with him not to go for a run but staying inside all day was driving him crazy.

He made his way into the living room and stretched in front of the big glass window overlooking the city. The early morning seemed to hold with it a silence that during these times was welcome amid both the internal and external chaos in Li's life. He looked into the bedroom before he left and whispered "I love you" to a sleeping Mei, then quietly unbolted their front door and made his way into the early dawn of Beijing.

Despite his better judgment telling him to keep his senses on full alert, he inserted a pair of small wireless earphones into his ears and tapped his glass band until he found an appropriate song for his early morning run. On the streets, he could see the flashing red lights of a Dispo unit turning around the corner.

Li took a deep breath and started his run, moving through the dark streets of a city he no longer identified with. While growing up here as a child, Beijing used to be so full of life. It felt warm, welcoming, and preserved the traditional aspects of what made it so great. However, over time, modern architecture, the need to develop, and globalization had all pushed Beijing towards something he no longer recognized. The city felt cold, no longer a place he was proud to call home.

As he felt his feet connecting with the hard pavement beneath, Li's heartbeat rose and a warmth spread through his whole body. Running through the dark city, he passed dead bodies and the occasional prostitute, still standing on the corner, hoping for one last client before the sun rose.

Li thought of the fact that someone might be plotting his death at this very moment. The thought pushed him to run faster. His long legs propelled him past buildings he remembered seeing as a kid. These days, many buildings had been fortified to ensure a "safe" environment, which had resulted in a less than pleasing esthetics on the outside.

Li could see the sun creep over the horizon. He continued to run, this time thinking of what Mei would say if she found out he had left the security of their home.

He heard a scream from an alleyway but knew better than to try to intervene. He continued running, trying to push past the part of him that told him he should help those in need. Sweat soaked the white undershirt he wore beneath his black hoodie. He looked at his band; it was 5:30.

The visible upper half of the sun made him realize with a sinking feeling that daylight was not an ideal time for him to be out in case someone wanted to finish him off early.

Still, Li paused for a moment along a bridge to look at the traffic that made its way underneath him. It was times like this that made it difficult to decide whether Contraception was a wrong choice. People were dying, which most would argue was a bad thing, but on the other hand, traffic was cut down, which resulted in less pollution. People were no longer fighting as the distribution of resources had once again leveled out, and the financial resources of the government were no longer being squandered on trying to create an equal standard of living, but were allocated towards advancements in technology, the improvement of educational systems, and increasing the efficiency of transportation systems instead of struggling to keep up with the demand.

He shook his head sorrowfully. No matter how he justified it, nothing was equal to a human life, and no one had the right to end one.

Li flicked his wrist to change the song, stretched his legs one last time, and then made his way through the early dawn back home. As he approached his front door, he paused, hoping that Mei was still sleeping. He scanned his eyes and the large door opened, and he smelled breakfast. This was not good.

"Smells good in here," he said, testing the waters before plunging into an explanation.

"Did you have a good run? I'm happy to see that the father of our unborn child wasn't murdered this morning."

Li smiled as he grabbed her by her hips from behind and spun her around to kiss her. After that, he looked into her big brown eyes and said, "Nothing bad will happen to me, expect maybe if I eat this breakfast. What are you cooking?"

"Eggs Benedict, although I may have fucked up the hollandaise sauce," she said with a frown. They both sat down at the kitchen table to discuss the day's plans.

As Li cut into one of his eggs on his English muffin, he said, "So, when do we get Sophie Xu, the teacher?"

"My idea would be before or after school," said Mei, as she took a sip of her coffee. "Any other time she's going to be locked up in that school or her apartment. Honestly, I think early morning; night time could be a challenge."

"Tomorrow morning, we need to do recon and get some questions answered, like what time does school start? And do we get her at her apartment, or during her commute?"

"I'll do it," said Mei. "A woman lurking near a school looks less suspicious." She had a point.

Li finished his breakfast, got up from the table and walked over to the big glass tablet on the wall. From his pocket, he took out the smaller tablet that held the identity of Sophie Xu and touched the larger one with it. Immediately, her profile appeared, along with the name of the school where she worked.

"Isn't this the weirdest conversation we've ever had?" Li said.

Mei, still at the kitchen table, shrugged. "Do what we need to do to get where we want to go."

The next day, wearing a pair of dark sunglasses, her hair in a ponytail, and coffee in hand, Mei made her way down the street of the school where Sophie Xu worked. She found a small bench within viewing distance of the school's gates and sat down. She took out the glass tablet and looked at Sophie's picture once more before putting it back in her purse. The fact that she was here to gain information on someone so she could end that person's life didn't seem to bother her so much now that she had committed to the idea.

Mei had always been a realist, ready to do what was necessary to further her own goals or aspirations. Still, the idea of killing someone had taken her some time to process.

As the street sprang to life, Mei focused on the section leading up to the school. And then she saw her.

Coming around the corner was a middle-aged woman whose black hair fell to her shoulders. Sophie Xu was wearing a floral dress and red shoes and carried a bright red leather purse.

Mei noted the street Sophie walked down and noticed that she clicked her band on a panel outside the gate to be let in. The gate, like all schools in China, had a security guard outside. Instead of the baton they used to carry years ago, they were now strapped with Daewoo Telecom K7 submachine guns, South Korea's contribution to child safety in China.

As Sophie went in through the gates and Mei watched the floral print dress flow out of sight behind the high hedges in the school compound, she knew she was ready. Her child was more important than whatever Sophie was or would ever become. Finishing her coffee, Mei tossed the paper cup into the garbage can, which immediately compressed it into the size of a coin. Then she made her way home to assess what she had observed.

In the apartment, she found Li sprawled on the couch, staring at the large glass screen on the wall and moving his wrist as he read through the news.

"I saw her; it's going to be easy," she announced triumphantly.

Li flicked his wrist and the screen went blank as he focused on his wife.

Mei walked over to the glass tablet on the wall, which displayed a smiling picture of Sophie Xu. She placed her band over the screen, and the street and gate of the school appeared. Using her fingertips, she traced a red line from the direction she remembered Sophie approaching the school.

"I walked past where she came, and it's a quiet street. I think if we get her on the way to school, it will be quick. There wasn't a lot of foot traffic. Some cars and buses, but technically, we're allowed to kill her, we have nothing to be afraid of."

Li looked at Mei and admired her determination. For months, it had been she who had been pushing to have a child. But now, it was he who was going to embrace the necessary steps.

"Tomorrow's Friday, and I'd rather not wait until the weekend, let's do it tomorrow. We'll use the gun, with a silencer. As I pass her, I'll shoot her, ID her, and be on my way," he said.

"There's no way I'm letting you do this alone," Mei responded immediately. "We're doing this together. You should have seen the dress she was wearing today; she should be killed just for that."

In the early hours of Friday, Li and Mei Hu both opened their eyes simultaneously as their alarm signaled it was time to wake up. The sun had not yet risen and out on the street there were just a handful of people. Men in shabby clothes delivered newspapers, bakers arrived at their shops to prep for the masses, and somewhere out there, Sophie Xu was getting ready to start her day teaching children.

With a wave of her hand, Mei turned off the alarm and rolled over onto Li. Nuzzling his neck, she asked, "Are you ready?"

"Let's get it over with," Li mumbled.

With minimal effort, he swung his arm over to the bedside table and his glass band automatically fit itself around his wrist. As the Hus dressed in all black, Li moved his eyes towards the kitchen wall and saw Sophie's animated face smiling back at him. Today would be the last time that she'd do that, he thought grimly.

From underneath the coffee table, he grabbed the briefcase Wang had given him and opened it with his wrist. He put a silencer on the Sig Sauer and paused before loading the clip. "What kind of bullet should we use? Poison?" he yelled out to Mei, who was still in the bedroom.

"As much as I'd like to poison her, we're going to be in close contact; there's no need for poison," she yelled back. "Either hollow tip, or electric shock to avoid blood."

Li looked back into the briefcase, wavering between the blue electric shock bullets and the bronze-plated hollow tips. He loaded the clip with alternating bullets of each kind as a precautionary measure and tucked the gun into his jacket pocket.

Mei came out of the bedroom. She was wearing her hair piled up on the top of her head, black studded earrings and gym clothes. She had a black track jacket and black yoga pants with a pair of black Nike running shoes. Li looked her up and down.

"You going to the gym?" he asked, trying to make light of the tense situation.

"People run, it will look less suspicious," she remarked.

Li stood up from behind the coffee table where he had been partially hidden from view. Mei saw he was wearing a similar outfit, black running pants, a black jacket, and black running shoes.

"Hypocrite," she said laughing

"Great minds think alike!" he remarked.

"Ok, let me have the gun," said Mei.

Confused, Li looked at her.

"You? Give you the gun?"

"Yes, I'm going to kill her."

Li looked puzzled. "And why do you get to kill her and not me?"

"Well, I did the recon, didn't I?"

"You wouldn't let me out of the house!"

"We'll flip a coin, the only fair way to decide."

"Are you serious?"

"You have a better alternative? Ready?"

Li nodded. From his pocket, he withdrew a coin he carried for good luck and said, "Call it in the air," as he flipped it with his thumb. The coin hurtled up and Mei said, "Heads." When it landed back in Li's palm, he turned it over to his wrist to reveal tails.

"Looks like the gun is mine, and I'll be the one pulling the trigger," he said as he patted his jacket pocket.

Although making light of the situation, Li felt it was his responsibility to kill Sophie Xu. Not only as the man, he felt it was something he *had* to do. Taking responsibility for his actions was something he not only theoretically believed in, but also worked to put into practice. For Li, it wouldn't be easy to kill someone, but that was the price for the choice he had made.

As the Hus waited outside their apartment for the elevator, Li, without looking at Mei, said, "I've only seen bodies, I've never actually seen someone die before. Do I just shoot her and run away?"

"That's pretty much the plan. You shoot, and I'll ID her," said Mei, touching her left pocket to reassure herself that she had the glass tablet that held the fate of Sophie Xu.

The elevator door chimed, and the Hus entered. A few floors later, it stopped for an old man with a cane and worn-out brown glasses that hung low on his nose. He was wearing a dark, blue-collared shirt and an old traditional Mao hat.

He nodded and in a low voice said, "Morning Li, Mei."

"Lao Shu, where are you off to so early in the morning?"

He smiled. "Everyone knows Mr. Zhao's has the best baozi (Chinese steamed buns stuffed with meat or vegetables), but you've got to get them before they sell out. And yourselves?"

"Um, you know, just an early morning jog."

Lao Shu casually said, "*shēng mìng zài yú yùn dòng,*"[3] and made his way to the back of the elevator.

---

[3] Life is motion; Physical effort is vital for our bodies to function

Mei gave Li a quick look before turning her face away. As the elevator stopped at each floor, the silence inside was deafening. Li could hear his heart beating while he noticed Mei was carefully releasing each breath before inhaling again. Lao Shu remained quiet in the back. Finally, after what seemed like an eternity, the elevator reached the ground floor.

The door opened, and as the Hus had one foot out the door, Lao Shu said softly, "Make sure it's worth it. Taking a life is never easy."

Li stopped dead in his tracks and looked back at Lao Shu. He couldn't find anything to say. He bit his lips and followed Mei, who grabbed his hand and pulled him forward.

They made their way out onto the street; the traffic wasn't too busy. Mei looked down at her band; they had one hour before school started.

"Let's go," she said.

Li patted his left breast pocket again to make sure the gun was secure as they headed towards the school. Jogging in silence they weaved in and out of Beijing's streets. Steam came up from the sewer and cooks in white aprons smoked cigarettes in the back-entrance alleys. The Hus continued to jog as the city woke up. The automated silver taxis flew by, gliding in and out of the lanes. Robots crashed far less often than humans. They also murdered hundred percent fewer humans.

As their feet hit the pavement, the Hus both pictured Sophie Xu in her floral dress and bright red shoes. As their feet flew, they were literally running towards the first of many moments that were about to change their lives forever. The look in their eyes was one of determination.

The buildings and trees seemed to fly by, and they ran towards the school where Sophie would soon be approaching. They made their way to a corner and Mei touched Li on the shoulder.

"Here," she said. She looked across the street and saw the bench she had sat on the day before. The sun had risen, bouncing off the shiny metallic walls and glass that now covered the city like a wave of locusts.

"She'll be coming from that street soon," Mei continued, pointing with her finger. "I think our best opportunity will be if we come out from the alley and cross paths that way."

Li looked to where she was pointing. A dark alley untouched by the sunlight cut the street from which Sophie Xu would soon come down. They walked into the alley, their black clothes blending in with the shadows created by the towering buildings on both sides. Li reached into his jacket and took out the gun. He was sweating, not from the morning heat but from the anxiety that ran through his body.

He took a deep breath. His back was pressed against the brick wall as the world around him grew silent, and the only thing he could hear was the beating of his own heart. His hand gripped the cool metal of the gun.

Mei peeked around the corner and from a distance, saw her – Sophie Xu.

This morning, Sophie was wearing a green jacket over another dress. This one had pineapples on it. Her green heels clicked on the sidewalk.

Mei had a look of disgust on her face as she turned her head and faced Li.

"Let me kill her," she pleaded.

Li shook his head, as if to imply no, but also to serve as a reminder to himself that this was the real world and he needed to snap out of it.

"You've got about 20 seconds before she's here," said Mei. "You can do this; you *have* to do this."

Li steadied his grip on the gun and looked down at his band. The seconds seemed to click by for what felt like an eternity. Then he heard the sound of the green heels on the pavement. He knew she was close.

Li waited until the clicks grew louder and he saw a shadow appear at the opening of the alleyway. He took a step onto the sidewalk and saw Sophie Xu, his first target. They made eye contact, both shocked at the suddenness of the moment.

Then Sophie, with her overdone eyes, looked disbelievingly at the gun Li was holding in his hand. She screamed and Li panicked. He placed his hand over her mouth and with the other hand, shoved her into the alley where Mei pinned her against the wall. As Li removed his hand from her mouth, Mei placed a finger on Sophie's lips to order her to be silent.

Sophie was shaking, the panic and terror of the situation was something she had never experienced before. Who were these people? They didn't look like they were after money. As her eyes darted back and forth between them, she finally understood. What else could two attractive, well-dressed young people want with her in this dark alley?

She stammered out, "M-my... my name came up, didn't it?" While she was talking, she furtively rotated her wrist three times, triggering the distress signal she had programed into her pass.

Sophie started to cry. Over a month had gone by since she and her husband had applied for a child at Contraception. She had taken the first week off, just as Li had done, spending all her time indoors.

However, with no attempts on her life, she was lulled into thinking her name may not yet have been chosen in the random selection and this, together with her passion for teaching, had made her venture out. As the weeks went on, she had worried less, thinking it could be a long time before someone, if anyone, came for her.

"Yes," replied Mei. "You understand, don't you? You would have done the same for your child."

Her tone was cold, not showing any sign of emotion or empathy for the woman pressed against the dirty alley wall. Sophie cried harder, causing her makeup to run down her face.

"My children need me!" she pleaded. The sight of this green-clad woman facing a moment she had never experienced before seemed to traumatize Li. He always felt bad for weak creatures. His heart was beating faster. In his mind he thought, it's her or your child. He double-tapped the side of the gun with his index finger to turn off the safety catch. The gun clicked, and Sophie cried louder, sobbing wildly as her life was about to be traded for another.

Li held the gun up towards Sophie's head, less than a foot away. Mei, in anticipation of his pulling the trigger, drew out the glass slate that held Sophie's name and profile. Li looked into Sophie's terrified eyes, seeing before him a whole lifetime she could never live. She too had dreams, someone at home who loved her, and a passion for doing something she enjoyed, which was rare to find in this world.

However, he also saw someone who would have been in the same situation as he was, given enough time. Her ambition to have a child must have been just as strong as his. Well, perhaps not equal, seeing as how she was the one up against the wall and he was the one holding a gun to her head.

Then the unexpected happened. A heavyset man in a suit charged into the alley like a bull on run, catching the Hus off guard. The man held a black stick in his hand that had bolts of electricity emitting from its end. Sophie's bodyguard had arrived. He moved forward like lightning and swung the baton down on Li's outstretched arm, causing him to drop the gun and fall to the ground in pain as the electric current coursed through his body. While Sophie stood frozen against the wall, Mei reached down and grabbed the gun, firing it at the burly man before he could deal another blow. The bullet flew and hit him in the neck, but instead of piercing the skin, it flattened out and turned red, emitting a paralyzing toxin. The man's eyes rolled into the back of his head and he turned stiff before dropping to the dirty alley ground.

Mei then positioned the gun back towards Sophie while darting a quick look at her husband. Li was conscious, but disoriented from the blow. He got to his feet unsteadily while Mei kept the gun on Sophie.

It was time to forget the revulsion over taking away someone's dreams, hopes and potential. She looked at Sophie dead in the eye and her finger on the trigger began to tauten, but before she could pull it, Li said, "Wait. I need to do this." His tone didn't brook any argument and in silence, Mei handed him the gun. Taking it with his other good hand, he pointed it at Sophie and almost immediately pulled the trigger.

The silencer muffled the shot as the bullet was expelled from the gun and flew straight into Sophie's forehead; however, no blood came out as the tip of the bullet lodged into her head. Mei looked at Li and then it happened. The tip turned a bluish color, and electric bolts could be seen running down Sophie's body.

Sophie convulsed violently as over a thousand volts shot through her nervous system. She fell over and continued to shake. Foam appeared at the sides of her mouth. Her eyes had rolled into the back of her head, leaving only the whites visible amidst the violent tossing of her head. After about twenty seconds, the convulsing stopped, the electric bolts disappeared, and Sophie Xu, former teacher, wife and daughter, lay dead in the alley.

Mei and Li both stared at the dead woman dressed in green. Li looked at the object protruding from her forehead and then back at the gun. He reached down and with a twist of his wrist, plucked out the bullet that had electrocuted her. There was a small hole in her skin where the bullet had hit her but other than that, there was no visible mark on Sophie Xu.

He put the bullet in his pocket, double-tapped the safety back on, and placed the gun once again inside his jacket pocket.

"So, what now? Do we leave her here?" he asked.

Mei was already busy with the glass tablet. With it in her left hand, she knelt down and placed one of Sophie's fingers onto the screen along with hers. After a second or two, the screen flashed "Authorized, deceased – Sophie Xu – Confirmed," and on the tablet, a large red X appeared over her face. One down, two to go, Mei thought.

Li couldn't look away from the body lying there, from which he had just taken its life. He had prevented Sophie Xu from achieving any of her goals ever, from being a mother, and from ever experiencing happiness again.

On the outside, he looked calm, but inside, he was battling both sides of every conversation he had had about right and wrong. Was this the right thing to do? Justifications came from the right and left, seeking to ease the guilt within him.

Mei stood up and said, "Ready?"

Such a funny question, he thought. Ready? Was he ready to live his life with the guilt of what he had just done? Was he ready to face the consequences of his actions? Often, people got vengeful when their loved one was murdered, and revenge murder, although not legally sanctioned like Contraception deaths, sometimes occurred. Would Sophie's husband come to find him, he thought.

Clutching his bruised forearm where the bodyguard had struck him, cold sweat collecting on his forehead, he replied, "Ready."

The couple stopped for a second to catch their breath and then approached the entrance to the alley where shadows met light. The sun had risen now, flooding the streets with light as the bustling cars and pedestrians made what had just happened seem like a normal occurrence.

Without looking back, the Hus jogged towards their apartment. Despite doubting the moral integrity of what they had done, they both knew it was worth it to have a child, and moving forward was the only way to deal with it.

At home, Li stripped off all his clothes and turned on the shower. He thought washing himself would somehow wash away the atrocity he had just committed. He stepped into the shower and felt the hot water hit his skin, wincing as it came in contact with the large purple bruise that had now formed on his arm. Mei had also finished taking off her clothes, and she slid the shower door open and put a hand on his back. She kissed his shoulder and stepped into the shower as well, closing the glass door behind her.

"What have we done?" asked Li, who had one hand against the shower wall as the hot water cascaded down over him. The image of Sophie, lying lifeless on the ground in some dark alley, refused to leave his mind. He had pulled the trigger. She was gone because of him.

"We did what had to be done. This is the world we live in, and we will move on," Mei said, in a tone that was softer than usual. Her pragmatic and logical viewpoint did not always fit the emotional needs of Li, who although logical, let feelings sometimes cloud his judgments. Her forehead was nestled on his back as the water continued to cascade down. The Hus were at the start of their journey, but not there yet.

After the shower, they got dressed, then lay together on their gray couch, with Mei's head in Li's lap.

"We have to do that two more times," whispered Li. "What if we don't go to the hospital? What if we have the child at home? Then we wouldn't have to kill anyone else."

Mei looked up in surprise. "You know what will happen if we do that," she said.

Illegal births were a workaround to Contraception. Only the hospitals and the officials at the Contra office could check whether a person's three kills had been confirmed, so having the baby at home was a loophole.

When Contraception was first implemented, the number of births declined, but the enrollments in primary schools and the number of people who purchased baby products online remained about the same. Curious about this, Contra officials did their due diligence and discovered that women were giving birth at home around the world, a situation that needed to be dealt with.

The pass system was therefore implemented to ensure that those who had home births would never be part of society. Without a pass, life was impossible.

Mei could tell that Li was thinking about it. She continued, "What kind of life would that be for our baby? No education, no healthcare, no opportunity to ever reach his potential in life. That's no life at all."

Contraception had thought about this problem many times. How to prevent illegal births? A meeting had taken place with every leader of the world to discuss possible solutions to deal with those who had found a way to circumnavigate the Contraception Initiative.

"Just kill the people who aren't tagged with a pass," suggested the Austrian President. The Chinese delegation had also agreed with the idea.

It was, however, Germany that had offered the now implemented idea. "We'll put restrictions on those without a pass. Restrictions so profound that the thought of death will be more appealing than allowing their child to live in a world it can never be part of. No education, no access to medicine, and restrictions on travel – the child will be an outcast until the day they die. Sure, they can live, but what kind of life would it be? We won't look like the bad guys because, as from the start, Contra will never get its hands dirty. The system was designed for society and society is the regulator."

Leaders from around the world nodded in agreement. And so, it came to be that each baby that legally came into this world after three confirmed kills was given a pass that allowed them to be members of society and enjoy the benefits that came along with that.

"Should we see who is next?" Mei asked.

"I suppose so," he said, swinging his legs off the couch to walk over to the table where the remaining two tablets were. One was still blank while the other had a new picture and profile.

Mei, who had followed him over to the table, read over his shoulder. "Chen Xin, a thirty-year-old police officer."

Mei sat down in one of the chairs and Li sighed, sweeping his hair back with one hand.

"So, we just killed an educator and now we have to kill someone who upholds the law," he said gloomily. "How are we expected to kill a trained police officer?"

"We'll figure it out, just like we did with Sophie," she said, reaching up to place her hand on his back.

"I know, I just…" Li's voice trailed off. "The thought of killing someone again isn't easy."

"We're doing this for us," she whispered as she stood up, hugged him and closed her eyes. The actions of the morning weighed on them both, but the determination within them outweighed the guilt.

7. BERLIN

Rome, Italy + Berlin, Germany

29.8% of Contraception applicants hire a hitman to kill at least one of their targets.

▪ Victor sat on his hotel room bed flipping a coin between his knuckles. His slick black hair matched the black V-neck t-shirt he was wearing. In front of him were two glass tablets, each containing the face and bio of two people whose fate was in his hands. Victor looked at them by turns, trying to come to a decision. For some reason, he couldn't seem to make up his mind. He got up and looked out of his window, taking in the evening scene of Rome.

The city lights illuminated the ancient city that had tried its best to avoid modernization. However, like most places in the world these days, it had succumbed to the implementation of technology and the forced habits that Contraception instilled in people. He saw barricaded windows, bodyguards following individuals on the street, and cameras almost everywhere.

Like everywhere else, for those who hadn't applied to Contraception, life was easygoing and happy. They walked the streets without the fear that someone was coming for them. For others, however, happiness meant having a child, and they hoped the fear and guilt of what was required would be worth it in the end. At least that's what Victor thought they believed. He never understood why someone would be so foolish as to risk their life for that of a child, especially an unborn one.

He thought of a couple who had risked everything to kill three people by battering their heads with baseball bats, and then their child was born with a cognitive brain disorder. The irony of it made him laugh.

From a young age, Victor had never felt he was part of society, staying detached, and when he grew older, through sheer luck, had found a job that required a man like him. He forced his mind to return to the objects in front of him; he wasn't in Rome for the sights, it was a stopping point between him and his next target.

Victor was a hitman. He had trained in the PLA as special ops from the time he was eighteen, and now, at twenty-eight, he was a lethal killing machine, thanks to the rigorous training and discipline that his commanders had instilled in him during those years.

People knew he was different from the time a boy at school had pushed him and he fell and broke his nose. Without making a noise, blood dripping from his face, Victor grabbed a stick and had beaten his attacker so badly that the boy was in hospital for months.

He felt nothing for humans, beyond that of perhaps fleeting gratitude for helping him get a paycheck after he had killed them. Money ensured his survival and bought him the luxuries he had grown accustomed to.

He reached for the gun on the bedside table, the same one he had used to kill Lisa, and disassembled it. He took each piece apart carefully and placed them on the bed. Then he took out a cloth and a cleaner from his travel case and wiped them thoroughly, knowing that if he took care of his equipment, it'd make sure the job was done without any hitch.

Again, he looked at the two glass panes. "Well, who's going to be first, guys? You, Mr. Hu, the college professor, or you, Pang Pang, the elusive hacker?"

Victor enjoyed a challenge. He reasoned that the professor could wait since his profile now indicated that he was a Contraception applicant. However, even before he applied to Contraception, Li had showed up on "the list" and now that he was in the Contra system, standard procedure would take over. By now, someone had his details and would be targeting him themselves. As Victor saw it, he would give someone else a chance to kill Li Hu before he took matters into his own hands. He picked up the glass tablet that held a mobile image of Pang Pang.

He read the profile: "Notorious hacker, dissident, spreads Western propaganda. Aged 26. Hometown: Shanghai. Last known location: Berlin, Germany."

Victor was excited about this one. Pang Pang was one of the best-known anti-China hackers in the world. Victor didn't consider himself a patriot but he had no sympathy for those who were stupid enough to fight against their own government, especially when that government was as strong as China and one of his best-paying, regular clients to boot. There was no cure for stupidity and he considered he was doing the world a service by fixing such stupid people.

He held the tablet in his hand, contemplating what would be the most satisfying way to end Pang Pang's life. He also thought about Berlin, a city he hadn't been to for some time. It would be nice to return to a country that valued order and efficiency. He set the tablet down and continued to clean his gun, whistling tonelessly under his breath. The mechanical procedure was something that soothed Victor as he had done this hundreds of times in the past.

Victor never contemplated the purpose of life. He found the whole thing to be rather mundane. The only thrill he got was from the hunt of his targets. The killing was the easy part; it was the thrill of the chase and the planning that went into it that was exhilarating for him.

As a hitman who killed people whose names were sent to him anonymously, he found business to be booming since Contraception came into being. Many people didn't have the fortitude to kill someone, yet still wanted to reap the benefits. Look at society these days, he thought, shaking his head contemptuously. So weak and yet as greedy as ever!

He checked his tablet again, which was displaying the face of a young, chubby Chinese man who was under Victor's control now. It was so simple to end one's life.

From time to time, Victor's personal tablet signaled that an incoming contract had been added to "the list," displaying the hologram of the target, a full profile, and who had posted it. However, in most cases, the sender remained anonymous. Most of his clients were Contraception applicants but didn't have the balls to do the killings themselves. Victor would accept the contract, and since the victim needed to be identified by an authorized party, he would send the location of the dead target to the client so that they could scan the dead body, and he would be on his way.

However, there was some uneasy similarity among some of his recent clients that Victor sensed but couldn't yet place and it bothered him. He had been paid almost double to take care of those names, compared to his regular assignments. Again, an anonymous sender, but one with deep pockets and power.

During his first kill for this client, after he had sent the location, to his surprise, he received a message to scan the victim with his glass tablet. Upon doing so, his glass tablet displayed the "Authorized" message with the logo of Beijing Police. Victor wasn't one to ask questions, however, his mind was in a whirl trying to figure out what was happening.

Only two parties had the authority to scan dead bodies without the police being alerted – either authorized applicants of Contraception who had been assigned the target or authorized law enforcement officers. With Victor's tablet given the identity of an officer of the law, he could scan the targets this client sent him without any untoward incident. He had killed at least 15 people for this anonymous sender, whom he simply called "Banks" in his mind due to the client's unquestionable wealth and power. He didn't question who Banks was, but knew it was someone with connections. If his tablet had been programed to assume a police officer's identity, he knew he was dealing with something very, very serious.

He thought about his recent victims for Banks – a nurse, half a dozen free speech activists, three professors, a few politicians, NGO workers, and a sanitation worker. The last one seemed to be out of place. He wondered what kind of person would want these people dead. He wasn't too concerned though. If the money kept coming, Victor would kill whoever was on "the list."

As the black metal gun finally shone from his meticulous cleaning, Victor moved his wrist and a map of Berlin appeared on the big glass tablet hanging on the wall in front of him.

He looked at the city and said, "Where are you, Pang Pang? Hiding behind a computer somewhere?" He flicked his hand, and the map zoomed in. Tomorrow he would set off for Germany and begin his hunt. Pang Pang, in his mind, was as good as dead.

The next day, wearing a black suit and dark sunglasses, Victor got off a private plane, carrying a small black duffle bag in his right hand. He looked around, spotted the black Mercedes that was waiting for him, and got into it. Without speaking, the driver took him straight to Hotel Adlon, and Victor checked in. Victor didn't risk his life killing people to live like them. He couldn't understand why people settled for less than what they actually wanted.

Entering the suite, he set down the bag, undid the zipper, and took out a pair of black leather gloves and a small cylindrical object, about the size of a prescription pill bottle, which he put into his jacket pocket. Then he left the room and made his way outside. After reaching the street, he went to Unter den Linden, one of the main streets of Berlin, and walked until he found what he was looking for, Metzgerei Müller, one of the city's most famous butcher shops.

Before entering, he put on the leather gloves and then pressed on the glass door to open it. He looked around. Ham, meats and fish lined the cold cases while loaves of bread and canned sauces were shelved on the walls behind him. A large fat man in a white apron stood with his back to him. As the bell rang upon Victor's entrance, the man turned around, displaying an apron covered in blood. He had a large round face with red cheeks and golden-brown hair. When he saw Victor, his face darkened and he clenched his massive hands convulsively.

Victor said in a calm, cheerful tone, "Hello Gregory, my old friend, it's been too long!"

The giant butcher locked eyes with Victor. There was both anger and fear in his face. He lunged towards the bloody cleaver on the counter, but Victor held up a finger in warning.

"No, no, no, not such a good idea, Gregory. Remember what happened last time? Today, on this beautiful afternoon, we can do this either the easy way or the hard way."

His hand reached into his breast pocket and removed a tablet, turning it to face the large man, with the screen displaying a value of 5,000 euros before setting it on the counter.

"I just need the location of someone in Berlin," he said.

Gregory was the man to see if someone needed to be found. The German's connections with the military and work done for the 'Ndrangheta, the Italian mafia, had made him, for lack of a better word, knowledgeable.

Victor looked at Gregory, "What do you say, big guy?"

"Fuck you!" came the shout in his German accent as Gregory picked up the cleaver and lifted the counter separating him from his customers in one fluid motion. He came out and stood in front of Victor. There was rage in his eyes as he caught Victor looking at his left hand – which had only four fingers now. Although these days he wasn't as active as he used to be, Gregory was still massive, standing over two meters tall and weighing at least 120 kg. His wide shoulders were still rippled with muscles.

"Ah, Gregory, still salty about last time? I will never understand why you always choose the hard way."

Before he could finish, Gregory had lunged at him, swinging the cleaver. Before the giant could reach him, Victor took out a black cylinder from his pocket and with a flick of his wrist, the object extended into about half the length of a pool cue. As the German's momentum flung him forward, Victor sidestepped him and struck the back of his left thigh with the metal rod. There was a sizzling sound and the German let out an agonized scream.

He looked down at his thigh as the smell of burned flesh filled the air. There was a rip in his trouser leg and an angry sear mark could be seen through the gaping hole. The German looked at the metal rod in Victor's hand in incomprehension.

"Do you like my new toy? Five hundred degrees of fun," Victor said.

A slower Gregory swung the blade again but Victor, like an acrobat, dodged it with ease. As he ducked under the horizontal slash Gregory made in the air, he swung the black rod at Gregory's stomach and once again there was the stench of burnt flesh and cotton. The German gasped as he fell on the floor with a thud. Victor stood astride over him, sliding his thumb against the black rod in a downwards motion, turning off the heat. This time he placed the rod on Gregory's neck.

"Now, you're going to tell me the location of a man named Pang Pang, a Chinese hacker living in Berlin. I need his whereabouts."

A couple approached the door and Victor, seeing them in the reflection from the glass countertop, flashed them an apologetic smile and in perfect German said, "Sorry we're closed."

They went away hurriedly and he turned back to Gregory, who was silent. Victor slid his thumb up the black rod. It grew hot and the skin on Gregory's neck turned dark red, blistered by the heat.

"You know, I've never turned this thing all the way up, but I'm told it gets pretty hot," he said conversationally.

The German made loud grunting sounds, trying to kick Victor. Victor took the rod out from under his chin and then slammed it down on Gregory's left knee. There was an audible crack. The German stopped flailing his legs. He looked at Victor in sheer hatred, struggling not to show his agony.

"Ja, I've heard of Pang," he gasped. "People say he's hiding out in Berlin Cathedral, Mitte Borough. That's all I know."

"Hard way, easy way – we always end up the same way, don't we? Anything else I should know?"

He winced and said, "His left arm has a tattoo, a microchip. It glows green, like electricity running through it."

"Keep the money and get yourself to a hospital, we don't want those burns to fester."

Victor slid his thumb down to turn off the heat, double-tapped the base, and the rod once again became the size of an innocuous pill box. Victor carefully put it in his pocket and looked down at

Gregory, who was clutching his throat. He smiled in satisfaction and walked out of the butcher's shop humming.

He knew the church Gregory had mentioned, a big neo-Renaissance monstrosity that loomed over the city as a testament to the days when religion had reigned supreme. Now, it housed an underground black market when it wasn't busy doling out communion to those who still clung to religion to find meaning in their lives.

Victor adjusted his jacket, repositioning it to make sure the gun holster was easily accessible. Inside the holster was an IMI Desert Eagle in matte black, one of his favorites. He hailed a cab and entered the coordinates of the church. As he watched the city fly by through the window, he felt disgust for all the people in the streets. No purpose, no ambition, no bigger picture; simple-minded people leading simple lives.

He noticed children laughing as they walked with their parents. Victor had never wanted children as he felt they served no purpose. Who had the patience to wait around to see what they might become one day? He felt indifferent to Contraception.

When its inception had been announced globally, Victor, along with billions of other people, had watched the scenario unfold. Most were shocked, stunned, and even angry that this was deemed the "best" solution out of countless others. Victor just nodded and accepted that the world was about to change.

As he sat in the robotically driven taxi, the only thing on his mind was death. Death, for most intents and purposes, was a means to an end. It had solved many of the world's problems caused by overpopulation, and for Victor, had provided him with a lifestyle he reveled in.

He had joined the PLA as a job for his skills but soon discovered that it had no prospects and certainly, no money. He was expected to follow orders all the time and risk his life for fat generals who were not only corrupt but incompetent as well. He had excelled at all his training and upon finishing, had disappeared from the grid with a lethal set of skills. Taxes, insurance, a family – these were things for ordinary people, and Victor was not ordinary.

He looked out the windshield and saw the shadow of the church before he saw the building itself. Standing mighty against a bright blue sky, adorned with large domes and high arches, the massive church on the corner had remained unchanged for hundreds of years. He paid with the glass tablet as he exited the cab.

Victor didn't wear one of the glass bands that had become so ubiquitous around the world. The removal of his ID pass was a necessity for training in special ops. When China was involved in top secret missions, the authorities couldn't afford to have soldiers flagged as operating under government orders. Chinese special ops were non-existent beings with no family, no baggage, and no connection to the outside world.

During the first week of training, all recruits were strapped to a metal chair and their hand was inserted into a clear tube. The army surgeon, or "The Operator," as he was called, began the process to remove the pass.

He pressed a button, and hundreds of robotic pincers, about the size of a needle each, shot out from the tube. With the recruits' hands locked in place, the needles methodically went into the wrist, injecting tiny amounts of titanium. The process took ten minutes as the titanium cooled around and within the bones in the wrist.

The result was a titanium bracelet that covered and insulated the installed pass. As both a durable metal and a weak conductor of electricity, titanium blocked the ability of a person's pass to be recognized or be detected by any scanner around the world.

Standing on the street, Victor involuntarily touched his left wrist, thinking of the sacrifices he had made to be where he was now. The operation had left no visible scars, but Victor could still feel the cold metal that was now a part of him.

For a moment, he stared at the big oak doors of the church that had big black bolts before walking up the stairs and entering. To an average person, the church looked like any other church with its rows of pews, paintings of saints and apostles on the ceiling, and candles lit at the far end, where a priest would later speak about forgiveness.

He walked down the red rug past the pews until a bald old priest with a white and purple cassock approached him. Victor held out his hand to shake the old man's and as he did so, he noticed a black raven tattoo on the old man's inner wrist.

He looked into the man's faded blue eyes and said, "Father, I'm here on business, if you would be so kind."

The old man let go of his hand and motioned towards the confession booth.

Victor entered, and once the door closed, a hologram appeared on the door in front of him, requesting authorization. He placed the glass tablet against the door, and a screen flashed, "Authorization approved."

The booth began to descend, and when it stopped, the door opened to what could only be described as the depths of hell. This was the Zeckenmarkt, a criminal flea market, the place where Europe's criminals and thieves gathered to trade, make deals, and often, find their targets. Men in suits intently scrutinized the stalls that lined the long hallway. Rooms, some with doors and some without, jutted out from the corridor. Victor adjusted his tie and made his way down the hallway. It was wider than usual, similar to a vegetable or fruit market, except that here, people were selling the latest in arms, criminal technology, drugs, women and skills.

Hookers, hitmen, and hackers – the triple H was something that the Zeckenmarkt was notorious for.

As Victor passed through the stalls hawking their goods, he saw rooms filled with a computer and cables running all over the walls. Usually, these rooms contained either a single person or a group of people; Victor had found the hackers.

Alongside them were women scantily dressed in glittering lingerie powered through electrical circuits to create moving images on them. These were the hookers. While Victor felt that a hitman's job was something that ought to be done by professionals, here, in this dirty bunker, the only hitmen he saw were thugs with no skill, just bulging biceps. People stared at him as he scanned each room, hoping to spot Pang Pang.

A woman with blue hair and wearing a garish sequined bra and thong approached him. "Hey there Mysterious, come explore me."

Victor paid her no attention. He made his way past grenades of all kinds, new types of bullets for an assortment of guns, customizable knives. You name it, the Zeckenmarkt had it all. Victor stopped. Loud shouts in Chinese were coming from a room ahead. He brushed past the people in the middle of the market until he came to a room with a door slightly ajar. Glancing inside, he noticed a shaven man sitting in a chair gesticulating. On his left arm, he had a tattoo, like the one mentioned by Gregory – a microchip that seemed to glow a neon green color.

A large Chinese man with dragon tattoos covering both arms stood near the door. He stared at Victor menacingly.

In Chinese, Victor said, "Hey brother, if you let me in there to do what I need to do, you won't die today."

"Fuck off," replied the big man, pulling out a gun from his back packet.

"Always the hard way," Victor said sorrowfully. While the man had been speaking, he had already whipped out his gun from his jacket pocket and fired two quick shots, hitting the man in the heart and head. As the shots rang out, the stalls started to close and giant metal barricades sprang up. Victor pushed the door open and swiftly moved inside. The eyes of all the men in the room were now on him.

He locked eyes with Pang Pang and said, "You can run, but you can't hide."

"The lights!" someone yelled. The room went dark, except for the dim light of a glass screen on the wall displaying random lines of code. The floor was strewn with beanbags and cushions. Victor could hear people scattering. With his gun still drawn, he moved across the floor in the darkness, carefully navigating his way through the mess of glass tablets and wires. Then a door opened at the back of the room and light flooded in.

Victor fired two quick shots. Someone ran out of the room. Victor lowered his gun and gave pursuit. He burst through the door and extending his gun out in front of him began running up the stairs where he saw his quarry vanishing. There was a gunshot from above but he continued his pursuit. He reached the landing of the stairway, once again finding himself in the main hall of the church.

He saw two men fleeing ahead and he ran after them, pushing past the priest. By now they were all on the street outside the church and as he sprinted after the two men, Victor took out a knife from his back pocket and in one fluid motion, tapped it twice with his finger and threw it at the quarry closest to him. The flying knife weaved in and out of other people and lamp posts to finally drive its sharp point right into the back of the man, hacking its way to his heart. The man fell as Victor ran past him. There was no need to confirm his death as there was no payment to be earned nor any penalty to pay for murder since technically Victor didn't exist.

"Pang Pang!" Victor shouted at his remaining quarry. He enjoyed a good pursuit, as it made things more exciting, pumping him full of adrenaline. He saw Pang Pang dash into an alley on the right. Victor did the same and saw Pang Pang had been stopped in his tracks by a fence. He was trying to scale it frantically when Victor pulled out his gun, loaded a paralyzing bullet into the cartridge, and fired it. Immediately Pang Pang's legs buckled and he fell writhing from the fence onto the filthy street.

Victor approached with the gun in his hand. Pang lay on the ground, clutching at his limp leg. The paralyzing bullet stuck out from his trouser leg. He was a young man, around twenty-six, with a shaved head. His tight black shirt had a clenched red fist on it.

"Power to the people, eh?" said Victor, motioning at the shirt with his gun.

"Who the fuck are you?" Pang snarled. Though he had never seen Victor in his life, yet he had a good idea why the man was there.

"My client has an issue with your hacking and political views that somehow seem to find their way online."

"I've never hacked any individual person, the only thing wrong with China is the government, for which I have gladly taken a stand."

"I don't get paid to ask questions or have an opinion. I do applaud your enthusiasm, though, for standing up for what you believe in, truly."

Victor meant what he said. He also knew that Pang knew he wasn't here for Contraception. Pang had been expecting to die sooner rather than later. Hacking a government's accounts and spreading political beliefs contrary to the official line was an offense punishable by death. For the past few years, Pang had been sleeping with one eye open at night, trusting few and making sacrifices for what he believed in. But Victor was the shadow he never saw coming.

"How can you do what you do?" he asked, no longer fearful of the thought of death. To him, it was inevitable, given the path he had chosen in life.

"Look, you've got a job, I've got a job, everyone's got a job to do. We do what is required of us. Think of me as the inevitable angel of death. I simply got here a little earlier than expected."

"Fuck you and fuck Chi-"

Before Pang could finish his words, Victor's hollow point had burrowed its way halfway through his head. Pang fell back into the alley where his blood mixed with the foul water that flowed from the neighborhood. Victor pulled out the tablet from his pocket and scanned Pang Pang, receiving the message: "Authorized. Deceased, Wei Pang Pang, kill confirmed."

Another notification popped up, showing that 1,000,000 yuan had been deposited into his account. Pang Pang's name disappeared from Victor's tablet.

Victor took out his sunglasses from his breast pocket and made his way out of the alley, back to the busy street. He knew the police would be here soon since Pang Pang wasn't a Contraception target and no one would scan his pass to authorize his death. He hailed a taxi, directing it to take him to his hotel. It was good to be back in Berlin, he thought. A city free from an oppressive government and free to express its individuality, which for Victor, was a nice change of pace.

Arriving at his hotel, he took out the tablet, with only one more name left in his itinerary – Li Hu. He knew Li's name had already been assigned to somebody at Contraception, who was doing his or her best to take him out. However, Victor was the backup. He served as the fail-safe, as most average people weren't equipped to take a life. Victor would get the job done.

Back to Beijing. He needed to check in on Li Hu and see if whoever had received his name from the Contra system had done what needed to be done. If not, Victor would step in and finish it. He felt calm despite the day's hectic work. He was built for this job.

He removed his suit jacket and placed the gun on the bed. Then he disassembled it again and began cleaning it in anticipation of the person who would be at the end of the barrel very soon.

8. THE STRATEGY

Beijing, China

*The number of guns sold around the world increased by 40%
during the first year Contraception came into effect.*

■ As Li settled into the routine that his life had now become, he
wondered if a child was worth it. The stress and anxiety of
continually looking over his shoulder was starting to take its toll on
him. For weeks, he had been cooped up in his apartment; thankfully
Mei had bought him a treadmill.

"It's too dangerous out there," she had said vehemently.

Li was on his eighth mile on the machine, but for him, it didn't
compare to the freedom that came from running outside in the early
morning. As his feet pounded away on the mechanical contraption,
his mind wandered.

From thinking of Sophie, these days, his mind was on Chen Xin,
the man they would have to kill next. Sweat dripped down Li's face
and proceeded to soak his blue shirt. Chen Xin was an officer with
Beijing Police who had been with the department for over five years.
He was a man of principles and had applied to Contraception with
his wife's consent three weeks ago.

"A fucking cop!" Li thought in frustration. "How am I going to
kill a fucking cop?"

The soles of his feet tingled from hitting the steel and plastic of the treadmill. Pavement was so much smoother.

For the past week, he and Mei had been discussing how to take out Chen Xin, who was one hundred and eighty-five centimeters, with the strength and agility of martial artist and trained to handle the city's worst. This would require more planning than an elementary teacher.

Mei was still in bed. There was something about the sunrise and the feeling of being productive while everyone else slept that appealed to Li. He continued to pound away on the treadmill, going over the possibilities of how to end Chen's life. He still wanted to use a toaster but doubted that Chen Xin was the type of man to take baths. He shook his head and beads of sweat fell to the floor.

The treadmill was next to the window, giving Li full view of the city. From up here, everything seemed normal, people walking, cars zooming by, dogs barking. Then the flashing red lights of Dispo caught his eye, which brought him back to the reality of the world. How should one kill a cop, he thought again.

In Li's mind, there were only two scenarios that would present the best opportunity. First, when Chen was off work and out of the house. Maybe he was careless and would decide to go to the store or the gym. Second, an accident. Everyone knew accidents involving cops happened frequently; life could be unpredictable.

Li reckoned that because cops had to be outside, either patrolling or investigating, killing Chen Xin while he was on duty and outside the station was an alternative. The mechanics and logistics of how it could happen still eluded Li as he kept running, placing one foot in front of the other. He knew that the sooner it happened, the less time he would have to spend living in constant unease and tension.

When the hologram in front of him displayed ten miles, Li waved his hand, and the treadmill slowly came to a halt. He hopped off and grabbed a nearby towel to wipe his forehead. Then he walked over to the kitchen, set the towel down, and made a cup of coffee.

The aroma of the ground coffee beans lingered in the air, making its way into the bedroom where Mei stretched her arms and opened her eyes. The only thing on her agenda today was a few sketches for a client. She got out of bed, brushed her teeth, and leisurely walked into the kitchen. She kissed Li and took the cup of coffee he handed her.

"Chen Xin," she said. "Tell me your thoughts."

Li explained to her what he had thought while running and she nodded in agreement.

"Don't the police patrol in pairs? If we try to get him while he's on duty, we'll have two of them to deal with."

"True, but he's at least guaranteed to be out in public. We don't know if his place is fortified, and if it is, waiting for him to go outside on his day off is a crapshoot."

"What about the wife?" asked Mei. "We could use her to get to him."

Li still found the difference between her physical beauty and elegance and her ability to be ruthless a little disconcerting.

"That's always a possibility," he replied. "However, I'd prefer not to get others involved. Killing a cop will be challenging enough. I'm still trying to come to grips with how I'm going to live my life after I kill a cop. First a teacher, and now someone who provides safety for the public."

"You'll live your life with me and our child, the sole reason we're doing this," she said, trying to boost his morale.

The phone rang in the middle of their conversation. Li glanced at his band, 8:00, a bit early for a social call. He waved his wrist, and a voice echoed through their apartment.

"Mr. and Mrs. Hu, how do you do on this fine morning?" It was Mr. Xi, their case leader at Contraception.

"Fine, thank you," said Li

"Glad to hear you're still alive, Mr. Hu. I hear you've got your first kill. Sophie Xu is confirmed dead, and only a few days after you've applied. Very impressive! Just two more to go and you'll be well on your way to a happy family!"

The upbeat way he spoke about murder was unsettling. It reminded Li of the way sociopaths mimicked social behavior, acting and speaking without any real sincerity.

"What can we do for you this morning?" asked Mei.

"I was just calling to check in. Part of my job, you know. How are things? Anything I can assist you with?"

Li thought for a moment before asking, "Has my name been selected from the database yet?"

"Mr. Hu, I'm afraid I'm not allowed to tell you whether your name is still in the candidate pool or has been selected and given out to another applicant. However, I assure you that should your name be given out, and be canceled for whatever reason, perhaps due to a lack of testicular fortitude, you will be informed. However, at this point, I have no news for you. Which means take care of yourself; a child without its father is unfortunate indeed."

"Thanks," Li said with heavy sarcasm. "We'll be in touch, Mr. Xi," and flicked his wrist to end the call.

"That guy creeps me out," he said.

"I told you it wasn't safe out there," Mei told him. Li smiled ruefully. Heeding his wife's advice made him physically safe, but mentally crazy.

Drinking his coffee, he put an elbow on the kitchen counter and said, "We've got to figure out Chen Xin today."

They both know any time spent waiting was a waste. There was no point in prolonging the inevitable. They had killed one person; they were already committed.

"When?" asked Mei.

"We need to figure him out – his schedule, his routine, his habits and from that, find a weakness. This one's on me, I'll do the recon."

Mei's face showed disagreement but she realized Li needed to get out of the house. He was going stir-crazy. She knew he would take every precaution.

After getting dressed, Li kissed her goodbye and made his way to the Central Police Station in downtown Beijing. He sat down on a bench across the street, wearing sunglasses and a hat with the brim low across his face. He pulled out the glass tablet containing Chen's profile and confirmed this was where he worked.

The sprawling complex resembled the many government buildings in Beijing – big, tall monstrosities that sometimes took up a whole city block. In front, huge gates barred the path of anyone without authorization. The two guards in military uniform on both sides of the entrance held black IWI ACE assault rifles, the design and components of which had been modernized to increase their accuracy and reduce their weight.

Li knew getting in would be a suicide mission. He had to wait for Chen to come out. Over the next hour, Li saw several police officers enter the station using their wrist pass. There was another entrance just for cars. It had a larger scanner that detected not only the pass of the people in the car, but also scanned the interior of the car for weapons, bombs, drugs or anything else not authorized to pass through the gates. Beijing police took their security seriously.

Li shifted his legs as the hard bench made prolonged sitting uncomfortable. Then something caught his attention. Two uniformed officers opened the door of the main building and chatting, made their way towards the front gate. Li recognized the man on the right – Chen Xin. Tall, broad shouldered and with black buzzed hair, he exemplified what a modern-day cop should be.

The men passed through the gate and made their way to a police car parked down the road. The top of the car had the number "11" painted on it. Chen got in on the driver's side and closed the door. The engine fired to life and tore down the street. Li got up from the bench, stretched his legs, and headed back home.

That night, Li opened the briefcase that Professor Wang had brought over. Hidden in the rounds of ammunition was a small box. Li opened it. Inside was a circular piece of clear plastic, about two centimeters in diameter.

Li picked it up and held it between his fingers. He had seen one of these things only in spy movies. It was a tracking device able to camouflage itself by taking on the color and texture of whatever it was attached to, making it undetectable. The absence of any metallic component ensured that it would pass through scanners without raising an alarm.

Li double-tapped the device with his thumb, syncing it with his pass to retrieve the location updates it would send. Then he stuck it in his pocket, put on a black coat and his hat, and went out.

As he walked through the dark cool passages of the city, he hoped he wasn't making himself too easy a target for whoever might have drawn his name. He could only wish that Chen was as foolish as he was; killing Chen on a cool night in an open street would be ideal.

Li continued down the street, passing street food vendors, dangerous men lurking in the shadows and people scurrying home, attempting to make safely to their loved ones.

He looked at the street sign, the police station was five blocks away. He put his hand in his pocket to make sure the tracker was still there.

While fiddling with the small device, he heard a scream in the distance, something which he had grown accustomed to externally, but which still caused him to shudder on the inside. Do what we have to do, Mei's voice echoed in his head as a constant justification.

As Li rounded the corner, he saw the blue lights that illuminated the station. He peered around, keeping his body out of sight, looking for anyone that might be watching. The street was quiet, almost frozen in time. It was lined with police cars that shone under the blue street lamps. Li came out from the corner and checked the top of the cars until he found it – #11.

He removed the small plastic device from his pocket and placed it on the underside of the rear bumper. The disk adhered to the car and turned white, the same color as the surrounding paint, and flattened out, leaving as little edge as possible. Li's band emitted a sound, signaling the tracker was now live.

He stood up from his crouched position, looked around, then headed back the way he had come. Anxiety and excitement pushed him to walk at a brisk pace. He made his way back to his tall apartment building, the lights from the street reflecting off the big metal panels that protected the building windows.

"If you're not safe, you're dead." This was a slogan that had appeared for one of the first companies fitting buildings with thick bulletproof and fireproof paneling. When Li first heard it, his immediate thought was that they needed a new marketing team. But as the city came to realize the real consequences of Contraception, the market exploded and that slogan became ubiquitous around the world.

Once up in his apartment, Li flicked his wrist and a tracking map appeared on the large screen on the living room wall. He clenched his fist and the screen read "Save coordinates." The blinking red dot on the screen showed the car still parked outside the police station. It was only a matter of time before the car would relay the life of Chen Xin back to Li.

He sat down on the couch and closed his eyes with his hands stretched out on either side. He would do what he needed to do, he thought to himself. He took a deep breath and thought how he could incorporate a toaster into his next kill.

***

Chen Xin had always felt that justice was better than mercy. Lessons needed to be learned and through experiencing the consequences of one's actions, one would grow to be a better person. This is what Chen's father had instilled in him at a young age and had led to Chen applying to the police academy. Now, as a police sergeant at the age of 30, he was well on his way to becoming a detective.

Chen was from the southern Chinese city of Shenzhen. His family had relocated to Beijing when he was a young boy because his father had found work at a steel mill. As an only child, typical of a Chinese family, Chen had been disciplined from an early age. School, homework, exercise, sleep, repeat. His father regarded things like dance, art or music as a waste of time.

Chen excelled in competition and discovered that he was a skilled football player at a young age. Through high school, he continued to shine at the game and was offered a scholarship at a university to play for them. But his father quickly dismissed the idea and persuaded him to enter the Beijing Police Academy – a place where Chen could bring honor to the family name.

After four years of training and rising through the ranks, Chen was now one of the most respected officers on the force. His drive, respect for the law, and focus were admired throughout the department. It was only recently that his mind had begun to wander and more important things were now running through his head.

Chen and his wife had decided to have a baby, which meant applying to Contraception. Chen had submitted his name and like most people, was struggling with the morality of murdering people. His sense of duty to society was in direct conflict with what Contraception asked of him.

However, the look in his wife's eyes when she had said, "A baby means everything to me," and her subsequent hints that she would be considering a divorce if he didn't see eye to eye with her, had convinced him that Contraception was a necessary evil, an inevitable part of the process.

***

When Li woke up, he first went to the living room and checked the glass tablet to see where Chen had been. For the past three days, this had become his normal routine. The coordinates with the most stops had been the police station, a coffee shop, a noodle restaurant, and an apartment building.

Li checked the location of the apartments, having agreed with Mei that it would be best to get Chen while he was off duty. Even though there were no assurances that Chen would leave his apartment, people were more likely to stick around their own neighborhood if they did. Li would need to decide if it was better to catch Chen at the apartment or this mysterious building.

"You free tonight?" he called out in the direction of the kitchen.

"Free is too subjective a term. I have time tonight, if that's what you're asking."

"We've got options with Mr. Xin, it looks like the best options are his apartment or his noodle restaurant."

Mei walked into the living room and looked at the tablet.

"Here and here," said Li, gesturing with his fingers. "We'll wait until he finishes work tonight and then follow him to wherever he might go. There have been some other places he's gone, but he pretty much sticks to his normal routine."

Mei nodded. She understood the necessity of recon and that the only way for this to happen was for both of them to do it.

Li looked at her. "He'll finish around six tonight, we need to be close to the station before then."

The day seemed to drag on as both Li and Mei had nothing to do but wait. The clock ticked by as if taunting the couple who were trapped by the hours of the day. Li had already done his treadmill routine, they had eaten breakfast, done laundry, and after that, Mei sketched building plans while Li flicked through the TV channels. He stopped at a news report.

"In a sign of protest, and perhaps detrimental to their entire culture, Switzerland has decided that no one living in the country will have any more babies. The move was sparked by the strong opposition to the regulations surrounding Contraception, which as we all know, require the death of three people before conceiving a child. In 2060, Switzerland voted in favor of the policy, but in recent years, has been a strong advocate against it. Their decision today is heard across the world, but their actions also align with the purpose of Contraception, which is to limit the growth of the world's population. Despite that, Switzerland's determination and symbolism are heard loud and clear."

Li thought about it, confused about the logic. He understood that by agreeing to not conceive, there would be no more murder in Switzerland, but Contraception would still prove to be useful by inhibiting people from having babies. What a weird world to live in, he thought. He closed his eyes and laid down on the couch, letting drowsiness overtake him, soon falling asleep amidst the faint buzz of the TV.

He woke up to Mei's gentle prodding. It was 17:30.

Mei said, "Time to go."

Li put on his shoes and the couple made their way out into the street. They took a taxi and gave it directions to the police headquarters. As they pulled up to the complex, Li put the taxi in turn-by-turn mode so that he could follow Chen's car instead of giving a final destination.

They waited in the back of the cab, which was parked on the side street a few cars behind Chen's. At 18:05, Li saw Chen emerge from the doors, scan his pass at the security gate, and get into the #11 police car. The car took off down the street, with the Hus following close behind.

The police car moved through the city, gliding in and out of the other cars on the road. The taxi wasn't as fast or nimble as the car ahead, refusing to take the same risks that a human might take. Li looked at his map, it appeared that tonight Chen was headed somewhere else before returning home. Li felt nervous but intrigued.

"We're nearly out of the city. Where do you think he's going?" he asked Mei.

She shrugged. "Maybe he's running a sex slave operation. Then, we'd actually be doing the world a favor by killing this creep."

"Seriously, what is a cop doing out in the bleak 7th Ring District?" Li wondered.

As Beijing had continued to expand, the necessity of a 7th Ring was felt acutely and it became a reality, with its completion in the year 2040. However, these days, it had turned into a notorious criminal zone, full of drug peddlers, and prostitutes, a general hangout for those with an affinity for crime. Beijing didn't waste its resources combating this. The government believed so long as these elements didn't permeate into the 6th Ring Road, it wasn't worth the effort or resources.

"It's possible he's corrupt. You know what cops make in Beijing, there's no way to raise a child on that."

Li nodded, his sense of intrigue growing as the taxi followed the #11 police car past the sprawling city. As they approached the 7th Ring, the biggest difference was the lack of lights. Streetlights hadn't either been built or were damaged beyond repair; businesses and shops remained black at night.

Even in the fading light of dusk, it wasn't difficult to tell that this area had been forgotten. Dispo units didn't patrol out here, nor did the police or sanitation crews. Contraception had eliminated the necessity of this area, which was abandoned as soon as property within the 2nd and 3rd Ring Roads became available. However, illegally born children, criminals and those with photophobia found it to be a safe haven; somewhere to live outside the law.

The police car flew down the highway and turned off a road that showed graffiti-riddled street signs. The Hus followed behind, but not close enough to arouse suspicion. Li looked at the map and again questioned himself what a police officer would be doing all the way out here. The taxi crept along the road with its lights off as it made the same turns that Chen made just 400 meters ahead. The streets were lined with garbage and the area was silent, making anyone who somehow found themselves in this desolate area feel acute uneasiness.

The once grandiose buildings of the "magnificent 7th Ring Road," as it was once referred to, now served as vacant property for junkies and those looking to live a life without the convenience of public systems like hospitals, education or transportation. These people didn't ask to be born without a pass; they had no control over their parent's choices. This was a consequence of not following the protocol of Contraception. The rules had been clear, and no exceptions were made. Thus, due to the desire to live that lives in all humans, these pass-less individuals strove to make a life on the outskirts of Beijing.

Li looked out the front of the taxi.

"He's stopped," he said. He directed the taxi to park on a side street and swiped his pass on the center console, paying a charge so it would wait for them. The Hus quietly got out of the car and made their way to the edge of the street, staying close to the walls of a brick building to keep out of sight.

Li looked around the corner and saw the bright taillights of the police car in front of a giant building that from the outside looked abandoned. The windows had all been broken, no visible lights showed from outside, and large piles of trash had accumulated around the perimeter. Due to the lack of light, it was hard to tell if the building was black or covered in filth.

"What the fuck is this place?" asked Mei.

Li looked up and from the faint glow of the moonlight, barely made out the faded logo of Huawei, a famous electronics company who had gone bankrupt in their attempt to develop a sentient AI, against the government's orders not to.

"I think it used to be some kind of factory or something."

The Hus watched as Chen looked around his dark surroundings, grabbed a bag from the passenger side, and approached the main door of the factory. He waved his hand in front of the lock and the door opened. He entered and the door snapped shut behind him.

"What do we do now?" asked Li.

"Let's go check it out."

They pulled their hoods over their heads and silently crossed the abandoned streets until they were next to the factory. The dirt and grime of poverty and neglect was visible on the outside of the large building. Li heard a faint cry from inside and moved close to the nearest window. He and Mei crouched low, peering in, but it was too dark to see anything. He turned to say something to Mei but she had already moved towards a set of stairs a few meters away. Li sighed and followed her, trying to move as noiselessly as possible.

Once they were both on the landing, Mei tugged the door handle but it was locked. Without a moment's hesitation, she pulled out a square piece of glass, and placed it directly over where passes were placed to be scanned for authorized entry. The glass became illuminated and a series of numbers and letters appeared, imitating an authorized pass.

"Picked this up from Lao Shu's tech shop, figured it would come in handy," she whispered to a mystified Li. The light on the door turned green. Silently, they made their way into the factory and found themselves staring down at a huge floor full of conveyer belts, twisted cables, robotic arms, and shipping containers.

Then the silence was broken. They heard Chen say, "Goddammit! How am I supposed to just kill someone!? I'm a cop!" The Hus moved along the upper floor until they saw a light coming from an area on the floor below. The place was surrounded with stacked shipping containers. Looking down, the Hus saw a disheveled Chen pacing up and down in a disturbed manner. He held a hammer in his hands. A single halogen light sitting on a nearby box revealed a young man chained to a large piece of machinery. He looked to be in his late 20s. He had no shirt and there was blood all over his face. Large bruises were visible on his abdomen. Li looked closer and felt there was something familiar about this man, he had seen him somewhere before.

With slow and precise movements, he reached into his pocket to pull out a glass tablet and pointed it in the direction of the chained man. Once the tablet focused on the man's face and identified him, a slew of results appeared on the screen.

"I knew I had seen him before!" he whispered to Mei. "I saw him on the news about a week ago, he had vanished and his family was offering some kind of reward for any information regarding his whereabouts."

"And that's him?"

"It's got to be, but why is he here?"

Li tried to fathom what was happening. Why would a cop be torturing someone? Was he paid to do so? Revenge?

"I have to do this," Chen suddenly screamed. "It's part of the rules. My wife, my family, our baby!"

The Hus watched in deathly fascination as Chen suddenly threw the hammer against the machine, inches away from his prisoner.

"Fuck!" he cried as he stormed away from the man, throwing the halogen light on the floor, leaving the factory in complete darkness. The Hus crouched down and stayed there till they heard the factory door slam.

Outside, Chen stood next to his car, running his hand through his hair and breathing loudly. Then he shook his head. Tonight, once again, he didn't have it in him.

He flung the car door open and tossed the bag back onto the passenger seat. The cop car roared to life, reversed in the direction it had entered, flinging dirt and debris into the air, then spun around to head back to the city.

Li and Mei both stood up and made their way back to the door and descended the stairs, both wondering whether they should help the man inside.

"Don't even think about it," Mei said finally. "This isn't our business, and if we mess with something, Chen will be suspicious and we could lose our shot."

"But we have to help him," said Li.

"We don't even know who he is or why he's here," exclaimed Mei.

Li thought for a moment before finally saying, "He can't do it. It's Contraception, the man inside has to be Chen's Contraception target and he can't bring himself to kill him! There's no other logical explanation."

Mei thought about it and agreed. "We need to go, now."

Li nodded, he knew Mei was looking out for their best interests, but he was once again faced with the inner turmoil of doing what he thought was right. What had happened to humanity? Was it lost in man's desire for personal satisfaction? Were humans unable to do the right thing for fear of forsaking their own dreams and desires?

The Hus sat in silence as their taxi headed back to the city, each preoccupied with their own thoughts. The remains of what used to be a sprawling metropolis now represented the very worst of a system that was, as their commercials claimed, helping society.

Li checked his band and saw that Chen was headed back to his apartment. He instructed the taxi to follow the same route. They needed to scope the area to figure out the best strategy. Pulling Chen into an alley like they did with Sophie wasn't viable, and besides, Chen was likely to be armed.

Half an hour later, they saw the police car parked outside a set of mid-income-level apartments. As standard in Beijing, the community had a gate with a security guard and a wall about two meters high. The streets around the neighborhood were quiet, with gingko trees spaced every meter. Li did a quick search of the community on the taxi's map and found that it had three gates, two of which accommodated vehicles.

From the profile on Contraception, Li identified the gray building Chen lived in. Now, it was just a matter of getting it done.

He looked at Mei, entered the location of their apartment into the taxi map, and they were swept back onto the city streets.

Arriving home, the couple crashed on the couch. It had been an exhausting ordeal but necessary. Far too many people simply rushed into their assigned targets and often wound up dead in the process. However, the recon, the emotional toil, and the pressure that came before a kill weighed just as much as the guilt that followed.

"Stay the course," said Mei. "And we'll get through this, together."

Li sat on the couch while Mei sprawled out, her feet in his lap. He rubbed his hands over her calves, deep in thought.

"This will be tough," he said. "Chen isn't exactly a schoolteacher. But then he's not invincible either. We must be precise, organized."

His voice trailed off and he said in a small voice, "I don't know what to do."

The darkness of night had made its way into their apartment, with a small lamp in the corner providing the only light in the room. This kept Li going. The metaphorical light at the end of the tunnel – their future child.

Everything he stood for, believed in, and worked to epitomize had now been shattered for the sake of a life he wasn't even sure would come into being. He had fought against Contraception and yet, here he was, participating in the very system he had once proclaimed was not the solution.

Mei looked at him with tender eyes, knowing the inner struggle he was facing. She too had her doubts, but knew being strong, both for herself and for Li, was more important now than ever.

As the Hus lay on the couch together, they both knew tonight would be one of many long nights ahead of them.

9. THE COLLECTIVE

Beijing, China

China was one of the strongest advocates of Contraception, creating marketing campaigns and making deals with other countries to garner support during the vote.

▪ Around 19:00, a young man in a suit hurried along the street carrying a black briefcase. Despite the cool night air, there were beads of sweat on his forehead. With an urgent, determined pace, he made his way past the rows of buildings until he approached a large imposing structure in downtown Beijing. The lights illuminated the giant red and gold emblem of the Chinese Communist Party prominently displayed on the front of the building. As he approached the gate, he hitched up his coat sleeve so that his wrist was exposed. The two soldiers on guard placed his hand in a scanner, and his credentials were approved. The heavy gate moved just enough to allow him to pass through.

The man made his way past the soldiers and continued through the security area, up the giant steps that led to the entrance of the building. Near the door, two more soldiers awaited him. One of them held out a glass tablet and scanned his face. Then the soldier nodded and tapped his wrist against a metal box on the wall, and the door opened. The man walked down the corridor lined with red carpet, with portraits of China's greatest political heroes hanging on the wall, while chandeliers hung high above him from the ornate ceiling. Mao, Deng, Xi and countless others stared at him as he hurried down the hallway. He found the elevator at the end of the hall, put his wrist against the sensor, and pressed eight.

There was heavy silence all around him as the elevator doors closed and he began his ascent. As the doors opened at the eighth floor, there was the red carpet once again. This time, he faced a decorated hall with large pillars and massive paintings portraying some of the events that had led to China's glorious ascent to power.

One depicted the Tian'anmen Square protests, which had been re-branded in the year 2039, their 50th anniversary, as a display of strength by the unified Chinese government, instead of the severe violation of human rights for which China had been continually criticized. The area the man walked past was where foreign dignitaries were received upon their visits to Beijing. Looking straight ahead, the man briskly approached a set of large French doors at the back of the hall. Silently, he opened one of them and made his way inside.

At the center of the room stood a large glass table, at which sat some of the most prominent and influential people in China. Politicians, military generals, business leaders and real estate tycoons. Many of them were smoking and drinking baijiu, a spirit that is somehow enjoyed by all demographics in China at most social events. The president of China stood at the head of the table, smoking, very much the leader of this gathering. Situated around the perimeter of the room were analysts, lower-tier government officials and computer programmers. This group of men were called a myriad of names, but they referred to themselves as "The Collective," short for "The collective group of men that controlled China."

"Gentleman, please, we have nothing to worry about," boomed the commanding voice from the head of the table. The Chinese president was a robust man with a friendly face. Someone ordinary men would feel confident about leading them into battle. The man with the briefcase made his way around the table, in between the thick plumes of cigarette smoke and towards the head of the table.

As he approached the president, he laid the briefcase on the table and swiped its top with his wrist to unlock the first set of locks. The president nodded, and the man walked towards the edge of the room, blending in with the rest of the individuals in black suits. The president also swiped his wrist over the briefcase, which popped up immediately. He raised the lid to reveal two glass tablets, each in a velvet-lined cutout.

"Gentlemen, your attention please. If this doesn't help resolve your fears and anxieties, then I don't know what will."

The president placed one of the tablets flat on the table. It immediately lit up, reflecting the image from the small glass tablet. The men gathered around the table, even those leaning against the wall at the end of the room, to see what was happening. The president swiped left, and a list of pictures along with names and job positions scrolled across the table. Hundreds of names flew by, revealing individuals that most members in the room either recognized or had heard of.

"We've succeeded this far due to our discretion and the fact that we keep our mouths shut." The president gazed around the room with a fierce look in his eye. He looked like a grizzly that warns its prey before attacking.

"We've not only made China a better place, but collectively, the world."

Around the room, there were shouts of support and the occasional "Hear, hear!"

"No one has caught on to us, and to preserve the harmony that China has now achieved, the same regulations must be followed. Am I understood?"

The room responded with a unanimous "Yes, sir!"

However, one man in the back had remained silent. He now stood up to voice his opinion.

"What we're doing here is wrong," he said. All eyes in the room turned towards the man who now stood in defiance of their entire operation.

"I can no longer continue to partake in these kinds of activities. We can't just make the world the way we want it. There will always be opposition in all facets of life. Who are we to remove that? As of now, my company and all affiliated business will no longer be involved in this collective. We will go back to doing business as normal even if it means losing shares of the market to our competitors."

The speaker had started a small manufacturing company at 21 and was now the CEO of one of China's largest state-owned enterprises. Along with that, he owned several large areas in western China that had developed massive solar farms and solar power factories. With heavy competition from countries like the U.S. and Canada, China fought to remain the market leader in solar panel manufacturing. Although The Collective had helped him remain the global market leader in this industry, the methods of achieving that had started to weigh on him.

The silence in the room was palpable. This was the first time that someone had decided to not only voice their opposition, but also decided to leave. The president remained calm, speaking to him with a smile.

"Mr. Feng, I understand your concerns. I see that you have found your moral compass. Though not a matter I can understand myself, however, I respect your decision. We thank you for your contribution to The Collective and wish you all the best. If you will, please."

The president gestured to the exit as two large men in suits opened the large doors. Mr. Feng bowed and then slowly made his way around the table. All eyes in the room were on him but no one dared to say a word. As Feng approached the end of the table and faced the open doors, the president nodded to one of the large men who followed Mr. Feng out, closing the doors behind him.

Once the doors were closed, the men inside all turned to face the president. He smiled at them reassuringly. Then they heard a gunshot, followed by the thud of something falling. The president's smile widened as he faced the remaining men, all of whom understood that their survival depended on their compliance.

"Anyone else having doubts about what we are doing?" the president asked, knowing not one man in the room would dare challenge him again. If not carrots, then sticks, he thought in grim satisfaction, before turning to the last arrival.

"Mr. Diao, how are things going with the Contra tablets?"

The man who had handed the president the briefcase now stood up to make his report.

"Everything going as planned, sir. So far, all chips have remained undetectable and from the intelligence gathered, no suspicions have been raised. My team and I are taking every precaution necessary when dealing with our Contra insider. We expect that within a few months, all names will be fully operational."

He sat down after finishing his report. Diao ran the tech team that handled the logistics of what The Collective was working to achieve.

"Alright then. For the rest of you, as mentioned earlier, please continue to follow the protocol for submissions, which will then be assessed by analysts and researchers. So far, despite issues of morality, we as The Collective have achieved a better future for our people – and for China."

The president slowly looked around the room, secure in the knowledge that no matter how much money or power these individuals had, he had them under his thumb.

"A toast, gentleman, to the future."

The men around the table stood and raised their glasses, "To the future!"

With a resounding clink, they cheered and drank their baijiu.

For The Collective, nothing felt better than consolidating their power and fortune, and they would continue to do so by whatever means necessary.

10. THE PARTY

Beijing, China

Fewer than 5% of Contraception applicants are single.

▪ The morning sun shone through the big windows of the apartment, illuminating the papers and maps that were spread out across the kitchen table and taped to the walls. Li and Mei had been working day and night trying to figure out how to kill Chen yet had not been able to come up with any idea that offered a high chance of success. The dark circles under their eyes and their pale skin indicated their state; they were exhausted, both mentally and physically. The strain of trying to create a foolproof plan coupled with late nights and little sleep had caught up with them. This morning, they slept in late. When the alarm clock rang, it was noon. Li yawned as he got up and then shook Mei to wake her up. As they both got ready for the day, a bell rang in the living room; they had received a video message.

Mei walked to the living room and flicked her wrist to play the video on the glass tablet on their wall.

"Li, come watch!" she yelled. The video displayed a smiling couple, around the same age as the Hus. They were Jack and Vivien Huang, a couple from Macao who had become friends with the Hus since they moved to Beijing in 2065. Jack and Li had met at the gym and had since formed a friendship based on their similar ideals and common interests. They soon introduced their wives and the next they knew, they were couple friends.

As Li came into the living room, the video started. "Hey guys! We're so happy to be sending you this message, as we have some big news!" said a smiling Vivien.

Jack said, "That's right, we're having a Contrabration party! It was tough, no doubt, but we're going to be having a baby!"

The couple's happiness seemed almost faked but then, the amount of turmoil they had suffered to get to where they were now was a good reason to be so ecstatic. The Huangs continued to beam, holding hands and looking like the stock photo of a happy couple coming in with a photo frame at the store. Mei cringed when she heard the word "Contrabration."

One of the first people to complete their kills when Contraception first came out was interviewed on local TV. The reporter had asked the woman what she would do next, with the woman responding, "I'm going to celebrate Contraception. A Contrabration!"

The video went viral and these types of parties were now marketed and promoted as an incentive to complete the three kills.

"Li, Mei, we would love for you to come and celebrate this exciting chapter of our life with us. Tomorrow, around 17:00, at our place. We'll drink, eat, it will be fun. We'd love to see you guys!"

The video ended with the two of them waving at the camera. Li moved his wrist and the video closed.

"I'd made it a point to not murder people, and now I'm being asked to celebrate it," Li said darkly.

Mei looked at him, thinking how to justify it. "Think of it more as a celebration of the fact that they can have a child, and not so much as celebrating what they did to get there. You're going crazy by staying cooped up in the apartment, and it is driving me crazy too. Plus, Gao He will be there and we haven't seen him since…" her voice trailed off thinking about the tragic incident.

Li knew she was right. The constant planning and arguing over how best to take care of Chen needed to be put off, if for just one night.

Li tapped his band and said, "Send Jack message: Hey, congratulations guys! Mei and I would love to see you tomorrow!" His tone reflected how he should feel, but not how he actually felt.

Mei asked, "What are we supposed to get someone celebrating the murder of three people?"

"A clear conscience?"

"Let's just go with a bottle of nice wine. I can't be bothered to buy baby clothes now."

They spent the rest of the day watching movies and reading. It wasn't until after dinner that Mei received a phone call.

She looked at Li and said, "It's mom."

Li shrugged and mimed that he was not there, continuing to read his book.

"Hi mom!" Mei said, not quite in the mood for conversation, "How are you?"

"Your father and I are great, dear. Oh Mei, it's so nice to hear your voice! How are you? Have you and Li given any thought to our last talk?"

"Well, busy, to say the least. As a matter of fact, Li and I applied for Contraception the other day."

Li had turned around on the couch and stared at Mei in anticipation of her mother's response.

"Oh, honey that's just wonderful, we're so proud of you! Imagine, a little granddaughter, your father and I would be so happy!"

"We've already killed one person and are currently working on number two."

"That's great news, really so wonderful to hear you taking such an important step in your life. Your father and I have been looking forward to this for some time now."

"Well, as long as you're happy," Mei said in a sarcastic tone. "But really mom, thank you for your support."

"Mei, you are more than welcome. We're here for you. Well we'd better get going, your father is taking me to the opera tonight."

"Hey mom just one quick question,"

"Yes?"

"If Contraception were around during your time, would you have applied?"

There was a short pause before her mother said, "You know, sweetie, your father and I have discussed this a lot and if we're being honest, we just don't think the risk is worth the reward, so no, we wouldn't have applied. We're just lucky we had you when we did, huh?"

"Lucky me," she replied in a deadpan tone. "Well, mom, I'll let you go, have a great time at the opera! Keep in touch," and hung up.

"I love your mother," said Li. "I take it she brought up grandchildren again?"

"When doesn't she? Spoiler alert, she's thrilled we've applied."

"Well no surprise there," he remarked. "She's been wanting a grandchild ever since the day I met her."

"Her happiness for us still seems weird knowing what it takes to have a kid these days," Mei came to join him on the couch after taking a bottle of white wine from the fridge.

"The new normal," he said.

The rest of the night was spent without any untoward incident. Screams and gunshots rang out in the night but Li and Mei were still safe in their apartment, high on the sixtieth floor.

The next day, Mei picked up a bottle of red wine and a greeting card from a store. The card read, "You're a killer couple!" Corny, but fitting in an ironical way.

When she arrived home late in the afternoon, Li was getting dressed, buttoning up a blue collared shirt. He wore a pair of khaki colored chinos. Mei changed into a semi-formal black dress and soon, they were on their way to the Huangs' apartment. Li had argued that going out occasionally was needed, despite the safety concerns. Arriving at the Huangs' luxurious apartment complex, the Hus took the elevator to the top floor and knocked on the door of the apartment.

Vivien swung the door open and greeted them. "Hey you guys, come on in! Really great to see you!"

The Hus entered after putting the bottle of wine on the counter. Inside was a small group of people that they knew.

"Li! Long time no see! What are you, a marked man these days?"

"Actually, yes," he replied.

"That's incredible, so how many left?"

"Two. Mei and I are working on how to take care of the second one, a police officer."

Jack joined the conversation. "Oh, that's a tough one. My second was a lab technician. It was almost too easy; you'd think he wouldn't sit on a park bench eating ice cream in the middle of the day. Went there every Tuesday! Couldn't have been easier."

The other people listening laughed. Contraception had been around for a decade now. But despite it being a part of life, Li still felt uneasy discussing death or treating it like discussing a basketball game played with friends.

"Poor guy, I almost felt bad for him. But hey, my life, right?"
The others nodded in agreement. Li walked off to find Mei engaged
in a similar conversation with the ladies. He caught her eye, and she
gave him a look that seemed to express the same uneasiness that he
felt.

Mei asked Vivien, "So, Jack submitted his name with the
application?"

"That's right, what a gentleman," she said, looking at her
husband with a smile.

"And what's going to happen now?"

"Well, after we killed the last person on our list, we received
confirmation from Contra that our kills were completed, and now
the only thing is to have the baby and Jack will be removed from the
database. We've been waiting for this moment ever since we applied.
It's such a relief to be finally done with the hard part. Just need to
have our baby and we'll finally be free! Don't worry, one day you
and Li will get here, hopefully!"

"Are you concerned about revenge kills?" No one liked their
family members to be killed, legally or otherwise. Loved ones and
relatives tended to lash out and try to kill those who had killed
members of their family. Tracking people down was challenging, but
through surveillance systems, sometimes families could identify an
applicant and illegally take matters into their own hands.

The other wives looked horrified at Mei's question. But she
didn't seem to find it any more inappropriate than discussing killing
someone else.

Vivien tried to handle the question as best she could. "Well, we
have given it some consideration, but we've taken every precaution
to prevent it, and we don't expect it to happen."

Mei nodded and excused herself to go to the bathroom. Despite
her feelings towards Contraception, she too had applied and was now

a part of it. However, all the smiles, laughs, and reminiscing about past murders was something she could not support. For her, Contraception was a means to an end, and something she wished to finish and never look back on. Li and Mei both needed to grin and bear it; losing face was still a big cultural thing in China and despite their experience abroad, some customs never faded. As everyone sat down to dinner, the conversation turned to Contraception once more.

"You recently applied, didn't you Gao He?"

"That's right," he said, eating his rice without looking up from his plate. "I applied last week and so far, I've killed one of my targets." His tone was calm and strong.

"We're all so sorry about your wife," said someone else at the table. Gao had been married just six months ago. His wife contracted a rare disease while doing research in Zimbabwe and had been bedridden for months. All of Gao's friends had been supportive, especially after she died at the hospital.

"Why did you apply?" asked Mei.

All the heads turned back to Gao as he said, "Before she passed away, my wife made me promise I would have a child so I wouldn't be alone in the world. I'm doing it for her."

He picked up a piece of beef with his chopsticks and ate it to fill up the silence that now sat in the room. His wife's eggs had been frozen, and through IVF, he was planning to use a surrogate to carry his and his dead wife's child as soon as he had finished the three kills.

Zhang Xiaoli looked at him and asked, "But why?"

"Why what?" he responded, staring at her.

"Why do you want to have a kid? There are plenty of ways to not be alone that don't require killing people or putting your life in danger."

"I made a promise," he said with quiet determination.

Zhang Xiaoli continued to look at him before saying, "I suppose now you're all going to ask me why I've chosen to never have a child."

"That's right," laughed Jack.

"Look, I understand that with my father on the Contraception Board, I should be obligated to apply; but I don't. I think it's an absurd system and frankly, I can't understand why educated people would make the choice to apply. It's not worth it. And to top it all off, I don't trust it."

"Don't trust what?" someone asked.

"The system. There's no way it's not corrupt. A system designed to kill people and you think it's not being abused? I'm not convinced."

Mei looked up, "You really think so? How could someone possibly manipulate a universal system?"

"I don't have proof, or even a working theory, there's just something about the system and the process that screams 'abuse' to me. You've just applied, but I caution you to be careful. There might be more going on than you're aware of."

"Ever the conspiracy theorist. And all that coming from someone who has never had kids," Vivien said with a cold smile.

"Neither have you," shot back Xiaoli.

"All right ladies, take it easy. It's all in good fun. No one says you have to apply or not, it's a life choice," said Jack, trying to ease the tension at the table.

"Speaking of life choices," said another man at the table, one of Jack's friends, "those Dispo guys, what do they get paid? There's not enough money in the world to entice me to haul bodies off the street. It's not like everyone gets a clean shot in the head. Just the other day, I saw a man with an ax lodged in his skull!"

Another man said, "Well, someone has to do it. Besides, it's necessary for us as a society to maintain a sense of order and dignity no matter how gruesome the requirements of Contraception might be."

Others at the table nodded.

Jack looked at Li and asked him, "What do you think of Dispo?"

"I don't, really," he replied. "They've got a job to do just like anyone else."

As dinner proceeded, different topics were discussed, ranging from Contraception all the way to urban gardens. This group of friends enjoyed talking about ideals and theoretical solutions to problems, but few practiced what they preached. These days, it was easier to come across as a good person than actually be one.

Another person looked at Li and asked, "Weren't you a consultant on the Contraception project when it was first proposed?" All eyes now turned to Li.

"That's right, I was."

"And you argued against it, right?"

"That's correct," Li said.

"And how do you feel now, now that you're taking part in the very thing which you openly denounced and fought against?"

Li took a drink from his bottle of beer before saying, "It's the world we live in. I don't particularly enjoy the subway, having to pay taxes, or cleaning my house, but I do all these things because they're part of my responsibility as an adult. And if I don't do these things, there are consequences. Perhaps not life-threatening such as those from Contraception, but for example, I would have a dirty house or I'd be late to work. It's the same with Contraception."

"If I want to have a child, there are things I must do. I understand the nature and purpose of it, but on a moral and personal level, I disagree it with it. I understand the need for the death penalty and the use of torture during interrogations, but I still disagree with them on a personal level."

"But at some point," said Vivien, "You had to acknowledge that drastic measures had to be taken. The world ten years ago was different from the world now. As someone against Contraception, what was your solution?"

Li sighed. He had been asked this question before, and his response was never well received.

"I didn't have one." The guests at the table all looked at him puzzled. Finally, one of them challenged him.

"So, in your mind it was ok to criticize and go against a real, tangible solution but provide no solutions of your own to an internationally ongoing issue?"

"If two countries are exchanging hostile rhetoric, I don't need an alternative solution before I recommend not going to war. It's the same with Contraception. I'd rather deal with the issues of overpopulation than resort to murder. I don't need an alternative to murder before suggesting we don't do it."

"Well, it looks like you're no longer on that high road of yours. Got off the high horse after you killed your first one?" a voice piped in from the end of the table. The room chuckled unpleasantly as Li took another sip from his beer.

"Do what you gotta do," said Li. The room seemed to accept that answer.

"A toast, everyone," said Jack, as he raised his glass, "To those three miserable souls whose deaths have allowed us to create life!" Mei cringed. The rest of the dinner party raised their glasses, and cheered the Huangs for their success, with Li and Mei joining in a lackluster manner. The Hus still didn't understand the purpose of having such a party. For them, it was straightforward, kill the targets, have a baby, and move on. Calling it a victory seemed barbaric; but Contrabration wasn't a much better alternative.

After dinner, the party guests sat together on the couches, listening to stories, drinking wine, and rehashing old times. Vivien was showing off a baby shirt she had bought, that said, "Daddy would die for me." Mei speculated whether someone had made a shirt that said, "Daddy died for me." Too dark, she thought. However, death was the new normal, and she supposed a shirt reflecting dark humor was to be expected.

She looked over at Li, who had both his hands around his bottle of beer and appeared uninterested in whatever was happening. She looked at her band; it was getting late. She set down her glass of wine and announced that it was time for them to go home.

"Busy day hunting down number two tomorrow," she said drily. It was received with laughter. She looked at Li, who had set down his bottle and was adjusting his shirt collar.

"Congratulations again you two. You'll be great parents." The Hus waved goodbye, and as they stood in front of the elevator, Mei looked less than thrilled to have attended the party.

"I understand they're happy to almost be finished with their application, but they almost seemed to be…"

"Glorifying it?"

"Exactly. It was really off-putting." Contraception had changed people. Many couples, including the Hus, were no longer driven by morals or doing the right thing, their sole focus was on having a baby.

"You think we'll end up like them?" asked Li.

"Shoot me if we do. We'll just go through the motions and move forward. And definitely no Contrabration party."

Li put his arm around her shoulder and kissed her. They took a taxi and arrived home, wondering what life would have been like if Contraception hadn't been implemented. It would have been more crowded and polluted, but at least society would still have maintained some shreds of humanity instead of this dog-eat-dog mentality that now consumed the world.

11. CHEN XIN

Beijing, China

The majority of Contraception kills take place on Wednesday mornings before 9:00.

▪ Today was the day. After this evening, if everything went according to plan, Chen Xin would no longer be alive and the Hus would be one step closer to being able to have a child. In the cool and overcast afternoon, the Hus sat at the kitchen table, looking at the rough sketches of Chen's apartment and surrounding streets that Mei had drawn. Earlier that week she had gone to see the apartment below Chen's, feigning interest as a potential homebuyer. During that time, she had roughly sketched the layout of the place, knowing it would be the same as Chen's. Now sprawled across the kitchen table, the apartment was one of many sketches that Mei had created to better plan their kill.

"Ok, let's walk through it again," said Li. As Mei and Li had been figuring out how this murder could best be accomplished, one of their biggest inspirations was spy and action movies. Li argued that if it could work in a movie, then it had the potential to work in real life. Mei was doubtful but went along with it as it couldn't hurt to try. Through tracking Chen's police car, they could figure out his habits, such as when he came home and when he left for work, and the places he liked to visit or patrol.

They had decided that tonight would be the best time. Chen was off work and on Thursdays, he would always go to the same noodle place to pick up noodles for his wife before she got home from her yoga class. This was Li and Mei's window.

"I approach him in the parking garage and escort him into the elevator up to his apartment. You're waiting by the apartment door. We enter the apartment and sit him down in a chair in the living room."

"I still don't understand why we don't just kill him in the garage."

Li sighed, he had been through this with her before. "If we're going to take a person's life, I need to look them in their eyes. I know it doesn't make any sense, but there's something honorable about confronting someone directly before taking their life. Besides, what if someone sees us kill him in the garage and calls it in? We'll have an entire police force on us who I'm sure wouldn't take kindly to us killing one of their own."

"It's an unnecessary risk."

"Killing him in an open garage with witnesses is an unnecessary risk."

Mei nodded and continued, "Then I'll tie him up with zip ties, and you put one through his head. I'll scan him and then we're out of there before his wife comes home."

"It sounds flawless, but you know what they say, '*Móu shì zài rén, chéng shì zài tiān.*'[4]"

"Make sure you check him for weapons before you get into the elevator with him."

---

[4] Hope for the best, plan for the worst

"Right."

"And honey, try not to die," she said, placing a hand on Li's cheek.

Li laughed and squeezed her hand "You're not that lucky."

"What's the plan for getting into his building by the way?"

Mei looked at him and said, "I've been meaning to tell you, but there didn't seem to be a good time."

"Go on…"

"I bought an apartment in his building."

"You did what?"

"Well it was killing two birds, really. After I bought it, they authorized my pass to enter the building as I am now the sole proprietor of apartment number 36. Also, it's a great place for my parents to stay."

Li stood looking at her, "Where did you even get the money for something like this?"

"I commissioned a new government building design for the Saudi government and I used the fee. Look, worst comes to worst, we sell it, but right now, there's no point in debating it because we own it and tonight, it will serve its purpose."

"How much did it cost?"

"It's better not to ask."

As the sun dropped from the sky, the time the Hus had set to go after Chen was approaching. They both dressed in black clothes and Li opened the case containing the military weapons that Wang had dropped off. He picked up the metallic string, stared at it for a moment, and then placed it in his left pocket. He also took two clips, one with hollow points and the other with paralyzer bullets, and loaded the latter into the gun. The gun went into the inner breast pocket of his jacket.

The last item in the case was the self-targeting knife. He picked it up and handed it to Mei. She tucked it into her waistband, knowing it was an important precautionary measure. The nervousness both of them felt was stronger than it had been for Sophie Xu. They were fully committed to fulfilling the requirements of Contraception; there was no turning back now. If they failed to kill Chen, then it was over. A second attempt would be futile as Chen would then expect it, more so than before. His death represented much more than a requirement; it was about life itself. With Chen gone, the Hus were only one more death away from having a beautiful child they could nurture and share with the world. Both Li and Mei knew what was on the line, and knew tonight needed to be perfect. There was no room for error.

"For our family," said Li

"For our family," repeated Mei.

She kissed him passionately and then they both headed down to the street to catch a taxi. The night felt different than usual. It was cooler, and dark clouds had started to form overhead. There seemed to be a stillness about the night, as if time stood still in preparation for what the Hus were about to do.

The taxi swerved through the streets until it arrived outside Chen Xin's apartment complex. Li looked up and identified Chen's. Exactly as per the schedule they had worked out, the light inside the apartment went off. They knew Chen was heading out for noodles.

Li and Mei exited the taxi and approached the complex. Mei casually scanned her pass against the gate and it opened. She smiled at the guard as they passed through and positioned themselves around the corner of a nearby building until they saw Chen enter the parking garage.

"Showtime," said Mei.

"Be safe," said Li, kissing her as she walked towards Chen's building where she would go to the fiftieth floor to wait for the men to show up. Li walked to the parking garage, taking the stairs down to sub-level four, waiting for Chen to come back.

As he stood in the shadows opposite the now empty parking space, he realized he was perspiring profusely despite the cold night air. His heart beat faster and faster in anticipation of what was going to happen soon. Although he had never been here before, he felt familiar with the area because of Mai's sketches. He knew the elevator was to his right, about sixty meters from where he stood now. He also knew there were two sweeping security cameras on this floor, and he would have to time it just right to get into the elevator without being seen.

Then out of the shadows, he heard Chen's car, the unmistakable sound the French-made Alpine A310 made as it roared through the parking structure, the sound reverberating off the cement walls. The model had ended production in 1984, but China had commissioned Alpine to upgrade and enhance it for Chinese security forces. Chen's #11 police car rolled across the gray concrete floor and into the parking space across from where Li was hiding. The headlights turned off, and as the car door opened, with Chen coming out holding the bowl of noodles in his right hand, Li stepped out of the shadows and approached him from behind.

Chen felt something cold against the nape of his neck as the car door slammed shut and knew immediately what it was, the muzzle of a gun. Then the whispered command came from behind him. "You will do exactly as I say or I will kill you right here. We're moving to the elevator. Back up and let's go."

Chen moved backward with Li following. As they walked towards the elevator, Chen started to make conversation.

"You know I'm a cop, right? There's nothing to rob at home and no one is going to pay a ransom for me. Besides, the boys on the force aren't going to take kindly to anything happening to me."

Li didn't reply. He didn't feel the need to engage any more than what was required. As they approached the elevator, where the swinging camera was, he barked, "Stop!" Then counted to three and finally nudged Chen forward with the gun. Then he heaved a sigh of relief in his mind and pressed the elevator button. The doors opened, and the two men entered. The doors closed before the camera could detect them.

"Where are we headed?" asked Chen.

"Fifty," said Li, in a calm, cold tone.

As Chen reached up to press the small button, Li noticed his big, broad shoulders. Chen was wearing a navy-blue hoodie over a white undershirt and black running shorts. Li respected people who worked out; perhaps in another life, they could have been friends, he thought. But for now, Chen would remain a target; a means to an end. As the elevator proceeded to the fiftieth floor, Chen once again attempted to talk with Li.

"So, you're just going to shoot me then? That's the big plan, kill a police officer, for what?"

Then sudden comprehension dawned on him. "Are you planning to have a baby? I'm your target, is that it?"

Li, with the gun pointing at the back of Chen's head, replied, "You would have done the same."

"Sure, but with some dignity, not in the elevator of my apartment building."

"Dignity? Is that what you call chaining up a man in an abandoned factory? Is that how you show dignity?"

Chen attempted to turn around, but Li pressed the steel barrel against his head, indicating that he should remain where he was.

"You know nothing about me or what I've done."

"Enlighten me. You're going to die soon, maybe good to get it off your chest."

Chen sighed, he noticed there were only ten more floors to go.

"I couldn't do it. He doesn't deserve to die simply for my desire to want a family. But I have to. My wife, she… I just have to do it, and it's taking longer than I expected."

Li could empathize with this. Pointing a gun at a cop's head in an elevator was not something he had ever expected nor wanted to do, yet here they both were.

The elevator announced their arrival at the fiftieth floor. Li pushed Chen with the gun pressed against the back of his head, and they both proceeded out of the elevator. At the corridor, they turned left and he saw Mei at the end of the hallway. The apartment building was nice; white marble lined the floor accented by a light gray paint on the walls. The two men walked down the hallway as Mei leaned against the wall next to Chen's door. When the two men reached her, she nodded.

"Open the door," she said.

Chen looked at her and without hesitation said, "No."

"I had a feeling you would say that."

From her pocket, Mei pulled out a long, thin piece of metal and inserted it into the keyhole of the door. She double-tapped it and immediately, the inserted end turned a hot white color, and the sound of cracking metal echoed through the quiet hallway. Mei pulled the metal rod out of the keyhole, grabbed the handle and gave a hard pull. The bolt clicked and the door swung open.

She looked at Chen and flashed a triumphant smile. Chen entered first, followed by Li and then Mei, who closed the door behind her. Chen placed the noodles on the counter as the lights automatically turned on. Li kept the gun pointed at Chen, who was now facing him. Mei walked into the living room and sat on the couch. Chen was now visibly angered with the situation. His face showed no signs of fear or anxiety.

Li motioned to the kitchen chair across from Chen, "Sit down."

"Fuck you," replied Chen. Li had expected resistance but had not thought about how to deal with it.

"You've got three seconds to sit in that chair."

"You're not going to do anything, you weak motherfucker. Who are you to come into my apartment and tell me what to do?"

Chen was now incensed. As a police officer, many people had threatened his life, but now, in his own home, his anger over his own carelessness boiled over.

Li saw Chen moving his left hand and he pulled the trigger. The paralyzer bullet flew from the barrel and buried itself in Chen's hand, which turned limp. Chen let out an involuntary gasp as pain surged through his hand and flooded his entire arm. Then something happened that the Hus had not bargained for.

Chen yelled, "Lights off!" and the room suddenly went black, with only a faint light coming from the large window at the end of the room. When their eyes had adjusted to the darkness, there was no sign of Chen.

"Where is he?" asked a frantic Mei, who had jumped up from the couch and was looking around the room in a frenzy. Li's eyes had not yet fully adjusted to the darkness; he had a limited vision as he turned around. Then from the hallway connected to the living room came the unmistakable sound of a gun being cocked.

"Get down!" yelled Li. Both he and Mei hit the floor as Chen's shotgun roared in the apartment and a hail of bullets hit the wall.

"You come into MY house and expect to get away with it?" An enraged Chen moved in the direction he thought Li to be in and shot off another round. One of the shots ripped through the bowl of noodles, and the metal BBs lodged into the fridge in the kitchen. Li knew the effect of the paralyzer bullet wouldn't last long and soon, Chen's hand would be back to normal. Hiding behind the kitchen counter, he could see Chen's reflection on the steel toaster next to the sink.

Chen cocked his gun with his right hand and then nestled it in the cradle of his left shoulder as his left hand was as useful as a dead fish. Then he whipped around towards the kitchen, knowing Mei couldn't have gone too far. He saw her hunched behind the sofa.

"Stand up!" he barked. Mei rose up slowly, hands raised in the darkness, but showing no sign of fear. She looked at Chen in the eye as she waited for his next move.

"Any last words?" he asked.

"Toaster," she said.

"What the…"

Before Chen could finish, the toaster from the kitchen counter came flying through the air and hit him on the side of the face with the force of a knockout punch. He fell to the floor and his shotgun dropped beside him. Li came out, still holding the cord of the toaster in his right hand, He looked at the motionless Chen and dropped it in the now quiet apartment.

Then he made his way to the entrance and found the manual control for the lights, turning them back on. When he came back into the living room, Chen was still lying still on the floor. One side of his face was a bloody pulp, with crimson blood relentlessly flowing on the floor. Both he and Mei stared at the body in disbelief. Eventually Mei found her voice.

"You finally got to use a toaster" she said feebly.

Then she became pulled herself together and said, "Let's see if he's still alive."

Mei pulled out the glass tablet and held it to Chen's fingers. The device flashed red, "Authorized – Chen Xin – Kill NOT confirmed."

Mei looked at Li and said, "Next time you should try to swing it harder."

He rolled his eyes and motioned for her to help him get Chen into the chair as planned. They tied Chen's hands behind his back and his ankles to the legs of the chair. He was still unconscious. Mei walked to the fridge and found a bottle of white wine inside. After pulling out the cork and taking a sip from the bottle, she threw the remaining wine in Chen's face. Sputtering and moving his head side to side, Chen came to his senses. He opened his eyes with a groan and seeing his two captors standing before him immediately flexed his hands and tried to kick his legs free but the zip ties held.

"Do you have any idea who I am?" he rasped.

"Of course, we do," said Mei. "You're the man who is going to die for us to have a family."

Chen looked at her. His black hair was wet from the wine and blood dripped down his left temple from where the toaster had struck him. The red blood contrasted starkly against the black and white interior. Li locked eyes with Chen. He knew luck was the only reason he wasn't the one in the chair. He pointed his gun at the center of Chen's chest. He had loaded in the hollow points, making sure this time the damage would be permanent.

Chen stared at him with a fierceness that Li recognized. Chen wasn't afraid to die although his desire to live was noticeable. He wanted to have a child and live his life as not only a dedicated police officer and husband but also as a father. As Li stood there, with his finger on the trigger, his hand shook. Mei looked at him with concern. Li was not a killer and was struggling with the thought of taking another life. He had too much empathy and now, while staring at his target, was not the ideal time for someone to have doubts. Mei looked down at her band; they had been here too long. The fight hadn't been anticipated, and Chen's wife was due home any minute.

"Is it worth it?" asked Chen. "The guilt? Knowing every time you look at your child, you will think of me?"

Li started to lower the gun; he couldn't do this.

Mei moved with purpose, grabbing the gun out of Li's hands. Before either man could comprehend what was happening, she pointed it at Chen's forehead and pulled the trigger. A small sound came from the muzzled barrel as the bronze hollow-tipped bullet hit Chen's head. Both men were frozen, staring at the gun as the bullet reached its destination and bored a perfect hole through Chen's head. The force of it whipped Chen's head back and the bullet exited through the rear of his skull, piercing the glass wall behind him.

Chen's head lolled awkwardly against the back of the chair, his lifeless eyes staring at the shattered glass which rained fifty stories down on the pavement below. Without hesitating, Mei grabbed one of Chen's fingertips and placed it, along with one of hers, on the glass tablet, which now flashed green and read, "Authorized – Chen Xin – Kill confirmed."

She slid the tablet into her pocket, looked at Li, and handed him the gun back.

"We've got to go."

Li stood paralyzed, staring at Chen, who was now slumped in his chair, with a hole in his head. Blood dripped onto the white floor while the zip ties continued to hold his hands and feet in place.

"Li!" she yelled. He was jolted out of his trance and back to reality. They needed to go. Dispo would be here soon, neighbors would ask questions, and although Contra killings were legal, there could be grave consequences for them if Chen Xin's fellow officers came to know who had killed him.

Li realized he had the gun and put it back into his jacket pocket. Mei was already headed towards the door, and he followed. Mei swung the door open, adjusted her hair, and exited the apartment. Li followed, shutting the door as best he could, now that the locking mechanism had been destroyed. The two stared at each other for a moment and then rushed towards the elevator.

As the doors opened and they got in, the elevator next to them opened and two men from Dispo got out. Their bright red overalls resembled a hazmat suit, but were better fitting. One carried what looked like a toolbox while the other had a foldable gurney under his arm. Their hoods were off. The Hus heard only the tail-end of their conversation before the elevator doors closed.

"All I remember is walking up the stairs and hearing, 'It's a two for one special!' and then two large thuds hit the floor." The elevator doors closed before the Hus could hear the rest of the conversation.

Li and Mei stood in their elevator, glad not to have been there at the time Dispo showed up. The type of men working for Dispo tended to be uneducated, brash, and somewhat disconnected from the world. Every day, their sole job consisted of transporting often mutilated and bloody bodies. They would need to identify the bodies, call their emergency contact, and then at some point, cremate the corpses if they were not claimed. This was not a job for the fainthearted. However, it was a job that needed to be done and paid better than most other blue-collar jobs.

As the elevator reached the ground floor, they could hear sirens in the distance. It was standard protocol for the police to be notified if a cop's pass no longer emitted a signal. Chen's death had prompted a call to the force, who were now on their way to investigate. Sanctioned by Contra or not, police did not take kindly to the death of one of their own.

"We've got to get out of here fast," said Li. They were now outside the apartment complex, contemplating the quickest and least conspicuous way out. Mei thought about the diagrams and pointed towards the south gate. Before reaching the guard in the small sentry box, they slowed down and walked through, with Li giving a silent nod to the watching man. Once on the street, their hearts pounding, they waited anxiously for a taxi. Adrenaline pumped through them, creating a heightened sense of their surroundings. The sirens grew louder. Neither dared to look back at the apartment, seeing the image of a slumped Chen tied to the chair.

Finally, Li managed to hail a cab just as the flashing blue lights of Beijing Police flew around the corner. They had no legal reason to fear, but the police in this city were not known for adhering to rules; it was better to avoid confrontation. The taxi sped away and Li tried to control his breathing. He rolled down the taxi window and let the night air whip against his face. Mei placed her hand on his knee. She understood it wasn't more difficult for him than it had been for her, and she loved it that he was willing to make sacrifices, not only for her but for their family.

"Two down, one to go," she said. "Should we see who is last on the list?"

Pulling out the third tablet, she held it in front of them and they both looked at the profile and picture that had just downloaded to the tablet. As Li squinted at the piece of glass in front of him, he was speechless with disbelief.

In a hushed tone, Mei said, "Is that...?" as she pulled the piece of glass closer.

"That's Ronan!" Li said, finally finding his voice. "From Boston! Don't you remember him? Ronan and I used to debate ethics at the bar where we met. I haven't spoken to him in years! And now I'm expected to kill him!"

Before she could respond, Li was frantically dialing Mr. Xi back at Contra.

"Hi, this is Li Hu."

"Yes, of course Mr. Hu. Congratulations on killing your second target! We just received confirmation. Making good progress so far! What can I do for you?"

"There's seems to be some mistake. Our third target is someone who used to be a friend of mine, we've known each other for years."

"That happens periodically, I'm afraid. Each target is selected at random from the database by the system, and our contract explicitly states that any relationship to a target is nothing more than a coincidence. Contra is not liable for the selection of said targets. Any other questions?"

"No, that will be all, thank you."

He turned back to Mei.

"It's not a mistake, just an 'unfortunate coincidence.'"

Mei was reading Ronan's bio. "It says he's back in Sweden working as a political activist. I don't recall him ever being interested in girls, he was always so obsessed with the idea of reform in China. In fact, I even wondered if he could be gay. Did he get married?"

Li looked out the window of the taxi, not sure how to process the idea of killing someone he knew.

"We drew three random names! What are the odds we have to kill someone we know? This is inconceivable! I can't kill Ronan, we're friends!"

His breath quickened as the question of right and wrong stirred in his head again. Was having a child worth killing his old university friend? True, they had gone out of touch over the years as he and Mei had moved back to China and the routine of daily life had taken most of his attention, but losing touch did not justify killing Ronan.

"We have to," said Mei. "What are we doing this for?"

Li placed his head in his hands and took a deep breath.

"I can't kill Ronan," he said.

"We just killed a pre-school teacher and a police officer to have a baby. I will not let someone you knew in university stop us from having the life we want," she said louder than normal. Mei understood the conflict of interests, but she had made her decision the instant she recognized Ronan's face on the tablet. As soon as Mei had decided she was in, she meant it.

"We're going to need to talk about this," he said, looking out blankly. Outside, a serene moon shone on the cold metal that covered the city's buildings. The decreased population in China had led to the closure of many factories and resulted in fewer cars, which had caused pollution to fade away.

"I know." She was also friends with Ronan, but not like Li. She was sure that if it were someone close to her, she would also have an issue with it, but in her mind, there was only one goal, and nothing would stop her from achieving it.

The taxi drove through the streets and pulled up to their apartment. Upon opening the car door, they heard the distant shot of a gun and hurried to get inside the building. As they waited for the elevator, Lao Shu scanned the front door and shuffled inside to wait beside them. He noticed Li's shaking hands. Mei saw what he had noticed and caught Li's hands in a firm grip with both of hers silently warning him. Then she turned to Lao Shu and smiled.

"You're out late tonight, glad to see you made it home safely!" she said

"Not everyone did," he said.

Li give him a look. "What do you mean?"

"When the night falls, only the strongest survive. For example, people like you" he said, gesturing towards them.

Then he also pointed at himself and said, "And myself included."

The elevator door clicked, and the three of them went in. The Hus were confused about what was going on. They noticed blood on Lao Shu's left cuff. Lao Shu followed the direction of Li's eyes, and then looked pointedly at Li's disheveled appearance and the blood on his black jacket.

"I suppose we both did what we needed to do," he said.

"But you're over sixty. Would you apply to have a child?"

"My son was never fond of blood. He and my daughter-in-law applied but spent months working their way through the list. Couldn't quite handle the last one, so I offered him a hand." The door opened and Lao Shu walked out.

Without turning around, he added, "And congrats to both of you!"

The doors closed. Mei looked at Li.

"Can you imagine him swinging a toaster around and knocking someone out with it?" They both laughed hysterically at the image. It was easier than accepting the reality that anyone, at any point in time, could kill you. The kill needed to be authorized using the verified applicant's fingerprint, but the actual murder could be done by anyone. Contra understood this loophole but didn't try to block it as their only goal was to see a decrease in the population. They weren't interested in who pulled the trigger, so long as someone technically had the right to pull it.

As they entered their apartment and took off their blood-stained clothes, Li thought of Lao Shu's revelation. "You know who we should persuade to kill Ronan for us?" he asked Mei. "Your mother."

"Or, better yet," she said, "let's have your dad do it. I bet he'd love to get out of the house and shake the dust off that old rifle of his. He'd be in Stockholm in a heartbeat." Li's father had been a sniper in the PLA and had always scoffed at Li for wanting to continue his studies.

"The classroom is no place for a man," he would say. As time went by, the two drifted apart, and his father now spent his days with his old army buddies, a military advisor who now, thanks to Contraception, did not have much to contribute. With the stability of resources and the balance of distribution restored, nations had little to quarrel about.

"Let's talk about it tomorrow," Li said as they both entered the shower and the hot steam fogged up the glass. They had a single thought – only one more to go now.

12. RONAN SÖRENSEN

Stockholm, Sweden

The biggest reason why many people don't apply to Contraception isn't because they don't want a baby, it's their fear of dying during the process.

- "Don't let them fool you, China is not a democracy, nor do they ever wish to be," the well-dressed, confident man said. His gray suit was tailored to his swimmer-style physique and his curly light brown hair was swept back to reveal a high forehead. His bright blue eyes twinkled behind his horn-rimmed glasses as he looked out over the audience of tonight's presentation. The invitation had read "China's Ascent through Deception," a speech by renowned international relations theorist Dr. Ronan Sörensen. As he looked at those in attendance, Ronan felt proud of all that he had accomplished.

"The Chinese rhetoric sounds good, and I do credit the speechwriters and those in charge of disseminating the propaganda. It even fooled me for a while! However, the world must not remain ignorant of the facts. China's rise through the past couple of decades has been achieved through deception and lies, both domestically and internationally. At all levels of government, both home and abroad, from *Zhongnanhai*, the seat of the Communist government, to the UN, China is corrupt, and we must no longer let them get away with it. What happened to accountability and preserving the integrity of our systems?"

"The Contraception Initiative was widely supported by China, and their population has decreased at an alarming rate. I posit that China has ulterior and sinister motives behind a majority of their decisions, including their strong push for Contraception to be implemented. It is with this contention that I urge all of you, and the world, to no longer put faith in a country that continues to dominate and control the world's economy through oppressive and shady tactics."

The applause came as Ronan smiled to signify the end of his speech, with both hands gripping the podium. This was among the hundreds of talks he had given about China, all pushing a similar agenda. His views on China were shared by many of his peers and government officials; unfortunately for him, he was more outspoken than his counterparts, which had led to his name being added to several watch-lists. Speaking one's mind, especially against the most powerful country in the world, didn't come without its own set of risks.

Ronan came down from the lectern and took his place back among the audience, who congratulated him on his speech. As someone who spent a lot of time around politicians and lobbyists, he had grown accustomed to the lack of sincerity in such praise. Since graduate school at Harvard, Ronan's interest in China grew into curiosity and perhaps something even stronger: a belief concerning China's involvement in world politics.

This turned almost obsessive, manifesting itself in the form of research, interviews, speeches, papers and investigations into what he believed was corruption on a much grander scale. For Ronan, China was at the heart of most political scandals, manipulating world affairs, and a thorn in the side of the United Nations, an otherwise smooth political machine that benefited almost every country around the world.

His main point of focus now was China's role in getting Contraception accepted by other members of the UN. For a country that had always looked out for itself, they had made many alarming allowances to garner the vote of other countries to support Contraception. He remembered the news almost ten years ago when China had formally given up the islands in the South China Sea to curry favor with Vietnam, the Philippines, Indonesia, and Singapore – who had all voted in favor of Contraception. Understanding that China had one of the biggest populations in the world was a logical justification for why they would push so hard for a population-reducing policy, but for Ronan, it still didn't seem to add up.

Due to his curiosity and the publicity he received concerning this perspective, Ronan had made headlines around the world and was labeled a "China critic," which had so far not caused him any damage beyond the anonymous threats that one could expect.

After the presentation, he hailed a cab to return to his apartment in downtown Stockholm; giving speeches in his hometown was something he always took great pride in. As a little boy growing up on these streets, the style and feel of the architecture, nature, and his surroundings had always been of great importance to him. He thought how the world had seen simpler times. Nowadays, fear ruled the world, with Sweden being no exception.

He saw Swedish Dispo units race by with their flashing red lights, signaling yet another body was in need of retrieval. As he thought about the flashing lights, Contraception, and his speeches over the past few years, he wondered if any of it was making an impact. The city swept by him as his taxi raced through the streets, revealing a city that had faced a turbulent past decade of violence and crime; much like every other major capital in the world.

The surging population over the past few decades had seen capitals grow into something humongous that not even the word "megalopolis" could describe – overflowing, crowded, dirty and crime-ridden. There was only so much available resource and man's natural instinct to survive manifested in a very animalistic way. Once Contraception was implemented, the capital cities were the first to see the population decline. At first, people were assigned targets only in the cities where they lived, but as the Contra application database grew, receiving the name of someone in a different country became normal.

Capitals also became less populated due to the fear of being an easy target. Many people moved to the countryside to live a simpler life and found the bliss of solitude in not being surrounded by potential killers. This was also an easy way for governments to maintain their agriculture industry. Many people gave up lives in the cities to start farms or raise livestock, which was an easier alternative than living in the hotbed of crime that capital cities had become.

As Ronan arrived at his two-bedroom loft apartment, his eyes were scanned, and the bolts unclicked. The giant metal door swung open, revealing a minimalist interior that resembled an old IKEA catalogue.

As he entered the foyer of his apartment, he was greeted by the familiar sight of the pictures hanging on the wall – his diploma from Harvard that read, "Master of International Relations," a photo of him as a child skiing with his parents, and a group photo with his friends, including Li Hu, at a bar in Boston. There was a smile on his face as he remembered the many late-night discussions he had had with Li over realism versus constructivism and the inherent nature of man. He imagined Li's reaction if, with Contraception being in effect for over a decade, he were to ask him, "So, man is inherently good, right?"

As a 40-year-old, Ronan Sörensen never saw the appeal of having children. They were bothersome and expensive and didn't offer much to his life. Ronan got a beer from the fridge and sat down on his black couch, He double-tapped his glass band and the TV turned on to the global news channel. These days, it was challenging for individuals or organizations to be anything but transparent. The overwhelming integration of technology into daily lives, and the mass means of information consumption had cut down on scandals, cover-ups and sinister plots that dominated international politics in the past. However, Ronan wasn't convinced that such things didn't exist anymore.

A man in a gray suit appeared on screen. "Tonight, we bring you an update on Contraception, one of the world's most controversial, yet effective policies. Since its inception in 2060, the world has achieved a 34% reduction in waste, a 56% reduction in emissions, and a 45% increase in agricultural and farm products. The world, as we know it today, enjoys cleaner air and water, and as a whole, is a more harmonious society."

"Harmonious?" Ronan scoffed, as he took a drink from his beer. At what cost? Ronan thought that although he could make his neighborhood quieter by burning his neighbors alive with a flamethrower, the little peace and quiet that came with it wouldn't even compare to the consequences of what he had done at a moral level.

For those without qualms about killing someone, society might be seen as being better off. Contraception and the resulting decline in population had brought with them a cleaner environment, less traffic, a more comfortable living environment, the ability to innovate in science and tech, and more benefits for society, including more public facilities and parks, and improved infrastructure. Much of the money that was being spent on welfare programs and initiatives to deal with population control had been re-allocated and pumped back into society. Killing people might have scarred people emotionally and made them question their ideals, but it also had a tangible benefit for those left to enjoy it.

The news continued: "As Contraception continues to be an important part of everybody's lives, today we have with us Deng Yi, China's premier advocate of Contraception and UN representative. Thank you for joining us sir."

"My pleasure," replied Deng.

"So, let's start with China, a country with one of the world's biggest populations and the world's largest economy. Why was China so passionate about Contraception?"

"As China has strived to transform into a global leader and subsequently, be recognized as a developed country, we looked at what was holding us back. It is not the Chinese fashion to speak in a direct manner, but we as a country realized that the answer was clear: our population. We could not continue to forge ahead as a leader in developing technology, higher education or innovation, so long as our focus remained on building public housing, figuring out how to educate a massive population, and how to feed our citizens. As China continued to play a bigger role in today's globalized world, we realized what needed to be done if we were to be a leader in pushing the boundaries of mankind."

The reporter nodded and asked, "So, Contraception was China's answer to that?"

"Precisely," said Deng, "It was an upfront and innovative policy that still gave people a choice, albeit one with consequences. But which choices in life don't come with consequences? Not only has Contraception curbed China's population, but it has also cut down on those holding our society back, and allowed the stronger and more intelligent individuals to prosper and live full lives in a more abundant and prosperous society."

"True, the population has decreased, but if we look at who is dying, we see that lower-class, uneducated individuals make up a majority of those killed. What do you think causes that?"

"Speaking for China's situation only, I think money. Cleverness is also a huge factor when hoping to successfully complete one's kills. However, those that you label as lower class and uneducated also applied to the same system that rich or educated people did. True, money might make things easier, but all classes of people are presented with the same requirements and are required to abide by the same rules. As for its impact on society, I can't comment on if things are better or worse, they simple are what they are."

"In the past, critics of China accused your government of manipulating the Contraception system for your benefit. Would you care to comment on this?"

"As stated time and again, China takes Contraception seriously and has and continues to abide by all regulations that were put forth by the UN and the board of Contraception. Any allegations about China concerning 'abuse' or 'manipulation' of the Contraception system are solely based on a personal bias with no proof nor substantiating evidence."

"Last, Mr. Deng, do you see a time in the future when Contraception will no longer be a viable or necessary protocol for our world?"

"It's impossible to predict the future, and frankly, the answer to such a question remains unknown. However, in China, we say '*zhuī běn sù yuán*, [5] which means tracing a source back to the problem. The issue our world had faced before Contraception was overpopulation,

---

[5] Trace something to its source, find the root of the problem

which was primarily caused by uneducated and poor people. Now there are requirements for having a child, much more than just the physical act of making a child. Our world can continue to thrive, both as a civilization and as a species. To summarize, I don't see a future in which Contraception won't be a necessary measure."

"Thank you so much for your time and your insights into Contraception."

Ronan swiped his wrist and muted the TV. He hated listening to Chinese politicians, always skimming the surface and taking the high road. Ronan knew what was going on beneath the surface but couldn't yet prove it. He wasn't surprised at Deng's answers; he expected just as much from someone representing China. A lot of big words, a planned defensive strategy, and continued support for this murderous mechanism. He had heard it all before.

But what he couldn't place his finger on was why China was still so enthralled with Contraception. Now that it had been over ten years why did China still find Contraception to be useful?

He stared at the wall to his left, which looked like a scene out of a detective movie, with pictures, red strings, and maps and sticky notes scattered around them, asking unanswered questions. Ronan knew intuitively that there was more to the matter and being a visual thinker, having it all laid out before him helped him absorb the information.

He stood up and walked over to the wall, looking at the almost indecipherable timeline of Contraception – its inception, the deaths of famous politicians, activists, celebrities, civil rights leaders, everything important that had happened since Contraception came into being. Not much about the system had changed in the last few years. He had to admit, despite the methods, that the policy was air-tight when it came to loopholes and covering what happened in each particular situation.

The requirements of the initiative were clear, it was how an individual went about fulfilling those requirements that brought a certain unpredictability to the equation.

He took another sip from his beer and loosened his tie. The big glass window twinkled with the night stars and city lights. Ronan gazed out, wondering how many people on this very night didn't realize that it would be their last. As he took another sip of his beer, he was glad he had chosen to live a life where that thought needn't be a constant source of fear.

13. DISPO

Beijing, China

On average, the Dispo unit of a city of at least one million people will dispose of ten bodies per day.

▪ As far as he could remember, Da Zhuang had always been looked down upon. His father had always told him he would never achieve anything. But as Da Zhuang now loaded up the dead body on the gurney, he reveled in the fact that part of his Dispo paycheck went toward paying for his father's medication.

Da Zhuang had grown up in the countryside and moved to Beijing in search of a better life. Without money for further education, he had worked odd jobs around the capital, anything that would allow him to continue surviving.

It wasn't until a few years later that an opportunity came his way. Contraception had been introduced and with that came the Contraception Disposal Unit, with positions that needed to be filled. Growing up on a farm, Da Zhuang had no problem dealing with blood, as his family killed, cooked, and ate the pigs and chickens they raised. Contraception changed his life.

Da Zhuang smiled every time he put on that bright red uniform, believing he was making a difference; adding value to society. *"Zǎo shēn yù dé,*[6] he often said. Being part of Dispo was also much more lucrative than any other job he had before. When his father had fallen ill, it was Da Zhuang who stepped up to pay for the old man's treatment. He continued to work hard, day in and day out, not only to provide a better life for himself and his father, but also for his wife.

They had met a year ago at a bar. She was sitting in a corner with her friend, drinking a gin and tonic, while he and his friend had come in for a beer after work. He caught sight of her as they entered the bar and he couldn't take his eyes off her. Eventually, he and his friend went up to the young women, introduced themselves and struck up a conversation, which led to dinner, more meetings, and eventually, a marriage proposal.

Da Zhuang was happy. In his mind, he had made it. He had left the countryside and moved to the capital to make a life for himself and in his mind, he had achieved it. The only thing missing from his life was a child, something which he thought was one of the greatest things a human could do – bring life into the world.

Contrary to Li and Mei, Da Zhuang and his wife were eager to have a baby and applied at Contraception soon after they had wedded. Da Zhuang was no stranger to the beast that Contraception brought out in people. Each day, he saw gruesome corpses mangled in new and unique ways. He and his shift partner would often try to piece together what had transpired, trying to understand the story behind the body.

Due to this experience, Da Zhuang thought himself to be clever and had been planning how to kill Li Hu for a while. Li was his second target and was proving to be a challenge to take down. Li didn't appear to have any set routine, nor did he often leave his

---

[6] Cleanliness is next to godliness

apartment. Da Zhuang had discussed with his wife what would be the best approach.

"It's best if I get him during work. I've learned that it's often more convenient to kill someone outside, either early in the morning or late at night. Doesn't need to be fancy, just need to get the job done."

His wife supported him, but had taken no part in the murder herself. She felt it best to let Da Zhuang handle it as he was the so-called expert. Besides, she didn't think it was right for a woman to involve herself in such affairs. Da Zhuang knew since Li didn't have a routine, he would just have to patrol the area around his quarry's apartment and hope he would get lucky. And on this morning, he would be.

***

Li needed to clear his mind. It had been three days since he had killed Chen and staying cooped up in the apartment wasn't helping. His mind had raced, conjuring up images of Sophie and Chen that, combined with his cabin fever, left him restless and irritable. Mei did her best to comfort him, but the guilt wouldn't fade. He tried to drink, exercise, distract himself with TV, but nothing worked.

Li also kept thinking about Ronan, avoiding talking to Mei about it. He knew she would do anything to have a child, but she didn't know Ronan like he did. Li couldn't kill his friend and rob Ronan's wife of her husband. He wouldn't just be killing a friend; he would be killing a husband, a son, a brother, and a future father.

These thoughts rolled around his mind, bringing him to the verge of madness. He needed to get out of the house but knew Mei would never go along with it. He needed to breathe, to feel the air against his face, to physically let go of all the stress, anger and regret he continued to hold onto.

The next morning, Li woke before sunrise, and without making a sound, put on his running clothes before sneaking out of the bedroom. He put in his headphones, grabbed his black hoodie from the closet, and left the apartment. He knew it was dangerous, but the urge to feel free had consumed him.

Upon exiting his apartment building, Li took a big breath of the crisp morning air and set off down the street. With each step, he felt lighter, as if a weight was being lifted off him. He continued to run through the dark streets, seeing nothing but the occasional Dispo truck pass through the intersection. He thought nothing of it. Dispo worked whenever they got a call; it wasn't uncommon to see them at all hours of the night and day. Li breathed the Beijing air, which of late was cleaner and less polluted. In his mind, he admitted that Contraception had improved some things, including pollution. However, the thought soon passed as he tried to clear his mind; he didn't want to think about anything. He kept running, pressing on through the streets, winding his way past skyscrapers and closed shops.

As he ran, Li noticed another red Dispo unit fly by. He caught sight of the back of the car and noticed a white "2" painted on it. He wasn't sure if that was the same one he had seen before. As he kept running, sweat poured down his face and the metal and glass structures reflected his image back at him. In the passing glass of a bank building, once again he saw the Dispo unit with the "2" painted on it. There was no mistaking it. Three times in ten minutes.

Li felt a shiver run through his body. It was clear that someone was following him. He felt his stomach contract as anxiety and fear gripped him. He cursed his stupidity, thinking of Mei who had warned him of this exact situation. He continued running, trying not to show that he knew he was being followed, driven by the feeling that he needed to get out of the open.

He swerved left, turning down a small side street where he knew the truck wouldn't be able to follow. With his right hand, he double-tapped the glass band which connected him to Mei in the apartment. The ringing woke her up and she pressed her band to connect.

"Li, where are you?"

"I went for a run, and now I think I'm being followed. I keep seeing the same Dispo unit."

Li continued to run but now he was more conscious of his surroundings. As he came to the end of the side street, he stood still. Mei remained silent on the other end of the line as Li looked around. The streets lay quiet and dark as most lights remained off at this hour. He turned around, trying to assess if the street he was in was too narrow for a truck. He turned back and looked ahead, shocked at what he saw. The red Dispo truck pulled out of the shadows and came towards him, its bright headlights illuminating him in the otherwise dark street. Li felt a sense of panic.

"He's here," he said. With nothing standing between the two men, he could now see Da Zhuang sitting in the blood-red truck, less than fifty meters away. Both men knew what was happening. Li had expected someone to come for him, but now that it was happening, it was different than how he'd imagined it.

"Li! Talk to me!"

"I have to go, baby, I'll handle it." He tapped the band on his wrist to disconnect from Mei and took a deep breath. Li had known his time would come one day, but he had never expected it to feel this intense. This was what Contraception was all about.

As he stared at the man in the vehicle, he felt a sense of empathy. This man was only doing what Li had done twice now – that which was required for him to have a child. However, now on the receiving end of the situation, Li felt his survival instincts take over. He knew it was him or the man in the truck, and he was not about to let his life slip away for a Dispo worker.

Li took a deep breath while maintaining eye contact with the thickset Chinese man. Then suddenly he turned around and took off, sprinting back down the side street, heading toward downtown Beijing. He heard the roar of the engine behind him as the vehicle tore after him down the narrow street, knocking over garbage cans and anything else in its way. Li turned right, and behind him, heard the Dispo unit skidding around the corner in pursuit. Da Zhuang revved the engine and swerved right in an attempt to hit Li, who leaped onto the sidewalk.

Li kept running, knowing that his chances of survival depended upon his precision and persistence. He pressed on, pushing his legs and rounded the corner, turning right into Beijing's downtown as the sun rose and reflected off the buildings. Da Zhuang whipped his Dispo vehicle around the corner, taking out a number of metal hologram machines situated on the corner that projected the daily morning news for anyone around. There was a grinding sound as metal hit metal, but the truck straightened out.

Ahead, Li saw laborers were unloading bags of grain and had obstructed the sidewalk. He slowed down, with the truck right behind him, closing the distance. Before reaching the laborers, at the last second, he jutted out into the road and dashed in front of Da Zhuang, barely avoiding being crushed. He could hear Da Zhuang curse from the open window and continued to run down the street while his pursuer remained stuck in traffic at a red light.

Li knew it wasn't over. He was at a disadvantage and he was well aware of it. He recognized this area; he was far from his apartment. It would be foolhardy to try to return on foot but staying out in the open wasn't smart. At the next intersection, he took a right, and then an immediate left down an alley. He hoped he could lose Da

Zhuang, as he had no other options. In the alley, he hopped the fence at the back and was now on a new block of the city. He noticed an intersection at the end of the street and didn't see any signs of the Dispo truck. He took another big breath, wanting to believe he had lost the truck and could now return home safely. Li double-tapped his band, and Mei picked up immediately.

"What the fuck!? Are you okay?!"

Li could hear the worry and fear in her voice.

He did his best to reassure her. "I think it's okay, he's gone now."

Li stood with his back to the wall, looking both left and right.

Then he stepped out of the alley and into the morning light, saying, "I'll be home so…" but the blare of the red Dispo unit cut him off. He looked behind him and saw his assailant tearing up the street, less than two hundred meters behind him. Li ran like mad toward the closest intersection, which now had a green light. He ran with everything he had, flexing his muscles and pushing off the ground with each step. He flew down the street, not bothering to get on the sidewalk because he knew this was his last chance. The sun was rising in front of him and Li ran toward it like his life depended on it. He was now a hundred meters from the intersection. The man was right behind him, closing the gap. He could hear the blare of the Dispo siren as he continued to run.

As he approached the intersection, Li saw the light turn yellow and then red as he pressed on. Straining his legs, he flew through the intersection. Da Zhuang pushed his luck too and tried to stay with Li through the red light. As he ran across the street, he heard a deafening crash and turned around to see what had caused the sound. What he saw made him stop.

A construction truck coming from the opposite direction carrying steel beams hadn't noticed the red light due to the sun shining off the metal and glass buildings, and tearing through the intersection, had collided head on with the Dispo truck, hitting the driver side at full speed. The metal beams rained all over the road, covering it along with shattered glass from the windows.

Li could not believe his luck. The entire driver side of the Dispo truck had caved in. Both the drivers were slumped over their steering wheels, with blood on their airbags. Li wondered what would happen now. He heard sirens in the distance signaling that the police were on their way. He felt another twinge of panic and decided it was best to not be there when the police showed up.

A crowd had gathered, as was the custom for Chinese when something happened. However, this was a significant enough event to warrant a crowd. It wasn't every day that two vehicles collided at full speed in an intersection. Li turned his back to the cars and walked off, away from the crowd that had now started to take pictures. Most cameras these days were installed in one's eyes, as that was deemed the most useful and efficient way to see and capture a moment. People just needed to tap their glass band and a picture would be taken and then saved in their database.

As Li walked away, questions filled his mind. Was the Dispo driver dead? And if he was, did that mean Li was off the list? Was he free? Speculation drove him crazy as he sprinted back home. As he reached his apartment building, he paused to catch his breath. This morning had involved a lot more running than he had initially planned. He also knew he would have to face Mei and explain to her why a morning run was worth destroying everything they had worked for.

He opened the door to the apartment and was met with Mei rushing into his arms and clutching him fiercely. He wrapped his arms around her, and when she pulled away, Li could tell that she had been crying, something that she rarely did.

"What in the hell were you thinking?" she said at last in a choked voice. "Do you know what could have happened out there? You could have died! And what was I supposed to do? Just wait to be called by Dispo? How could you do this? We've already killed two people, and you were just going to put that in jeopardy because you wanted to go for a run?!"

She gestured toward the treadmill, "And what is that for then? I explicitly told you not to leave this apartment because it was dangerous and I had a feeling that your name had been given out. And what did you do? YOU LEFT THE APARTMENT!"

Li didn't let her continue with her tirade. He held her firmly by the shoulders, looked into her eyes, and said with patent sincerity, "I'm sorry, my love."

Mei knew he felt guilt for what he had done and yelling at him was not the solution.

"It's okay; it's out of my system now, I'm just glad you're alright. What happened?!"

As they sat down at the kitchen table, he told her the events of the morning.

A look of excitement came into her eye and she said, "So he could be dead? This is fantastic news!"

Li understood her reaction, but still a man – two men – were possibly dead somewhere.

"I'll call Mr. Xi to confirm."

Li scrolled through his contact list, double-tapped their application manager, and a familiar voice answered the phone. "Mr. Hu, how are you this morning? Early start to the day I see."

Li never understood how this man could be so ebullient, especially in his line of work.

"I have a question for you," he said without preamble. "A man tried to kill me this morning but was involved in a car accident. I am curious if he died in the car crash. If he did, what would be the status of my Contra application?"

"Yes, we heard about the collision, but fortunately for our applicant, he is still alive. He had surgery this morning for internal bleeding and appears to be recovering. It's fortunate for you too. As things stand now, you aren't back in the database because your name still belongs with the man in the hospital as his target. Until he dies or rescinds his application, your name will not go back in the database. But if he dies, then your name will go back in the database and will be given out to someone else. So as long Mr. Da Zhuang remains hospitalized, I'd say this is the best-case scenario for you."

Li ended the call and looked at Mei.

"It's not over," he said. "He didn't die in the crash, I'm still his target."

Mei was the first to recover.

"Well, at least he's out of the game for a while. If he's recovering from surgery, there's no way he'll be able to come after you immediately. And a Dispo worker can't afford a hitman, so for the time being, you're safe."

Li tried to stay calm. The stress, anxiety and moral conflict, not to mention the physical act of murder, was driving him insane. All this for a baby, he thought. I'm killing people to change dirty diapers and be woken up by shrill crying at 03:00.

He looked at Mei. "Do you think my parents would have killed three people for me?" This question had been going through his mind for quite some time. Even knowing what they now knew about him, everything he would come to do, be, and achieve, would they still have wanted him if it required them to kill three people?

"Well your mom would absolutely have wanted you, but I think it would have been your dad who would have done the killing. I think it might have been good for him, sort of stress relief. So yes, I think they'd have done it."

"And yours?" he asked

"I've thought about it too. They told me they would have, but I'm not so sure. You know my mom, very strong in her convictions about morality and what she defines as 'good.'"

"Well I used to be strong in my moral beliefs too until I decided our family was more important. Maybe if it was an actual choice and not a hypothetical question, she'd have murdered for you."

Mei appreciated his comfort, but still didn't believe him. She knew her mother wouldn't have killed for her, but she'd be damned if she didn't kill for her own child. As the Hus sat at the table, the events from the morning began to sink in.

One man had attempted to end Li's life, with no regard to who he was as a person; he was merely a target. Li reflected on his attitude toward Sophie and Chen. To him, they were more than targets, but to rationalize their death, much like humans have done throughout history, it soon became the classic argument of "us vs. them."

Li had known death before, he had seen his grandparents pass and a friend drown in elementary school. Death didn't scare him, nor the idea of an afterlife. What scared Li was leaving this world unfulfilled. Wasted potential of an untaken opportunity was what kept him up at night. These things were the primary motivators behind his decision to apply to Contraception. He preferred to avoid the question "What if…?" at all costs, instead choosing to live life, for either better or worse. He was content with at least making a choice instead of doing nothing at all.

However, Contraception was challenging the limits of what he deemed to be moral behavior.

Mei flicked her wrist, illuminating the large glass screen, and she opened a browser with a built-in VPN to check the news. China's censorship still remained problematic for reliable journalism. She first checked the daily news report about the day's deaths; a grim but popular service provided by Contraception.

"As you can see, Beijing this week ranked highest in Contraception deaths in China with a total of 1,274, much higher than in other major cities like Shanghai or Shenzhen." A smiling Chinese woman read it out in the same manner that one reported the weather. "Meanwhile, unauthorized murders or 'old-fashioned' murders if you will, have almost gone extinct. It looks like most people are just waiting for Contraception to catch up with those they wish dead."

Mei then swiped her hand and typed in Ronan's name, curious about their final target. She found a news report from the day before in which a man in a black suit and an expensive haircut said, "We're joined by Ronan Sörensen, a famous scholar from Stockholm, to discuss with us his views on the past twenty years with Contraception. How are you tonight, Mr. Sörensen?"

Li and Mei both straightened up as they saw their old university friend and next target on the screen in front of them. For Li, it was almost like seeing a ghost. Ronan smiled brightly and looked into the camera, as if right into Li's eyes.

"Great, thanks."

"Now that Contraception has been a part of society for ten years, what do you expect from the next ten?"

"That's tough. We've seen a drastic drop in our population, which was the ultimate intent, and we've also seen substantial improvements in pollution, resource management, and quality of life – for those still left alive. Going forward, I don't expect Contraception to be abolished, but I expect some changes. Although I disagree with the entire concept of Contraception, I understand its necessity. But still, to keep and maintain a healthy workforce, especially in the agricultural or manual labor industries, we're going to need people. And we can't meet those labor needs if we keep the current 3:1 ratio."

Li and Mei watched in fascination as the man they were planning to kill appeared right before their eyes. The host asked another question.

"As an outspoken expert on China and at times, critic, what do you believe is the relationship between China and Contraception?"

"It's definitely a favorable one. China, as I've said before, pushed hard for Contraception. I believe China to be a naturally corrupt nation and although it's only speculation, I believe China is, let's say, manipulating Contraception for their own benefit. That's all I can say on the issue."

"A strong accusation Mr. Sörensen. One last question for you: has the initiative been worth it?"

Ronan waited a bit before answering. He adjusted his tie and sighed.

"It depends on your priorities," he answered at last. "Every single person needs to ask themselves what's the most important thing in their life. Morality? Family? Or, is it bigger things, such as the environment? Or the overall well-being of their country, or the world?"

"Contraception has helped us solve these big picture problems caused by overpopulation, but at the expense of our morality and the nature of mankind. Ten years have passed and people talk about murder the way one might talk about going to the grocery store. Contraception has desensitized us to where I fear we won't be able to go back to what was considered pre-initiative normal."

"Is it worth it? I can't say. Do we deserve it? Absolutely. We brought this upon ourselves, as a world, through our reckless neglect for what was happening and feeble attempts to deal with the issue.

So, ten years ago, a system was designed for us to murder people to conceive. It's a horrendous policy, but it's what we deserve for our lack of responsibility in dealing with the issue before it became a catastrophe."

"Thank you, sir, we appreciate your views and look forward to hearing more about China when you have something to back up your claims. That's all from us here about Contraception, and now, on to the weather."

The TV was tuned out as Li and Mei now pondered what to do. It never seemed to end. Kill two people, escape death from a Dispo driver by a hair's breadth, and now the last man on your list appears on international news on a completely different continent. Seeing Ronan after so many years brought back a flood of memories for Li. He knew there was only one thing to do, but thinking something and doing it were completely different things.

"He was right there! Can you believe it?" he said, not expecting an answer.

He knew Mei was also wondering what Ronan was doing on the news and perhaps, how they were going to navigate through Stockholm to kill him. Her mind was on finishing the job and in her mind, it was all that Ronan was, a job. She knew they needed to discuss what to do next, but also needed to approach the topic with tact. Ronan's time was coming and it was imperative that Li didn't hesitate when that time came.

14. THE DECISION

Beijing, China

According to worldwide research after five years of Contraception, 73% of respondents said they support the initiative, claiming the benefits of a lower population outweighed the moral consequences of killing someone. The remaining participants condemned the initiative, claiming it was not only wrong on a moral or religious basis, but it also violated the Universal Declaration of Human Rights adopted by the United Nations General Assembly.

▪ Over the past few days, Li and Mei had been discussing if and how they would kill Ronan. Mei had pushed for the kill, arguing that their family was the most important thing and that old friendships die, though making sure not to use that exact word.

Li had argued, as usual, that it was morally wrong and in addition, he didn't want to be put in a position where he had to choose between having a child and keeping his friend.

"Then what would Sophie and Chen have been for?" asked Mei. She had a valid point. They had gone through an incredible amount of risk and effort and with only Ronan left to kill, it would be a complete waste of it all if Li baulked now. Also, it would mean giving up on their dream to raise a child.

"What am I supposed to do?" Li asked in despair. "Fly to Stockholm and say, 'Ronan, long time my friend, good to see you, uhh, sorry about this, but I've got to kill you because having a child is more important than our friendship or your right to life?'"

"I would phrase it differently," replied Mei.

Li walked around the room, massaging his throbbing temples, then stood near the big window overlooking the city. The morning sun had risen high and it was now close to lunchtime. He looked out as far as he could see, imagining Ronan in Stockholm, living a life that Li was now contemplating to end. From his apartment, the cars and the people on the street looked like tiny insects, almost as though if they were erased, it wouldn't matter. Li's life wouldn't be impacted if the tiny man in the blue shirt on the street below was wiped off the face of this earth.

This was how he was trying to rationalize the murder of Ronan. If Ronan died, Li would be sad and feel guilty, but his life wouldn't change, except being allowed to have a child. He sighed. He knew that Mei was awaiting his answer and he knew what she wanted to hear. Li walked toward the couch and gestured for her to come sit with him.

Without looking at her, he said, "If we do this, we'll have to go to Stockholm and we'll need to plan this out. We can't have another Chen-style situation on our hands. If it weren't for that toaster, who knows where we might be now."

"Of course," responded Mei. Chen letting off his gun in his apartment was not a situation she wanted to find herself in again either.

As they sat on the couch, they knew their trip to Stockholm would forever change their fate. There would be no denying the fact that they would have murdered three people, but those resourceful enough to achieve that went on to have a baby and just kept their eyes on the future. Everyone's past contained secrets and no closet was complete without a few skeletons. However, society still carried on.

Ten years ago, someone known to be a convicted murderer was shunned by the world. They couldn't gain employment, had few friends, and were judged harshly by society. Now, however, if you killed three people through Contraception, you were deemed clever, strong and fit to be a parent. These people were congratulated and looked upon as doing something beneficial for the world.

Li looked at Mei. "But even if we do kill Ronan, we're not going to have a Contrabration."

"Absolutely not. We'll just have a baby. A beautiful baby who will hopefully cure cancer one day or set an Olympic record. Because after all our efforts, an average baby isn't worth it," she said.

Li laughed, put an arm around her and hugged her tightly. "Our baby will be perfect." He kissed her and lifted her chin to meet his eyes.

"But seriously, do you think our child will make a difference in the wheel of life or even create a new wheel, so to speak?" Mei said slowly. "Or will our kid be just another cog in the machine? Not everyone can be a leader; the majority of people are followers. Is that what we're doing this for? Having a baby that can grow up to be average?"

He looked at Mei tenderly, tucking strands of her tousled hair behind her ear.

"We're having a baby because we are in love and we both believe a baby is the most beautiful thing we can leave this world long after we are gone," he said with a gentle smile. "Whatever our child does in his or her life is up to him or her, we can only provide love and support and share our mistakes with them, hoping they don't make the same ones we did."

Mei felt the warmth of his exploring hand on her face and the sincerity in his words. She nodded contentedly.

Li looked out the window for a moment but then turned back resolutely and said, "I'm in. Let's kill Ronan." He grimaced while he said it, but continued with what he had thought out in his mind, "It sounds horrible to say it, and it won't be easy, but our family comes first and will always come first. I'm willing to do that for us and -" he looked at her flat stomach, "our future cog."

Mei smiled. She knew it was hard for Li to do this, but it meant so much to her.

She kissed his cheek and whispered, "I love you."

With the decision now made, it was time to plan. Li and Mei knew Da Zhuang was still an existing threat and they needed to kill Ronan as soon as possible. Mei was praying that Da Zhuang had complications in his operation and would remain in hospital as long as possible. She knew it was wrong to think this, but backing her husband over a Dispo worker was an easy choice. The Hus had decided that again, surprise would be the best element, and had chosen to not contact Ronan for fear of arousing suspicion.

"Ronan works for the Swedish Institute for Security and Development Policy, but often travels abroad to attend seminars and conferences, mostly concerning China," said Li.

"I guess some people never change. He was always so opinionated about China."

Again, the Hus had decided to kill him at his home, as it was the place least likely to drawn unwanted attention. However, they were in conflict about how best to get into his home.

"Look, killing Chen wasn't smooth, but getting him from his car to his apartment was the easiest part of the whole process!" remarked Li.

"I think it would be easier to play it like we were vacationing in Sweden and just ran into him. Then he'd invite us into his apartment and we can catch him off guard."

"But what if he suspects something? What if he senses our nervousness and the whole thing gets ruined? I think we should surprise him and either get him to his place under duress or break into his apartment."

They were at a stalemate. Both their plans had their pros and cons, and since they did not want a repeat of their last kill, it was a tough call to make. They needed another opinion. Li made a phone call and very soon, there was a knock at the door. Li answered it.

"Lao Shu, thank you for coming."

The old man stood in the doorway, dressed in a grey sweater and loose khaki pants. Slowly he came inside and sat on the couch. Mei offered him a cup of tea, which he readily accepted.

Without any pleasantries, Lao Shu remarked, "So I hear you're at a bit of a crossroads with your next kill?"

"That's correct," said Mei, trying not to show her astonishment that he knew why he was there. She went on to explain what had happened with Chen, with Li interjecting to explain his relationship with Ronan.

"A difficult situation indeed. I couldn't imagine killing my friend, but I do suppose that the old saying holds true 'Xuè nóng yú shuǐ.'[7] Now about the logistics."

Li smiled. Lao Shu was like his father, focused on the details and the tangibility of a situation, and not so much the abstract parts.

"You're going to be in a foreign country. It's going to be a new environment and will present its own challenges, different than those

---

[7] Blood is thicker than water.

here in the capital." Lao Shu took a sip of his tea before continuing. "Having said that, I would recommend to go with what you know."

Li wasn't sure what the old man meant. "What do you mean?"

"If you try to kidnap someone and take them to their apartment to kill them in a foreign country, where you aren't entirely sure of society's reaction to Contraception, it could present a flood of challenges. However, if you go to Stockholm as a tourist, and wait for the right moment to arise, you may be out of your element as a tourist, but not as a murderer. I side with Mei on this one. You might feel bad playing the part of a friend, but I think it will be the easiest route."

"But we *are* friends!" a defiant Li said.

"Of course," replied Lao Shu, as his blue eyes held Li's stare. "That's why you're going to murder him."

Li wasn't sure if it was sarcasm or food for thought. It was too late now; he had made up his mind and promised to Mei. He couldn't turn back now. As she had said, just move forward.

They continued to drink tea, discussing in details their plan of action to tackle Ronan's case. It was finally decided that they would fly to Stockholm and stay there a few days before calling Ronan and setting up a dinner.

"If we're already there for a few days, it won't look like we're flying there specifically for him," said Mei.

The two men agreed. Li felt safe at the thought of leaving Beijing, as the odds of Da Zhuang leaving the hospital and following him to Europe were not high. However, there were still many other things that needed to be figured out.

"I can't exactly take a gun on the plane," said Li. "So, what do we do? We're vacationing, we meet Ronan for dinner, and then what? I cut his throat with a broken wine glass?"

Mei looked up. "What about that metal string? Surely we could get that onto an airplane and then use it to…"

"To what? Decapitate him?" Li recoiled in horror.

Lao Shu leaned forward to stop the argument. "Dead is dead," he said in a tone of finality. "The only thing that matters is the result."

Li got up and began to walk around. He needed to move to think. He understood the logic of taking one of the weapons that Wang had given him, knowing the metallic rope would be the only thing to pass an airport security check. The alternative was to fly to Sweden empty-handed and then work to get a weapon or kill Ronan with his bare hands. The latter would never happen.

He gave in. "Ok, we'll take the metal rope," he said at last. "It's not the cleanest method, but as Lao Shu said, the only thing that matters is that he dies."

The conversation made him sick to his stomach.

Lao Shu nodded and finished the last of his tea. He stood up and thanked both Li and Mei for inviting him to their home. As he approached the door that Li had opened for him, he slowly turned back to face them.

"It is a great honor to bring a child into this world, and I'm sure you will both be fantastic parents. We all make choices in this world, but it's better to have tried and lost, than never to have tried at all."

With that, Lao Shu left their apartment and Li closed the door behind him. Mei looked at Li with a puzzled look on her face.

"Why does he always give advice at the doorstep? Is that his trademark?"

Li laughed as he remembered Lao Shu doing the same thing at the door of the elevator.

"Perhaps it adds to the allure and mystery of his wisdom. Or maybe old age has caught up with him and he forgot what he wanted to say while sitting on the couch. Either way, I'm grateful for his opinion as I don't think we could have settled this by ourselves."

As the Hus got ready for bed, they were both imagining what would happen in Stockholm. Would it be a flawless murder? What challenges would they encounter? Could they go through with it when the time came?

These questions preyed on their minds as they lay down in bed together and prepared for what awaited them the next day.

***

"Did you remember to pack socks?" Mei yelled from the bathroom. For some reason, socks were the one thing that Li always forgot when packing.

"Of course!" he yelled back. Quickly looking in the direction of the bathroom to make sure she couldn't see him, he opened the top drawer of his cabinet and grabbed a handful of socks and stuffed them into his suitcase. The Hus were getting ready to leave for Stockholm under the guise of taking a much-needed holiday. Li was still on his summer vacation, and Mei was doing only freelance work at the moment. Their trip could not have been better timed.

Li checked his band, they had only an hour left before their flight departed, but these days, that was plenty of time.

"Time to go!" he yelled as Mei walked out of the bathroom, looking beautiful. He stared in wonderment at her for a moment, thinking how lucky he was that he had her in his life, notably this last month. Her decisiveness and commitment to their Contraception application had been qualities that helped Li do what he had done.

With their bags packed, Li looked around the apartment wondering if they had forgotten anything. Then it came to him, the metal rope, or as he called it, "the strangler." He reached under the coffee table and pulled out the black case that contained the metal string. He took it out and looked at Mei, holding out his hand.

"Wear it like a bracelet. Just wrap it around your wrist."

Mei looked at him, shocked. "And what if it gets activated? I'm going to lose my entire hand." She had a point, and she stared at him with a look of defiance.

"It's activated only by my touch. As long as I don't double-tap it with my thumb, which won't happen accidentally, you'll be fine."

With a reluctant look on her face, Mei took the shiny silver metal and wrapped it around her wrist a few times until she could tie the loose ends together, forming what looked like a strange bracelet. "If we need anything else, we can pick it up there."

They took one last look at their apartment, not sure if they would ever see it again. Their journey to Stockholm was their last chance to start the life they had been dreaming of for years, but the trip also presented a unique set of challenges and risks.

Mei checked her luggage to make sure she had the last glass tablet given to them for Ronan by Contra. Li pressed a button outside of his luggage, and it immediately compressed, squeezing out all the air within and transforming his once bulging suitcase into what was now the size of a gym bag, which he slung over his shoulder. Mei did the same with hers.

Due to the increase in population over the last 50 years, physical space had become a precious commodity. Airlines charged exorbitant fees for carry-on items due to demand for space. Innovators that were tired of paying more than their fair share figured out a solution. Special air-proof suitcases were now everywhere. With the click of a button, a mechanism within the fabric condensed and squeezed the contents within to expel all the air and save much-needed space when flying.

At first, the technology acted like a trash compactor, breaking everything within, but now, sensors in the fabric detect hard and soft objects as well as pliable and non-pliable materials, learning where to apply pressure and what to avoid during the compression process.

Once the bags were compressed, both swiped their bands across a small circular piece of glass attached to the zippers of the tags. This linked their contact information and flight details so that the bags could be sorted correctly. Mei slipped the strap of her bag across her chest and opened the door of their apartment. Li followed her and without looking back, closed the door.

Out on the street, he looked around before telling Mei, "The closest tube station is on Fifth Street."

The tube station was the transport and security system able to scan an entire person and their luggage before shuttling them into a high-speed train that would take them to the airport. These days, with the decline in population, travel had become an enjoyable experience again. However, decades earlier, airports saw the worst of what an overpopulated planet meant. Changes had been implemented so that getting into an airport was allowed only for airport personnel, security teams and passengers. Pickups and transport from the airport, just like in the years past, could be made outside, but going inside to wait was no longer an option. Crowd control became vital in dealing with the surplus people and limiting who was allowed inside an airport was just the start.

As the Hus rounded the corner, they found the tube station. Two guards stood on either side of a staircase that went underground. Between the guards stood a table with two scanners, one on each side. Li stood on the left and Mei on the right, scanned their bands and proceeded down the stairs. Mei had bought the tickets online the day before, authorizing them to enter the tube station. Sensors on both sides of the stairs scanned for weapons or explosives, and both of their bands flashed green with the words "Clear."

They walked toward the area marked "International Departures" and saw hundreds of clear tubes that extended from the floor all the way to the ceiling. They placed their bags on a large conveyor belt that would take them to the sorting facility. The bags would be scanned by their own security system, and then the small glass circle with their flight details would also be scanned before all cargo was loaded onto a separate train to the airport. Upon arriving at the airport, all bags would be sorted according to their destination and automatically loaded onto the plane before the passengers arrived.

After sending their bags off, Li and Mei went to stand in line in front of a large transparent tube, much like that used in banks to send checks from a car to the teller. This time of day wasn't too busy, and although there were still lines queuing for the hundred tubes or so, it was nothing compared to ten years ago.

Li held Mei's hand. He knew that although she put up a tough exterior, she was nervous inside. Then he let go of her hand and entered the large tube in front of him, whose door had now slid open. As he entered, along with his carry-on bag, the door slid down, and his body and bag were scanned for weapons, drugs and other prohibited objects.

Airport security had been significantly upgraded to make things more efficient for the masses. As his band flashed green, signaling he was clear, the platform beneath him shot up, transporting Li through the ceiling to the train which would take him to the airport. After their platform had taken him to the train station, a new platform slid into place, and the door opened, allowing Mei to enter and begin her security scan.

The whole process took just a few seconds, minus the time someone needed to get rid of a prohibited article. However, this was a rare occurrence as most people didn't want the embarrassment of the tube turning red due to prohibited items. Society had realized that due to the sheer quantity of people, holding up a line was a cause for outrage and violence.

Li admired the new system, not only for its creativity but also its brilliance in both efficiency and design. He had seen someone's band turn red before in the tube. The entire tube would turn a faint red, and a hologram would appear on the door facing the traveler, detailing the prohibited item in their bag or on their person. The passenger would then be instructed to remove the item and place it in a box protruding at the rear of the tube. If this scanner detected a threat not picked up by the stair scanners, such as a weapon, drugs, or explosives, in less than a second the tube would send the person to a secure room below the station to be dealt with by airport security forces. The tubes were bullet, fire, and explosion-proof and so far, had a ninety-nine percent success rate in preventing any threats, dangers, terrorist attacks or catastrophes since their implementation.

As Li and Mei both reached the top of the platform, Li looked at "the strangler" on her wrist.

"Glad to see you've got both your hands with you," he laughed. He thought they were lucky that she had got through without being detected and that the innocent looking "strangler" hadn't malfunctioned and sliced off her hand. He silently thanked the PLA for the innovative ability and quality of weaponry.

The platform they now stood on was huge, with high-speed trains leaving the airport every three minutes. Full or not, the train doors would close and shoot off towards the airport, allowing the passengers to get where they needed to go. Gone were the days of dealing with physical tickets or long lines in security. People's bands contributed to the convenience of modern travel and not having to deal with people-to-people interactions. There was no need for passports, boarding passes, or any forms to fill in when traveling overseas. Everything was done through a person's pass and the corresponding glass band. Li and Mei stood in front of the empty track waiting for the next train to arrive.

"Excited for our trip?" he asked.

"Certainly! A little sun, Swedish food, beautiful scenery, oh, and killing your friend from university. Nothing like a vacation to refresh the soul."

Though she meant it to be a joke, it set Li thinking once again what would happen in the next seventy-two hours. The train pulled up to the platform, and they entered and found their seats. The train whisked through the city on the tracks built high above the streets and wound its way through buildings until it increased speed on reaching the main line to the airport.

It was an overcast day, with gray clouds looming above, threatening to rain. Looking down the train window, they saw streets they had known for years, but which at that moment looked different. Perhaps the streets had changed, or maybe it was they who had, and they now saw things differently.

Li tried to relax as he felt anxiety building in his stomach. The feeling of a knot forming in his gut and the same thought running fixatedly over and over in his mind was something that he simply could not control. He knew the only way to get relief from this sensation was to take care of the thing that was causing his anxiousness – Ronan. As the train arrived at the airport, the Hus grabbed their bags and got off.

Most airports had remained the same as before, but the layout was different. Airports were no longer in charge of security, nor did they undergo the process of weighing each bag and the monotony of printing out a boarding ticket. As Li looked around for their gate number, he realized it had been a while since his last trip. He noticed how relaxed the airport had become. Not only had the drop in population made traveling more pleasant, but airports now offered a greater variety of amenities to travelers. They had gyms, spas, showers, robotic massages, fortune-telling, and upscale restaurants, bars, and pastry shops.

Mei took a moment to check the holographic sign for departures projected from the ceiling and found their gate number. As they made their way there, Li wondered if anyone else that he saw was at the airport for a similar reason. Perhaps they too had received a target not in China and were headed abroad to end a life. He hoped that they too didn't need to kill a friend or someone they knew. The thought whirred in his mind as he and Mei found a coffee shop and sat down.

Li ordered a flat white and Mei a black coffee. Neither was big on sugar.

"This is going to sound terrible," said Li, "but what if our kid is born with a mental disability?"

Smiling, Mei told him, "One, you worry too much. And two, we'll love our child no matter what. After this whole ordeal, just having a child, disabled or not, will be a blessing."

They continued to sit at the coffee shop, discussing their plan for Stockholm and Ronan and sipping their coffee until it was time to board their flight. When their flight was announced, they made their way to the gate, swiped their bands on the scanner by the door and boarded the plane.

The time had finally arrived for them, and although perhaps not ready, they were willing, which was the first step in making any choice. Once all the passengers were on board, the plane pulled out of the boarding area and made its way onto the runway. This was it – the last target on their list. In a matter of days, they would be face to face with not only their friend from university, but also their biggest challenge yet.

15. THE DISCOVERY

Stockholm, Sweden

The average lifespan of a baby born illegally, outside of Contraception, is only 16 years. Many of these children die due to malnutrition. However, scientists have also argued that lack of societal integration, education, and the ability to live a free life also impacted their physical health.

▪ Sitting at an open-air restaurant in downtown Stockholm, Li and Mei enjoyed a glass of wine with their shrimp salad. They had been in Sweden for two days now and, despite their purpose there, were actually enjoying the trip. This was their first time in Sweden, and everything enthralled them – the architecture, the food, the way people dressed and the ease with which they smiled and made conversation, and the cleanliness.

"Why didn't we ever move to Stockholm?" he asked. This was a question he had been asking over the past forty-eight hours on multiple occasions. He took another sip of his wine.

Mei answered pertly, "Someone wanted to teach at a prestigious Chinese university, because, and correct me if I'm wrong, 'shaping the minds of the future is more than work, it's a duty.'"

Li smiled as he recalled saying those words to her years ago. He was happy with his life then, but after each trip he took abroad, he had always thought a little more about permanently moving out of Beijing.

He looked at his band, 18:45. They were right where they needed to be. As the sun faded and the cool night air crept in from the north, the Hus were expecting Ronan. Over the last two days, they had located and followed him, searching for a pattern in his behavior.

It turned out that for the past two nights, Ronan had a drink along with some lutefisk at the same bar. The bartender had informed Li that this was a common occurrence.

As the Hus sat at their table along the road, less than a block from where Ronan was assumed to be headed, they continued to wait, trying to hide their intense anxiousness.

It was Mei who first noticed the tall, slender man in a gray suit walking down the street. The sun at his back outlined him and his silhouette seemed to float on the street. His long legs carried him past the big windows of the shops, and Mei took her eyes off him, looking at Li.

"It's him," she whispered.

Though he was dying to turn back and look, Li didn't turn back. He could now hear Ronan's shoes hitting the cobblestone street. The steps became slower and then came to a halt as Ronan spotted Mei. Mei watched him turn back and make eye contact with her and she smiled.

"Mei!" he said warmly and his mouth formed a wide smile. Mei flashed her teeth, and her eyes seemed to light on seeing a good friend after such a long time. Finally, Li turned around to face the man with whom he had spent many a long night conversing and drinking.

Both men smiled. "Li! I can't believe it's you!" Ronan shouted. The two men hugged each other as Mei pulled up a chair for Ronan.

He sat down and the attentive waiter brought another wine glass for him.

"What brings you to Stockholm?"

"I'm on summer holiday," Li said easily. "And Mei wasn't too busy either. So, we thought it best to get out of Beijing for a while. I remember you always talking about how beautiful Sweden is in August, so we thought we'd come and see for ourselves."

"That's so great to hear. Man, it's been ages since we were last together in Boston. You should have let me know you were coming! It's such a surprise you just turning up like this."

"A bit of a last-minute trip," commented Mei, smiling.

As the three of them sat at the table drinking wine, laughing and catching up, it was hard to imagine that the Hus had set up this rendezvous with an ulterior motive. For anyone on the outside looking in, it was just three friends talking together, enjoying the evening as the sun crept below the horizon.

"We saw your interview online a few days ago; I see your notions about China's 'hidden motives' haven't changed."

"It's nothing personal. I just believe China isn't all that it wants the world to believe. Without transparency, corruption runs rampant. Until that veil over China is lifted, I refuse to believe the lies."

"Corruption exists everywhere, we've seen it in your country, and almost every country in the world," retorted Li. He wasn't angry at Ronan's remarks, they had had this discussion many times before.

"Of course, but I'm talking about Contraception. Something about China's push for it, and the events that have transpired over the past decade lead me to believe something else is going on. After decades of fighting for the South China Sea, they just gave it up to get votes for the initiative? That doesn't strike you as strange?"

"Always the conspiracy theorist," laughed Mei.

The idea didn't surprise either her or Li as China had issues with corruption in the past. However, these days, it was tough to find evidence of corruption as technology and the methods used were a lot more advanced and often, sneakier.

As the night wore on, Ronan suggested they check out another place. So, after paying the bill, the three of them set off down the street. A cold autumnal wind blew from the north. Summer was coming to a close and fall was sneaking in, presenting a new beginning for many people. Students would start school, people were starting new jobs, and if things went as planned, Li and Mei would be free to have their child.

As they walked down the quiet street, Ronan rolled a cigarette and lit it, inhaling the blue-tinted smoke and exhaling into the cool night sky. The moon had just risen and along with the evening stars, illuminated the street below. They reached their destination, *Akkurat*, a local bar and restaurant that Ronan often visited after a late night of conferences and interviews.

The trio found a spot for themselves on the roof and Ronan ordered three glasses of akvavit, a yellowish alcoholic drink distilled from potatoes and flavored with herbs and spices, giving off a sweet smell, but leaving a bitter after taste. He also asked for six potato dumplings filled with seared bacon and onion and served with melted butter and lingonberry sauce. The smell of the sweet berries and charred meat filled the air as the candle on the table danced in the wind, providing just enough light to illuminate Li and Mei's faces as they drank and enjoyed their so-called holiday. There were a few other tables in the room, with the other guests huddled in conversation as the star-lit sky shone down from above. The quiet murmur from the surrounding tables and the quiet footsteps of the passing waiters seemed to break the silence without being too loud.

"You guys will love Stockholm; the food here is fantastic. Speaking of which, I've been cooking a lot and take it with a grain of salt, if you will, but I'm not half bad," Ronan boasted.

"Well we're in town for another two days, we'd love to try it," said Mei, seizing the opportunity they had been waiting for.

"What about tomorrow night then?" asked Ronan. "I'd love to cook for you guys, and we'll talk, and maybe, just maybe, I'll convince you I'm right about China," he said well-humoredly.

They laughed and Li nodded.

"That sounds fantastic! *Skål*," he said, raising his glass to the center of the table. Looking at Ronan, he said, "To old friends," and then added, "And new beginnings," this time looking at Mei. The three clinked glasses and took a sip of their drink, each enjoying the toast for a different reason. Ronan was delighted to be reunited with old friends, Mei was thankful they had found their last target and their plan was working, and Li appreciated the current moment, resolutely focusing on it.

Whatever might happen over the next twenty-four hours, the fact that he was there, with Mei and an old friend were important to him. He wondered how many people had lost their lives to Contraception and never been able to see their loved ones or friends ever again. Da Zhuang's life had nearly ended but somehow, he was fortunate enough to survive.

Li smiled absentmindedly as the others set their drinks back on the table. They continued to drink and eat for some more time till Li noticed Mei getting sleepy. She had a habit of staring off into space when she was tired, which helped her from nodding off. Ronan asked for the bill, and as the three of them walked outside, they said their goodbyes.

"So, tomorrow night then, let's say 18:30? Does that work? My place for the best Swedish meatballs you've ever had! Here, let me send you the address."

He and Li both extended their wrists, and Ronan lightly tapped Li's with his own, transferring the address into his band.

"Sounds terrific, we'll see you then," said Li, as he and Ronan gave each other a farewell hug. Ronan then held Mei by the shoulders and kissed her on the cheek.

"Fantastic, really fantastic to see both of you! Until tomorrow," he said and took off down the street.

Mei looked at Li and shook her head, "What are the odds of us drawing his name? What a crazy world," she said, yawning.

"Let's get a cab and get you back to the hotel. Someone looks like they could use some sleep."

Li hailed a taxi, and the driverless car took them back to their hotel. After getting ready for bed, they climbed into their bed. Li put his arm around Mei, cuddling her.

They lay like that for a while, staring out of the window opposite. "Tomorrow's the day," Li whispered.

"We're not bad people," said Mei, "It's just that sometimes, life happens." Then her eyes closed and she had fallen fast asleep.

Tomorrow was an important day for them, and they needed to be well rested and have all their wits about them. Li closed his eyes too but images of Sophie and Chen swam in his mind. He tried to clear his head, but an image of him floating in a blood-red ocean seemed to trap him, he feeling unable to escape from it. Li at last embraced the dream and gave in, succumbing to the waves, unwilling to fight any longer.

***

Li woke up first, after having slept late due to the feelings of security of being out of China and on vacation. After making a cup of coffee and stretching in the spacious hotel room, he went out for a run through Stockholm, a city that had also felt the impact of Contraception but not as much as Beijing.

As he ran, he saw Dispo units like those in Beijing, the white vehicle with the triangular Contra logo on the back and both side doors. If there was one thing about Contraception that he liked, it was the work of their graphic designer.

He continued to run, enjoying the chilly morning as he whizzed past farmers' markets, coffee shops, banks and bookstores. Sweden was cleaner than Beijing, but Li wondered how much blood had been spilled on these streets. He thought of Switzerland refusing to have any more children, as they had said in the news, and wondered if any other countries would follow suit. He thought it unlikely.

Humans were selfish, and ultimately, their personal lives and dreams would trump any obligation they might feel to their fellow man. The more he studied, researched, or experienced life firsthand, this was a commonality he had discovered and held to be true. Humans would always choose their self-interests above anything else.

His feet flew over the sidewalk and his black running jacket rustled in the wind. When in a new place, he always felt he was a stranger until he had run there.

With the stimulating physical activity of the run combined with all his senses, he felt relaxed, like he was a part of where he was. Stockholm's biting cold wind, the smell of the ocean mixed with the smell of cut wood, the sounds of a foreign yet beautiful language, the modern architecture blended with the ancient, and the lingering taste of coffee in his mouth filled Li with a sense of peace. After his run, he returned to his hotel, feeling balanced and ready for the day.

He found Mei sitting in a chair with her legs drawn up to her chest and a cup of coffee in her hand. She looked at Li, who was sweating and smiling as he stood near the door.

"Let's move here from Beijing," she said.

"It's certainly tempting, isn't it?" he said, looking out the window at the city. "But no matter how many new places I experience, for some reason, Beijing keeps calling me back."

"You ready for tonight?" she asked, putting her coffee cup away.

"I don't think 'ready' describes it. I'm prepared to do what I need to do for us."

She knew it was a hard thing to talk about, and a severe challenge to go through with, but she needed to know they were both on board. They hadn't flown all the way to Sweden so they could have second thoughts.

"So tonight..." she said.

"Right," said Li, sitting down in the chair next to her. "We'll meet Ronan at his place this evening, and then maybe after dinner, we'll either use the strangler or something in his apartment."

Both knew tonight was one of the most important nights of their lives. As soon as they were dressed, they went off to explore the city. They had lunch at a small bistro and sat outside, enjoying the sunshine and the fall wind. Despite what was to come, the Hus spent the day enjoying a freedom they hadn't shared together for a while. The day seemed to fly by as they strolled through the city square, visiting bookstores and walking through parks.

The fall air surrounded them and reminded Li of his first time walking through the doors of Peking University as a new teacher during his first semester. It was a mixture of nervousness and excitement, with an energy in the air from all the eager new students experiencing what they had dreamed of since childhood. For as long as he could remember, fall was a new start, for him it was the start of a new semester, either as a student or more recently, as a professor.

However, this fall brought with it the feeling that something much bigger was going to happen than anything he had experienced before. As the wind whipped his face, he looked at Mei, who was admiring the trees in the park, and thought about what their life would be like with a child. This time, the new beginning would be theirs; starting a family was something they had both wanted since they met.

Li and Mei finally sat on a park bench, taking in their surroundings. In that moment, they finally felt a sense of peace, having come to terms with what they had decided on. On the other side of the park, close to the street, they noticed a young man walking through the park in a bright yellow running jacket. He was smiling, enjoying the late afternoon just as the Hus were doing on the other side of the park. From the opposite direction, a man walked towards him, pulled a large knife from his pocket, and slammed it into the man just as he was within distance. The man in the neon jacket fell to his knees as blood spurted out of his mouth. The man withdrew the knife and again stabbed it into the man who now lay on the sidewalk clutching at his bleeding abdomen. The man with the knife pulled out a tablet, scanned the man's fingers, and then stood up and walked off like nothing had happened. From across the park, the Hus stared at the dead man in the bloodied jacket, with neither one of them saying a word.

"We should go," said Li quietly.

Mei nodded. She knew they were no better than the man with the knife but seeing the violence with what had just occurred made her feel uneasy.

She glanced at her band. It was 17:00.

Ronan had contacted them earlier to verify that they come over around 18:30. They made their way back to the hotel by foot and began to get ready for the night they had been waiting for and dreading.

"You take the strangler. Wear it on your wrist just like at the airport," he told Mei.

"What are you going to take?"

"If need be, I'll improvise," he said.

"Right, because that worked out so well last time," she said with a flash of annoyance.

"In that case," Li said as he finished buttoning up his shirt, "what would you have me take?"

He picked up the TV remote and held it up. "Perhaps a television remote? Or maybe this?" he asked, picking up a coffee mug.

"I've thought this through," he continued. "He must have knives in his kitchen, or at least a blunt instrument, and if that thing on your wrist doesn't finish the job, we'll find another way."

Mei seemed to accept the answer as she stood up from the bed and adjusted her all-black dress. Li was wearing khaki pants with a white-collar shirt and brown Sperry boat shoes. His hair was brushed and slicked back while Mei wore her hair in a tight ponytail. The metal weapon on her wrist shone under the light, reminding her of its power.

"This is it," she said, looking at Li. He took a big breath and exhaled slowly.

"After tonight, everything changes," she continued.

"I love you," he said, gripping her hand before kissing her bright red lips. They held each other for a moment after the kiss, before they opened the door and let it close behind them.

Ronan's place was too far to walk, so they hailed a taxi. It took them through Stockholm, arriving at a block of modern-looking apartment buildings. Mei swiped her band to pay the fare, and they got out.

Decades ago, cities all over the world were quick to adopt China's version of a "cashless" society, using mobile phones like bank accounts, transferring the globalized "credits" quickly and securely. Physical cash and coins were phased out first, with mobile phones following suit a few years later. A person's pass facilitated the transfer of funds. Technology could transact every kind of transfer, from bank to app, from Bitcoin to bank, and from app to both bank and Bitcoin. Paying was as simple as a swipe over a company's glass tablet or another individual's glass band, following which funds were transferred to the designated account.

They looked at the soaring complex where Ronan lived, a twisting formation of glass, metal and white trim. As the population had grown, so had the buildings. The only place where cities could expand was upward, and so many buildings, particularly apartment buildings, were constructed with at least 100 stories. This complex seemed to climb into the sky. There were eight main buildings aligned in two rows of four, thus forming a support for the four larger buildings situated above the original eight. They finally found Ronan's building and made their way to the elevator. As they waited, Li gave a nervous grin

"I can't help but think that as soon as these doors open, Lao Shu will be standing there."

Mei laughed. "And right as the doors close, I'm sure he'd have some invaluable advice for us."

The doors opened to reveal an empty glass elevator, and they both stepped in. They were headed to the seventy-first floor. The elevator shot upward and they could see the sprawling city out in front of them. The sight of the city bathed in the light of the fiery sun transfixed both of them for a moment. As they both stared at the sprawling metropolis below, time seemed to freeze. But then the moment was over and the elevator had arrived at Ronan's floor, the doors opening to let them out.

They stared for a few seconds more at the city below them. The decrease in population had drastically reduced pollution, and the sunsets had once again become truly spectacular. Li and Mei walked to the end of the hallway and found Ronan's apartment. Soft jazz could be heard from inside and as soon as they knocked, Ronan flung the door open. He was wearing dark blue chinos and a burnt orange sweater with the sleeves rolled up to his elbows.

"You made it!" he said, welcoming both in, shaking hands with Li and kissing Mei on the cheek. Li held up the bottle of wine he had brought and Ronan smiled.

"This will go perfectly with the salmon!" he exclaimed, setting the bottle on the kitchen countertop. Li and Mei entered the apartment and looked around. The apartment could have been pulled straight from an advertisement for IKEA. Most of the furniture was white, except for the dark blue sofa, and everything had a modern and minimalist feel to it. There were a few framed photographs around, most of them of Ronan with the famous political figures he had met. Other than that, the only color in the apartment was Ronan's sweater, which provided a stark contrast to the white kitchen where he now stood.

"Take a seat, let me pour you a glass of wine. Dinner should be ready in no time. I've got some gravlax ready, it's salmon cured with salt, sugar, and dill."

"Fantastic, thank you," said Li. "I don't remember you being much of a cook back in school. If I remember correctly, most nights ended in us ordering pizza."

Ronan laughed. "A lot has changed since then! I'm on the road a lot, always going out to dinners or staying in hotels. So, when I'm back in Stockholm, I like to cook for myself."

"And your wife?" asked Mei.

Ronan looked at her, raising his eyebrows quizzingly. "No wife," he said.

Li looked at Mei with a hint of confusion in his eyes.

"Girlfriend?" he asked

"You'd have to be more specific," Ronan laughed, stirring the mashed potatoes on the stove. "On a lighter topic, how's the Chinese government these days?"

"Oh, you know, open, inclusive, transparent as always," Li retorted, a part of his mind wanting to press Ronan on his previous answer, but then decided to move on. "Tell us about your big TV interview, superstar."

"Ah, the interview," said Ronan. "Yes, people love a good conspiracy, don't they? I'm working on another book concerning that conspiracy, so it's always good to get free press. Get my name out there while the masses still have a decent attention span. What did you think?"

"My first thought was 'typical' Ronan. But different from your other conspiracies, you don't seem to have any proof about China's corruption related to Contraception. Some people believe Harry Potter and Hogwarts are real, but just saying that doesn't make it so."

Ronan nodded as he cut a loaf of sourdough bread. "You live in Beijing, what do you think?"

"China has had a history of corruption," said Mei. "But I don't see how anyone could influence or find a way to corrupt Contraception. The system was created to be an airtight and universal policy. How could China, or any country for that matter, impact or alter it?"

"That is the question I am hoping to answer," said Ronan. "But so far, it has proved to be a challenge. Every time I think I'm getting close, the trail ends. People refuse to talk to me, or they die. Which I think speaks for itself. And on that happy note, dinner is served!"

Li and Mei helped Ronan carry all the food to the table. Dinner was grilled salmon on a bed of mashed potatoes with a garlic-infused cream sauce served with sourdough bread and a side of roasted asparagus. The apartment smelled fantastic as the three sat down at a wooden table.

Ronan raised his glass in a toast, "To my dear friends, may life bless us with all we desire." Their wine glasses clinked as the soft jazz music continued to play in the background.

"So, you two," said Ronan while cutting off a piece of his asparagus, "Have you thought about having a baby? Could you go through with Contraception's requirements?"

Li choked on his piece of fish and took a hasty drink of his wine. "Funny you should ask, actually," he said.

Before he could finish his sentence, Mei interrupted, "We've already killed two people."

Li shot her a glance as if to tell her to stop talking but she went on. "We applied a few weeks ago, received our three names, and the first two have already been confirmed dead."

"In terms of wanting to have a baby, that's great news. But for humanity's benefit, I can't say I support Contraception."

"I agree," said Li. "However, it's something that needs to be done if we want to have a child. I'm sure you can understand making sacrifices, I mean, wanting your own family comes with its own set of challenges. Surely, you can see where we're coming from after you yourself applied."

"Applied for what?" asked Ronan in puzzlement.

"For Contraception," Li said, with a hint of incredulousness in his voice. Mei had stopped eating and listened intently. They both stared at Ronan who threw his head back and laughed.

"Apply to Contraception?" he said and continued laughing. Li and Mei sat at the table frozen, not sure what was happening.

"Why in the world would I apply to have a child? You think I want a little monster destroying this apartment? Coloring books and toys all over the place?" Ronan continued laughing as he took a drink of his wine.

Mei looked at him with glittering eyes. "So, you never applied to Contraception?"

"Of course not!" said Ronan, still amused at the idea of him wanting to have a child.

"Bullshit," said Li, who grabbed the knife next to his plate and held it in his left hand. Ronan looked at him and stopped laughing. "What are you doing? What's with the knife?"

Mei pulled the glass tablet out of her pocket and laid it on the table before Ronan. It showed his complete profile along with a holographic picture. Ronan froze as he sat there, looking at the piece of glass that had "Target" written on top in bright red.

"This can't be true," he whispered in disbelief. He looked at Li, who still gripped the knife, and then at Mei, who looked hard and merciless. As he realized what was happening, Ronan jumped up from the table and took a few steps backwards.

"You're here to kill me! My friends are trying to kill me!" he said in shock, looking at the people he had once considered friends. There was panic in his eyes.

"I'm sorry Ronan, but our family is far too important," Mei said in an outwardly calm manner that suggested that mentally, she had already come to terms with what she was about to do.

"But I didn't even apply! I don't have a wife, I have a few girlfriends, but it's nothing serious! Look at my apartment!"

At that, Li's eyes involuntarily moved around Ronan's apartment. Everything seemed to be in place, with no extraneous objects anywhere. The apartment, simple but elegant, showed no signs of female presence. There were a few photographs of women but they seemed to have been taken during professional meetings.

Li got up from the table and went into the bedroom. He looked into the closet and saw only men's clothes and men's shoes. As he walked back into the kitchen thoughtfully, Ronan was still standing where Li had left him while Mei still sat at the table, her eyes riveted on Ronan. Li put the knife back on the table and sank down into a chair. Then he picked up the bottle of wine and poured each a full glass and motioned for Ronan to sit down.

Ronan came back slowly and looked at them. "What the fuck is going on?"

Li raised his glass and gulped the wine down, "That's precisely what we need to figure out."

16. THE DISCUSSION

Stockholm, Sweden

Data from Contra found the average time for a married couple to finish their three kills was 28 days.

■ For several hours, the Hus and Ronan had been discussing how Ronan's name had ended up on the glass tablet that now sat in the middle of the kitchen table, taunting them with the mystery of the situation.

"So, walk me through the application procedure again," Ronan said, still trying to get all the facts before jumping to a conclusion.

"We went into the Contra building in Beijing, were directed upstairs by a lady at the reception, and there we met Mr. Xi, the man in charge of our application," said Li, telling this for the third time.

"And what was his demeanor like?"

"His demeanor?" asked Mei.

"Yes, like his posture, or his attitude."

"I know what demeanor means. I'm just not sure how that's relevant."

Li looked at her and shrugged. Turning to Ronan, he said, "I don't know, he seemed chipper, like oddly enthusiastic and welcoming."

"Interesting," said Ronan. "Go on."

"He then explained to us all the rules and intricacies of Contraception before sliding a painting on the wall out of the way and revealing what I can only assume was the database of names. There was a slot in the wall where he inserted the glass panel that held my agreement and it disappeared. Then three glass tablets popped out of the same slot, and they gave us the names of our targets."

"And one of those was my name, correct?"

"Correct," said Li.

"The question remains, why and how could my name end up in the database without applying to Contraception."

This was what they had been debating for so long. Ronan was sure it had something to do with China.

"I'm telling you, this was a setup," he had been saying.

"I'm sure this has something to do with China. No offense, you guys, but I've been outspoken about China for years and this can't be a coincidence."

Mei looked at Li and shrugged her shoulders. "It makes sense, but as of now, it's just a guess." Then she turned towards Ronan. "And as of now, you're the only thing standing between us having a baby or not."

Ronan spun around, unsure if he had heard her correctly.

"You can't honestly be considering killing me," he said, with a look of incredulity on his face. "Don't even think about it. If you kill me, and I haven't applied, number one, I'll be dead, which is something I'd prefer not to be. Second, we'll never figure out how my name ended up in the system, and third, you'll just keep perpetuating a system that for all we know is corrupt. But most importantly for you, since I haven't applied to Contraception, I am not a legitimate target. Therefore, you could be framed for killing me and that would mean no babies for you."

"We don't know it's corrupt," said Li. "For all we know, there was a mistake."

"Well, a mistake that may cost both my life and yours!" said Ronan, lifting the bottle of wine off the table and taking a long swig from it.

"What if," said Mei, looking at Ronan, "And just if, we entertain the possibility that your name was given out intentionally? It still leaves the questions of who, why and how. Furthermore, how deep and widespread is this? And even if we get the answers to these questions, what are we going to do with them?"

The night wore on with the three of them contemplating these questions, each drawing their own conclusions. With each new idea, a sticky note was added to the wall. Around 1:00, the three of them sat back on the sofa exhausted, looking at the wall in front of them that was by now covered with little yellow squares.

"Who suggested aliens?" asked Ronan in disbelief as he read the notes again.

"I'm just saying, it's possible, just not likely," Li said sheepishly. The notes on the wall ranged from broad terms such as "conspiracy" and "China," to more specific things, like the Prime Minister of Sweden or a very detailed note describing a crazy woman that Ronan had dated years ago and as he explained, the relationship did not end amicably.

"*Hé dōng shī hǒu,*"[8] he had said, justifying adding the note to the wall. As they stared at the sea of yellow post-it notes in front of them, Li came to an astronomical conclusion.

He exclaimed, "Do you realize what will happen if we discover the truth? Contraception will be over."

---

[8] Hell hath no fury like a woman scorned

"Not necessarily," said Mei. "When someone kills another person with a gun, what is ultimately to blame? The person, or the weapon?"

"A valid argument," added Ronan. "But that's the question, isn't it? Whoever illegally put my name into that system will be punished, but will Contraception also face prosecution for allowing it to happen in the first place?"

"There's no such thing as a perfect system when humans are involved," said Mei.

The two men nodded in agreement. People always screwed things up. Perhaps the larger issue was with people themselves. People stole, lied, cheated, became corrupt and dishonorable, and let greed get in the way. The systems they created were either influenced by man, or were constructed in such a way to allow them to be manipulated to man's interest, instead of the purpose they were designed for.

One discussion that took place during Contraception's inception was whether killing people was right or wrong. Then came the topic of whether man was inherently good or bad. Parts of the debate had been aired live on TV, the rationale being that since Contraception would affect the people, they had a right to see the proceedings. It was determined that although man could be good, he was, at the core, concerned only with his own interests and needed to be regulated to create a more prosperous society.

As they all sat on the sofa, Ronan turned to them and said, "In all seriousness, there's no scenario that includes killing me, right?"

Mei said, "The whole reason we applied was to have a baby, so…"

"Right, exactly. On the other hand, Ronan is a friend," Li said. "I suppose we could wait until we sort this out and then kill him." Li then turned towards Ronan, "That okay with you?"

"Funny as ever," replied Ronan feelingly. Li placed his hand on Ronan's shoulder.

"We're going to figure this out, together. And no one is going to die, I promise you that."

Mei checked her wrist and added, "And on that note, we better get back to our hotel. We'll meet you tomorrow. We'll figure this out, Ronan, we're with you."

Ronan walked them to the door. "It's been great seeing both of you, although I wish it had been under different circumstances. But you're here now. That's what's important. I've got something tomorrow, but what about the day after next? Let's say early evening? We'll have dinner again?"

"Sounds great and thank you for dinner!" said Li as he and Mei walked out the door. They took the elevator down to the first floor and made their way to the street to get a taxi.

"What an unexpected turn of events," Mei said as they waited on the sidewalk of the quiet street.

"What does this mean for us?" asked Li, knowing she didn't know the answer either.

"Whatever happens, will happen. As long as we're together and we make it out of this thing alive, that's what matters most," said Mei, as she kissed him with sudden passion.

An empty taxi passed, and Li stuck out his hand but it continued to roar down the street. Despite the advancements in technology, some things never changed.

The Hus managed to flag down another taxi and returned to their hotel. As they lay in bed, both thought about what the future would look like for them after this – what Mei had referred to it earlier as a complication.

Li decided that calling Mr. Xi was not in their best interests, as Xi was the one who had personally given him the tablet with Ronan's profile. The whole situation was mired in challenges, confusion and above all, corruption. Regardless of how Ronan's name had ended up in Li's hand, someone had tampered with the system. They had figured out how to bypass or manipulate the algorithm that randomly selected names from the database. The question now was who.

As the Hus drifted off into an uneasy sleep, the cold night air crept through the bedroom window while the stars shone above Stockholm, illuminating the glass and metal structures below. Tomorrow was another day and there was much to be done.

17. THE HUNT

Beijing, China

Initially, Contraception kept applicants in the database even after their child was born. However, due to a drastic decline in the population and low application rates, the policy was later amended to remove a person from the Contraception database if they completed their kills and had their baby. Following this change, the number of applicants increased, limiting the decline of the population to what Contra considered a more 'healthy' number.

▪ The past week had been a very frustrating one for Victor. After flying back from Berlin to Beijing, he had begun to hunt Li Hu, which proved challenging since Li remained inside his apartment most of the time. The one chance that had presented itself to Victor was thwarted by an incompetent Dispo driver, who had landed himself in hospital. Now, the time had come to finish off Mr. Hu.

For weeks, Victor had ignored Li, amusing himself with the others on "the list," partially because Li Hu did not carry the hefty price tag that some of Victor's other targets did. This was largely because Li still had a high chance of being killed by whoever had received his name from the Contraception list and paying a hitman to kill him seemed like a waste of money when someone else would do it for free. However, Victor had received a recent phone call, essentially making Li Hu his top priority.

"Victor, take care of this for us," the voice on the other end of the phone had said. Victor waited patiently while the details were relayed to him.

"The man tasked with killing Li Hu for Contraception, as you know, is now in the hospital on life support. Hu must be eliminated, and we think you'll find our compensation enticing." Then the voice went quiet and the phone was disconnected.

Victor pulled out the glass tablet with Li's profile and saw the price had changed from 75,000 to 300,000 yuan. He smiled in satisfaction. Li was now his main target.

Having left Berlin for Beijing, Victor arrived in the Chinese capital hoping for a quick kill. Contrary to his wish, Li had proved to be a worthy opponent. He stayed inside on most days, and when he didn't, he would go for a run at an unpredictable time in the morning.

The one time that Victor had stayed up all night waiting for Li, the professor did go for a run. Victor followed him and found a five-story building from which to set up his American-made enhanced sniper rifle with a digital scope. But the Dispo truck appeared out of nowhere and made it a challenge to get a clear shot as it went swerving all over the road in pursuit of Li. When Victor found an unobstructed shot, with the back of Li's head in his sights, a huge truck passed through the intersection, colliding with the Dispo truck just as Victor fired. He missed, and Li didn't stay around long enough for another shot.

For a few more days, Victor waited patiently for Li to leave his apartment again until he realized too late that Li and his wife had left for Sweden. He cursed himself for being so careless and decided to follow them there.

His taxi passed by a public airport security entrance. Victor's weapons helped him to perform to the best of his ability, and there was no way he would travel without them. He always flew private, and with enough money, he could carry anything he liked onboard. Reaching the private airfield, he got out of the taxi, a menacing figure in a long black coat, his black-gloved hands carrying a black briefcase filled with what he liked to call his "tools."

He nodded at the pilot before walking up the short stairs of his private aircraft and taking a seat. He removed his sunglasses and set them on the table. As he sat there, he thought about his job. He enjoyed it because he was good at it. People, and at times, governments, valued his skill set and paid large sums for it. It amazed him that people were still concerned about the moral consequences of what they did. Even as a child, Victor knew that he would do whatever was necessary for self-preservation. He understood the difference between right and wrong, but through his training and hard experiences, he had come to realize that the only thing important in life was survival.

If his parents were still alive, he wondered what they would think of him now. Victor felt proud of where he was in his life. People relied on him, he was successful, and he was rich, something he couldn't say for most of the comrades from the PLA; most were dead.

As the plane took off, he looked down at Beijing, a city he had never thought of as home, but a temporary place in which for brief moments, he experienced life. Victor never felt much attachment to family, belongings, or the idea of permanence. Everything in life, including people, was disposable. He smiled at the thought of what his job title would be on a resume, "The Disposer." He was often told by the voice on the phone to "clean up" a situation. Frequently, someone or some organization needed someone dead, and when the candidate for Contraception couldn't do it, Victor was put into action to make sure the job got done. He was a safety net, insurance, or simply, the guy you called to make sure shit got done.

He laid his head back on the seat, took his eyes off the news playing in front of him and glanced out the window. The clouds below him hurtled past as the jet flew towards Europe.

This whole situation with Li Hu irritated Victor. He prided himself on being efficient and the fact that he had wasted a week in Beijing not being able to kill Li grew into an irritation that Victor felt deep inside him. Time was money, and money was freedom. He didn't want to stop killing people because it gave him a sense of purpose. Having the money to disappear from the grid whenever he wanted was more valuable to him than anything.

As the plane continued to soar through the skies, Victor closed his eyes and thought of his next target. He was headed to Stockholm to kill Li Hu, and this time, there was nothing that would get in his way.

***

Stockholm, Sweden

The plane touched down in Stockholm during the late afternoon and Victor took his briefcase and put on his sunglasses before getting off. As the chilly wind whipped at his long coat, he glanced up at the bright blue sky before getting into the black car that took him to his hotel.

Victor was one of the rare people who needed to use a physical key card to open his hotel door instead of simply using his wrist, another reminder he wasn't part of society. However, he preferred it this way. How most people lived, the normality of life, it was all so mundane; killing people was much more fun. He always found it curious that so many people on his list had applied to Contraception. Why would someone want to have a baby? he thought. Sacrificing money, time, energy, and above all, freedom, didn't seem worth it to him. Victor enjoyed his unencumbered lifestyle and believed those foolish enough to have applied to Contraception deserved to die, either by their target's hand or his.

After entering his hotel room and placing the briefcase on the coffee table, he saw his sniper rifle lying on the bed in its sleek black case. Carrying it around was too conspicuous, so Victor had it delivered to wherever he was headed. He opened the case and ran his hands on the cool black metal barrel, remembering how many lives it had taken, and how much money he had made with it. He remembered that day in Beijing, sitting on that roof, staring down his sights at Li Hu's head and firing just as the truck got in his way. The thought irritated him, and as his hand continued its way down the barrel, he swore that he would not miss again.

His phone rang, and Victor answered it without saying a word.

"Update," said the voice, demanding, not requesting.

"In Sweden, doing recon now. The target will be dead within 48 hours," he replied.

"Good luck," said the voice before hanging up. Victor hated that phrase. "Good luck" was something that had been said to him all his life. Victor didn't believe in luck. He had always maintained that luck was the last dying wish of those who believed winning can happen by accident. He believed winning was a choice. Victor didn't spend years training in the PLA so he could put a 300,000 RMB target in his scope and base his success on luck. Luck was a cheap idea and for Victor, an undermining thing to say to someone.

That evening, Victor pulled out his tablet and made a call to someone he had trained with in the PLA. He wouldn't define them as friends, more as associates who helped each other out on occasion.

"I need a location," he said in a flat, calm voice. "Li Hu, Stockholm."

There was silence on the other end of the line. Then a gruff voice responded, "Last pass activity has him checking into the Grand Hotel."

"Consider us even for Tokyo," said Victor, and ended the call.

He put down the glass tablet and opened the black briefcase. From inside, he took out a black pistol, loaded a clip, cocked it, and placed it in a holster inside his jacket. He also took out the silencer and placed that in the other pocket. Although he was authorized to kill Li Hu by accepting the hit-list contract, he wasn't legally allowed to do so. As such, it was always better not to arouse suspicions. Taking one last look at his IKEA furniture-furnished room, he left the hotel and headed towards Li's hotel.

The hotel was famous throughout Sweden, known for its splendor and prime location. It was in a busy part of the city, by the waterfront facing the Royal Palace and the Old Town, which presented its own set of challenges but could also be favorable depending on the circumstance. Victor wasn't sure which floor they were on and knew that information would be critical for his success. He looked around at the buildings surrounding the hotel, many of the same height as the hotel, with a few parking garages, business buildings and shopping centers that weren't quite as tall. He walked toward the hotel entrance, gazing around the lobby and approached the reception desk.

"Good evening," he said in Swedish. The receptionist looked up at him, shocked to see her native language spoken by this tall, handsome Chinese man.

"Good evening, sir, what can I help you with?"

"I'm in a bit of a bind," he said. "I'm supposed to be meeting my brother here in Stockholm for our friend's wedding, but we seemed to have crossed wires and got all mixed up. His name is Li Hu, and he said he was staying here, but I've just recently landed and his phone seems to be having some issues. Could you help me, Adelana?" he asked, glancing at her name and flashing her a coaxing smile.

She smiled back and said, "That would be no trouble at all, sir." She typed Li's name into the computer and then looked up at Victor. "He's staying in room 5005. I hope you two have fun at the wedding."

"Oh, we will. Thank you. You have been ever so helpful," he replied and left the hotel. He made his way to a small park adjacent to the hotel and sat down on a bench. From his breast pocket, he pulled out a pack of tobacco and some rolling papers and rolled a cigarette. With the mechanical movements of an expert, the cigarette was in his mouth and lit within a matter of seconds. He thought about how he could ensure that Li would die this time. Taking a shot at fifty stories up was a risk, even with his top-of-the-line rifle.

Also, if he missed, he wouldn't be able to get down in time in case Li left the hotel, which in all likelihood, he would do. The issue, he thought, taking another drag on his cigarette, was that if he went into their room, he would also have to deal with the wife. Victor didn't advocate death, he killed for the money, and since Li's wife had no value to him, she was just a complication to killing Li.

Like his strategy in Beijing, he could wait until Li went for another run, but he had no patience to play another waiting game, hoping that Li would leave the hotel. He decided that killing Li from a distance involved too many variables that could lead to failure; so approaching this head-on was the best way. As he took another drag, he looked up at the fiftieth floor, wondering if Hu knew what was in store for him.

Victor knew that one day, his own life would likely end at the hands of someone else. But for now, he was the one dealing out fates, and tomorrow, Li Hu would meet his.

**

The next afternoon was cool. Victor was in his room, stretching and preparing for the night. His muscled torso bent over his legs, revealing a series of scars from his tough past. A knife fight, falling from a five-story building, PLA training; for Victor, the scars were a reminder that he had lived. For him, life was something that needed to be pushed and tested, and his scars were testament to those times when he had.

As he got up and took a shower, with the hot water flowing over him, he thought about Li Hu, visualizing exactly how he would kill Li and the fulfillment he would get from doing so, both personally and financially. Victor was a finisher, and he liked closure. For him, the satisfaction of killing someone came when he finally scanned their fingerprints or face, and the glass tablet flashed "Approved," signaling the end of a contract.

After the shower, Victor dressed in a new suit and put on his black gloves. He placed his gun and silencer into the inner pocket of his suit and then a thin metal wire. He didn't enjoy strangling people, but sometimes, it was the only way. After getting everything ready, he put on his sunglasses and left the hotel. Outside, he fired up the Indian Scout Sixty he had paid for with cash on arrival and revved the engine. The freedom and power that came with a motorcycle were something that Victor connected with. He chose not to wear a helmet as he figured that dying on a motorcycle wasn't the worst way to go; at least he would die cool.

He made his way to the park bench outside Li's hotel, parked the motorcycle, and waited. There was no telling where the Hus would go tonight, so he needed to be ready. As he sat on the bench and rolled a cigarette, the sun began to set. He kept a close eye on the entrance of the hotel. He took out the glass tablet from his pocket and checked the time; it was half past six. They would get hungry soon, he thought. He lit the cigarette and started to smoke when suddenly, he saw Li and Mei leaving the hotel. They looked around and then hopped in a taxi.

Victor took one last puff on his cigarette, flicked it onto the street, and then fired up the motorcycle in pursuit of the taxi. He stayed a few cars back in order not to arouse suspicion, preferring to kill Li inside rather than outside. The taxi stopped at a well-lit restaurant called *Rolfs Kök* and Victor rode past it as the Hus stepped out of the taxi.

As Li and Mei entered the restaurant, Victor turned right and circled back so he could wait. He parked across the street, entered the bar opposite the restaurant and ordered tonic water. As he sat there, sipping his drink and keeping an eye on the entrance, he had the same excited feeling he always felt before a kill. He checked the time on his tablet and knew that for Li to die, he only needed to remain patient.

***

Ronan spotted the Hus as soon as they walked in and stood up, waving. They walked over to his table and greeted him.

"This place looks fantastic," said Li, admiring the design of the restaurant.

"This is one of Sweden's newest restaurants and one of a handful of places in the country to receive a Michelin star," commented Ronan, "Seemed like I owed you guys."

"Owed us for what?" asked Mei

"Well, now we've agreed that you won't kill me, you can't have a baby," he said and took a drink from his glass of red wine. Li looked at Mei before answering.

"Ronan, we go way back, and we're not going to kill you because it's not legal. You didn't apply to the system, therefore, though your profile was given to us, you're safe, at least from us."

"But if you had applied, and we ended up with your name, we were prepared to kill you," Mei said.

Ronan looked at her a minute before saying, "Well cheers to that; I can't get mad at someone for following their self-interests!" The glasses clinked together, and soon, their first dish arrived, nässelsoppa, a nettle soup with hard-boiled eggs and crème fraiche.

As the three ate, they continued to discuss the revelations from two days ago, still unsure how to approach and find evidence concerning the suspicions they had. The "who" was still unclear.

"So, Contra draws from a central database of names, correct?" asked Ronan.

"Right," said Li.

"And usually, two names are given out domestically, and one international name?"

"Correct."

"So, we can't be sure who submitted my name, because once it's in the database, technically anyone in the world could have received it."

"Yes."

"Well for the record, I still think China is involved in my case, especially given the subject of my lectures and basically my life's work of hurling accusations at one of the world's biggest superpowers."

"And that's where we fall short. If somehow, we could present this before the governing board of Contra, we'd need proof, verifiable proof," Mei said. She was referring to the members who made up the board that oversaw Contra and the Contraception policy. At first, due to the universality of it, the board had included one member from every country. However, with almost 200 representatives in the room, it had made updates slow and inefficient. The governing board of Contra was established to be a balanced, impartial group who oversaw matters related to the Contraception policy and ultimately, decided on behalf of the world.

As the three continued to eat dinner, their minds were on the future, and what lay ahead of them. Ronan wondered how his name had ended up on a glass tablet while the Hus were more concerned with what this meant for their application. Li still argued that Xi be left out of this, as he suspected the official could be part of the corruption.

Dinner carried on, with Janssons frestelse, creamy potato and fish gratin, Hjortkött med björnbär, a venison served with a blackberry sauce, and a rabarberpaj, a rhubarb crumble, to end their evening.

"Truly spectacular, thank you," Mei said, smiling at Ronan.

"Thank you for not murdering me!" Ronan said in mock seriousness. "Since you leave in two days, you have got to have a drink with me at my place tonight."

Li shrugged his shoulders, looked at Mei, and responded, "Why not?!" They finished the rest of the wine in their glasses and Ronan insisted on paying the bill as a sign of gratitude for what had, and had not, transpired in the last 48 hours.

***

From his seat at the bar, through the window, Victor saw the Hus along with another man exit the restaurant and stand on the street waiting for a cab. Victor thought the man looked familiar but couldn't put a finger on who he was. He pulled out his glass tablet and held it up to scan the man's face. Once the face was recognized, a complete bio appeared, and a notification that Ronan Sörensen was on "the list" as a low-profile target since his name had been slipped into the Contraception system.

Victor had always thought that "the list" was a cheesy way to refer to something that held incredible power, but it worked. "The list" was a collection of names that people or organizations posted, and hitmen like Victor could scroll through it and accept contracts. For many, this made life a lot easier, able to work not only wherever they happened to be, but also killing those they felt they were capable of killing. For Victor, he felt fit to kill everyone. The face had looked familiar, and once seeing Ronan's profile on the list, he immediately recognized him. Victor hadn't taken the contract because he had never planned to be in Sweden, but now, fortune was on his side.

He clicked on the Contra logo to see who was tasked with killing Sörensen and started to laugh when he saw Li Hu's name. As he watched them walk out of the restaurant, he wondered if Li was here to go through with it. If Li was, then Victor knew he needed to hurry up to get paid before Li did the work for free.

"The list" functioned not only as a simple list of targets for hitmen to choose, but also as a backup measure to ensure that certain targets who had applied to Contraception would be guaranteed dead. Sometimes, Contraception applicants rescinded their application, or died while trying to kill someone else, and often, those unexpected circumstances caused great trouble for other people. "The list" served to minimize this trouble; if a Contraception target didn't die from their application, a hitman could accept their contract and finish the job himself. Now, Victor had both Li Hu's and Ronan's contracts from "the list."

A double payday, he thought, smiling as he placed a five-hundred krona note under his glass and exited the bar. He made his way to the motorcycle down the street as the Hus and Ronan got into a taxi. Victor adjusted his jacket before whipping the bike around and placed himself a few cars' length behind the cab. He hoped they were going to the same destination. If they split up, Victor knew he would have to stay with the Hus. Taking a contract from "the list" was a personal choice, but Li Hu had been given to him, and Victor knew his employers were not to be crossed.

The taxi, with Victor not far behind, raced through the city as the moon and stars shone down on Stockholm. Occasionally, a gunshot was heard, and Dispo units could be seen racing toward the sound.

The taxi turned right down a well-lit road, and Victor stayed at the intersection, waiting to see which apartment they were going to. He watched them get out of the taxi and head into the first of many large apartment buildings. Victor blinked his eye twice and kept an eye on the building. With the special contact now activated, he squinted his eye a little, zooming in on the upper stories of the building. He quickly shifted left as a light flicked on at the seventy-first floor. Zooming closer, through the large glass window, Victor saw Ronan and knew he had them. He blinked twice to turn off the contact, returning his vision to normal.

He left the motorcycle on the street and made his way to the parking garage below the apartment building. Victor walked slowly through the garage until he saw a young Chinese woman getting out of her vehicle. He slowed his pace further until she began to walk towards the elevator.

As she approached the elevator, she turned and said, "I've never seen you here before."

"Funny, I've never seen you before either." Before she could say something else, Victor grabbed her, placing one of his gloved hands over her mouth and his other arm around her neck, positioning himself behind her. He pushed her forward to the elevator scanner and tightened his grip around her neck until she stretched out her wrist, pressing it against the scanner. The light turned green, the doors opened, and Victor slammed the woman's head against the wall, knocking her unconscious. Once inside the elevator, he punched the button marked 71, adjusted his black leather gloves, and stared directly ahead as the door shut.

***

Li and Mei sat on the gray couch and Ronan was in his kitchen, mixing cocktails and moving to the sounds of the funk/soul music playing in the background. When he finished, he brought the drinks over to the coffee table and took a seat in the armchair across from them. The large window at the end of the living room provided a complete view of Stockholm's city lights below.

"What have we got ourselves into?" said Li, in near disbelief over the situation they were in.

"Ya, this is a bit weird, right? But if I remember correctly, you were always up for a challenge," said Ronan. "And I think our little predicament qualifies as a challenge."

The three of them took a drink of their Old Fashioned and Mei made a sound indicating she enjoyed it

"Ronan, you've certainly changed since university," she said.

He smiled and retorted, "Being single has that effect on people. Lots of time for self-exploration and time to invest back into yourself. I learned to cook, how to make drinks, have more time at the gym, met a handful of lovely ladies. In fact, I don't know why anyone in their right mind would apply to Contraception. No offense, of course."

"None taken," said Li. "I think one reason we applied was so we could be a part of something bigger than ourselves. Having a baby, a legacy, something to leave our mark on this world. Also, Mei was getting bored, so we figured a child would give her something to do," he said with a deadpan face.

Mei shot him a glance, and Ronan laughed. He raised his glass and said, "To each their own!" They cheered and drank as the music filled the room and the lights from the city shone bright against the dark of the night.

For a moment, while the music was changing, the room was silent with no one talking and not a noise to be heard. In this silence there was a knock on the door. The sound seemed to shatter the silence, and all three heads snapped up to look towards the big metal door. Ronan looked at Li and then at the clock. It was 22:00. Then the next song found its way on the record player and as the quiet funk music filled the room, Ronan, with his drink in hand, made his way to the door.

Li looked at Mei and knew intuitively something wasn't right.

18. LI HU

Stockholm, Sweden

Spanish-speaking countries were found to have the highest number of Contraception applicants, with Colombia, Mexico, Spain and Argentina placed in the top 10 for the first five years of the policy.

▪ Ronan approached the door, and for Li, sitting on the couch, time seemed to stand still. His eyes were locked on the door as Ronan looked through the glass to see who it was. All he could see was a man in a suit holding a police badge up to the camera, blocking out his face.

In Swedish, the man said, "Mr. Sörensen, this is Detective Inspector Larsson. We received news earlier this evening regarding a credible threat to your life, something to do with one of your speeches a few weeks ago."

Ronan felt a sense of relief, he had been through this process before. It wasn't the first time someone had threatened his life and the police came to check on him often as that was standard protocol when public figures received such threats. "One second, officer," he said.

Ronan looked at the Hus and said reassuringly, "This will only take a moment."

Before Li could say anything, Ronan had unbolted the lock and the heavy metal door swung open. Ronan found the cold steel of a gun's silencer pressed against his temple. His drink spilled to the ground and he stumbled backwards. Victor stepped in and quickly closed the door behind him. Ronan was in utter shock.

"Ah, I love parties," Victor said chattily. "What are we celebrating?"

With the gun still pointed at Ronan's head, he looked at Hu intently. "I've been waiting a long time to meet you face to face," he said with grim satisfaction.

Li had never seen the interloper before in his life and was mystified what he meant. Before he could get a word out, Victor motioned for Ronan to sit on the sofa with Li and Mei. He sat on the coffee table with one leg crossed over the other, his hands and gun resting on his knee. He tapped the gun barrel against his knee.

"You are a smart one, Mr. Hu. And you, Mr. Sörensen, what a surprise for me. Who knew I'd get two on the same day."

"Two what?" Mei asked before she could stop herself.

Victor looked at her with an expression of disbelief as if he couldn't comprehend how she could fail to understand what he had said. "Two targets of course," he said pityingly as he stared confidently at the three people on the sofa, all of whom were confused about who he was and why he was there.

"Well this is awkward," remarked Victor. "I'm not all clued in on the dynamic here. Let me take a guess." He motioned at Li with his gun and said, "I think Prof. Hu didn't have the balls to kill Mr. Sörensen, and the man tasked with killing Prof. Hu is in hospital. Still, did you really think you were both just going to walk away from this?"

"But I didn't even apply to Contraception!" Ronan whispered.

"Most times, that doesn't matter," Victor said in a condescending voice. "Contraception is a beautiful system when you think about it. In your case, it allows murder to merely appear legal and authorized."

As Li, Mei and Ronan tried to piece together what he had just said, Victor tapped the gun on his knee to show his impatience.

"Right, so I think I'll kill the Swede first and then you, Li. Fortunately for Mrs. Hu, she gets to live, though as a merry widow. It'll all be over in a matter of minutes."

Li found his voice at last. "Who are you?" he asked.

"You can call me whatever you like, but most just call me Victor."

Victor pointed the gun at Ronan and said, "Up you go, big boy."

Ronan stood up with a disbelieving look on his face. "What is this all about? What do you mean target?"

"For someone about to die, do the answers to these questions seem relevant?" Victor said impatiently. Then suddenly, his mood changed as he seemed to reach some decision in his mind.

"Alright, I'll tell you, anyway. Maybe you can get some peace of mind before I finish with you. Seems like a fair trade."

"Ready?" he asked, not waiting for an answer. "Your name was given to Li Hu through the Contraception system. It doesn't matter if you applied or not, your name ended up in there. Someone wanted you to die but didn't want to get their hands dirty. So, your name was added to "the list" to ensure that you die. But in case whoever received your name from Contraception couldn't go through with it, I was the insurance package. Now I'm being cashed in to ensure that you die. Li is also on 'the list' because someone wants him dead, and unfortunately, that Dispo driver couldn't finish the job. So now that responsibility falls on me."

As Li sat on the couch listening to this self-possessed assassin telling them what Contraception was being used for, he had surreptitiously turned his wrist so that his band was recording what was happening right in front of him. He had a feeling this information would come in handy in the future.

Ronan stood there looking from Li to Victor. "I have done nothing wrong!" he said and his voice shook.

It left Victor unmoved. With a bored look he pulled the trigger. The silencer muffled the sound of the exiting bullet to a soft plop and it went through Ronan's skull, making blood gush out in jets and hit the wall behind him. Ronan fell backward onto the couch as Mei put her hands over her mouth to prevent herself from screaming. Victor, indifferent to the fear and chaos around him, pulled out a glass tab.

Li realized what was happening. Victor was going to scan Ronan's finger and get the credit for his death. If the hitman was allowed to do that then he and Mei, in case they managed to escape the killer by some ploy, would still not be out of danger. Contraception would then assign them a new target. People died all the time due to a variety of reasons, from natural causes, or accidents, or in this case, by a hitman. If a person's target met his or her end due to any of these reasons, then a new profile would be sent out from the database. But if they could prevent Victor from getting the scan done and could do it themselves, they would get credit for the kill. It would mean no more plotting and planning to kill another person.

"Listen," he said in a rush, trying to divert Victor, "why am I on 'the list'?"

Victor stopped what he was doing and looked at Li. "Well, you're a professor, right?"

"Yes."

"Have you ever written or said something that the Chinese government might consider offensive or dangerous?"

Li thought about the books in his study. "I suppose one might label my books as offensive to China," he said slowly.

"Well, then, there you go."

"What do you mean 'There you go'?"

Victor put his gun and tablet down and turned back to face Li. "How do you think the CCP has kept power for all these years?" he said with a sneer. "You think it's in their best interest to have people disseminate information or views contrary to the party line? Absolutely not."

Li knew that China was corrupt, but was still shocked to hear someone admit it out loud. Something inside him knew that Contraception would somehow be manipulated, and Victor's admission justified those beliefs; he had just never thought that he would be on the receiving end of the corruption. Although his books were critical of the regime, he had never thought they exceeded the limit and caused so much anger that someone felt the need to end his life.

"You were also an outspoken critic of Contraception, if I remember correctly. I don't think that boded well for you; China loves Contraception and frankly, so do I," said Victor, holding up his fingers and rubbing them together to indicate money.

"So, I'm in the Contraception database because I applied, but how did I end up on this list of yours?"

"Oh, it's not just mine. I am just a 'utilizer' of 'the list,' if you will. Regarding who put you there, I have no idea. Though I have a good guess, I am not going to spend the whole night telling you all the Contraception secrets. I still have my little business to take care of, so tell me, Prof. Hu, would you prefer it if I killed you here in front of your wife or in the bedroom, out of her sight?"

Li looked at Mei. The expression in her eyes told him she wasn't ready to quit. It was the same spirit that had made him fall in love with her.

"No," said Li, with a firmness in his voice that surprised Victor. Li felt having come so far, he wasn't ready to die now, least of all at the hands of a hired gun.

"So, in front of your wife then?" Victor sounded incredulous. Li rose to his feet slowly, looking at Ronan, who lay motionless on the couch. Blood continued to gush out of the gaping hole in his head made by the bullet. In a trice, Mei too had jumped up and put herself in front of Li, shielding him and facing Victor.

"What gives you the right to kill my husband?" she snarled at him.

"A cash sum, frankly," responded Victor. "If you don't get out of the way, I will kill you too, but I'd rather not waste the bullet."

Li embraced her from behind and buried his head in her neck, as if in a final farewell. Only Mei could hear his faint whisper, "Let me go. I'll find a way out. Scan Ronan when I'm in the other room."

Mei sighed, then moved out of the way.

"Let's go into the bedroom," Li said grimly.

"As you wish." Victor motioned to the bedroom with his gun and Li walked in front of him. Before they went in, Victor turned around and looked at Mei, pointing the gun at her with quiet menace.

"Now, you behave in here, be a good girl," he said.

She stood still as if in shock but as soon as he had gone, she hastily took out the glass tablet with Ronan's Contraception profile from her pocket, and placed one of Ronan's cold fingers onto the screen along with hers. "Authorized. Deceased, Ronan Sörensen, Contraception kill confirmed," flashed on the screen. She quickly put the tablet back in her pocket and removed the bracelet around her wrist in one swift tug. Then with the silvery metal rope in her hand, she rushed toward the bedroom where the two men had gone. She could hear them talking, but couldn't distinguish what they were saying. Her heart beat faster and the blood pounded in her ears. She thought of the night when Li had re-programmed the weapon for her touch and felt grateful for his foresight. The strangler felt cold in her hand as she double-tapped it to activate it.

As she reached the door in one quick movement, she saw Victor raise his gun and point it at Li's head. She knew it was now or never. With her left hand, she pushed the door wide open, and with her right hand, threw the strangler at Victor with all her might. The metal cord spun through the air and the door hitting the wall caused Victor to turn around, lithe as a panther. Then things seemed to move in slow motion as Victor turned the gun towards Mei and fired. Mei had thrown herself on the floor and the bullets hit the door just above where her head had been. The silver strangler flew toward Victor, who put up his arm to block it.

As Li stood frozen in his place, unsure what to do, he saw the metal bracelet fly toward Victor and wrap itself around his forearm, right above the elbow, then tighten like a python's grip on its prey. The metal string became a tight tourniquet that cut through Victor's skin as he tried in vain to pry it off with his other hand. Blood poured out from his arm as the metal wire continued to slice through skin and muscle. Then there was the crunch of bones as the metal continued to draw itself tighter. Li looked at Victor and for the first time, saw a fear in the killer's eyes.

Victor fought the pain and in a last-ditch attempt, tried to take fresh aim at Mei. The sight galvanized Li into action. He ran towards Victor and slammed into him ferociously, throwing him to the ground. The strangler continued to grow tighter still and blood began to gush out like a sprinkler. Then before Li's shocked eyes, one side of the circular metal came to join the other side and a sizeable part of Victor's arm fell to the floor, writhing there like a creature in agony.

Victor fell on the floor, doubled up in agony, looking at Li with hatred and pain. Li brought his foot down on the killer's face, knocking him unconscious.

"Mei!" he yelled, running towards the door. He reached the hallway and found her standing there with almost no expression on her face. She looked numb, having just escaped death.

He held her in his arms, frantically running his hands over her.

"Are you hit?" he asked again and again.

"No, I'm fine. What happened in there?"

"The strangler cut off half his arm, and he's unconscious on the floor. What do we do now?"

"He has information, and if we expect anything to change, we'll need proof."

They went back to the room, hand in hand. Victor still lay on the floor, covered in a puddle of blood. For the first time in his life, it was his own. Mei ran to the bathroom and grab a towel, winding it tightly around Victor's amputated arm to stop the bleeding. They needed to keep him alive.

Li caught the unconscious killer by the shoulder and dragged him back into the living room, his bloody arm leaving a trail of blood on the floor. With Mei's help, Li hoisted him onto a chair. Mei ran to the kitchen and in one drawer, found duct tape. She grabbed the roll and tossed it across the room to Li. He caught it and used it to tie Victor's remaining arm to the chair's arm. He did the same with Victor's ankles and torso, making sure there would be no escape for the killer. Mei nodded in approval.

Then they stood facing the man who had killed their friend and had attempted to kill Li. He was a sorry sight as he sat tied to his chair, covered in blood, his expensive suit a mess. His black hair now hung matted over his face while he sat there hunched, still unconscious. Mei walked over to him and reached into his pocket, withdrawing the glass tablet. She placed one of his fingers on it to unlock the screen and found Li's profile staring back at her. Above his picture was some text in white that read "300,000 RMB."

"Did you scan Ronan?" Li asked

"I did," she said.

Li squeezed her hand. "So, we're done? We did it?"

"Almost. But you're still on that list and someone else could come after you now. Who knows how many more innocent people are being killed, thanks to the corruption in Contraception."

"That has nothing to do with us," he said.

"Well, your name is somehow on that list. I'd say we're pretty involved at this point. From what I understand, the only way off the list is death. We need to fight for your survival, and if we have the opportunity to do something, we should."

Li knew she was right. He wondered if this madness would ever end.

He looked at Victor and asked, "So do we wait for him to wake up?"

"Hold on; I saw this in a movie once." Mei walked to the kitchen and filled a glass with cold water. She went over to Victor and threw the water in his face. Nothing happened.

Li looked at her and said, "Maybe it wasn't cold enough."

"Let's wait. We also need to do something about Ronan; I can't bear to see him like this."

As Li sorrowfully looked at the lifeless body of his once closest friend slumped on the couch, with the wall behind him spattered wildly with blood and tissues, Mei ran into the bedroom again. This time, she brought a blanket and tossed it over Ronan.

"This will have to do until Dispo gets here," she said.

The Hus heard a faint sound, almost like the grunt of an animal. They both walked back to face Victor, and he slowly lifted his head.

He looked at his arm, the one which was missing half a hand, and said, "Well, this is a first."

"There's a first time for everything," said Li. "Now start talking.

19. THE CONFESSION

Stockholm, Sweden

Each government has the power to remove a person's pass, but only under extreme circumstances. Special departments of the military had their passes removed for covert missions, and there were even cases of a person's pass being removed instead of being given a prison sentence for a crime conviction.

"So, this is how it ends for me? Tied to an IKEA chair and killed by a Chinese couple! I had thought my death would be more heroic," Victor said, spitting a stream of blood on the ground.

Li had put his glass band on the table in front of Victor, and its dim white light showed that it was recording.

"Who do you work for?" asked Mei.

"Whoever pays me," Victor said with a grimace.

"What is 'the list'?"

"Ugh, do we have to go through this again? It's a database of names with price tags. If I accept a listing, I'm authorized to kill that person, and a sum of money will be transferred once the kill is confirmed."

"How do names end up on 'the list'?" asked Li.

"Powerful people have a way to get them there," Victor grunted. "Not just anyone can access it."

"How did my name end up on it?"

"I already told you, I don't know. Would you mind lighting a cigarette for me?"

Li looked at him searchingly. He knew unless the wound was professionally treated, it would be only a matter of time before Victor bled to his death. He felt he couldn't refuse a dying man's last wish.

"Breast pocket, inside of my jacket," Victor said with visible effort.

Li found the cigarettes and a box of matches. He placed a long thin cigarette in Victor's mouth and lit it for him. Victor balanced the cigarette between his lips and took a long drag.

"How did Ronan end up as a Contraception target even though he didn't apply?"

"Ah, now that's a question I know the answer to," Victor said and the cigarette fell from his lips. "For some time, Contraception was a solution to overpopulation. However, countries, like China, soon found that it was also a solution to their own problems."

"What kind of problems?"

"Well for China, the biggest threat to the leadership is losing power. The threat would be anyone who undermines the rule of the Chinese Communist Party. Who are likely to be the top choices? Dissidents, political activists, human rights advocates, and anyone else who is outspoken against the party."

Li looked at Mei, and they both thought about Ronan and his speeches about China and his theories about its corruption.

Victor continued, "So, instead of taking a big risk to eliminate these 'threats,' they thought that if Contraception applicants were killing people anyway, why not figure out a way to slip in the people they wanted dead? And that's precisely what they did."

Mei looked at him, almost not believing what she was hearing. Victor gasped and then was overcome by a fit of coughing. Blood started coming out of his mouth.

"But how could they possibly manipulate the Contraception database?" she asked.

Victor gave a weary grimace. "They couldn't, they didn't."

"Then what did they do?" asked Li.

Victor nodded toward the square outline of the glass tab in Mei's pocket. "The tablets," he said faintly. "They have an inside guy in the company making Contra's glass tablets and the guy inserts a chip or something in the tablet. I don't know the specifics, but somehow, whoever was behind all of this managed to hack the system and make it think that the profiles uploaded by the government were actual Contraception applicants."

Victor began to convulse. His body jerked wildly but the restraints kept him tied to the chair. The Hus watched him anxiously. It was painful to watch a man die under their eyes, even though someone who was a killer, but it was even more tense wondering if they would get to the bottom of the mystery before this man, who held the key to it, died on them.

It was some time before the spasms subsided and Victor could continue.

"The couple got their target, Contraception believed the kill was authorized, and everyone just kept their eyes forward."

"How do you know all of this?"

Victor spat out the blood welling up in his mouth and choking him. His teeth were red as he bared them in a wolfish grin. "You and I operate in different circles. I know people, and people talk."

"But you don't know who is behind the falsification of Contraception applications?"

"I told you, I have my guess, but you need proof. I'm sure your next question will be why I didn't try to find proof myself. The answer is easy, money. If I tried to expose what was going on, a majority of targets on the list would be gone, and I would be out of work."

Li and Mei looked at each other. They both wondered how many innocent people had died simply because someone wanted them dead. The only reason they had discovered this truth was because they had personally known Ronan and had a chance to speak with him instead of killing him right away. Li felt sick, wondering if Chen Xin and Sophie had also been illegally submitted names, instead of being actual applicants.

He looked at Victor who stared back at them. He looked ghastly, all color drained from his face, making it look ghastly. His makeshift tourniquet was now soaked, dripping blood onto the floor, creating a spreading puddle. Li knew Victor would die here and soon, but he still needed more information. He looked at his band that was recording everything that had happened.

Victor finally spoke up. His voice was so faint that they had to strain their ears to catch what he was saying. "Look, you guys got me, so now please just let me die. If you let me go, I'm still going to try kill you. Don't let me spend more hours strapped here, bleeding to death."

He looked at Mei fiercely and then nodded to the gun that sat on the table next to her. She looked at Li. Without saying a word, Li walked over to the table and double-tapped the glass band, turning it off. Mei picked up the gun from the table and raised it toward Victor's blood-soaked body.

"*Shì sǐ rú guī*,"[9] he said, smiling.

---

[9] To view death as a return home; not to be afraid of dying

Mei pulled the trigger, and the bullet flew from the barrel into Victor's chest, piercing his heart and taking with it the little life that was left in him. His head fell forward as one last fountain of blood soaked through the once white button-up shirt beneath his suit jacket. Li looked away. "Let's get out of here," he said.

Mei wiped her prints on the gun and tossed it on the couch next to Ronan's body. They knew Dispo would be here soon, as the tablet had alerted them after Mei confirmed Ronan's death. They didn't want to be around when Dispo found another man dead and taped to a chair. Besides, Victor's kill was not authorized. In normal circumstances, police would have been notified of his death within 15 minutes. However, since Victor's pass had been removed years ago, he was off the grid. But since Li and Mei did not know that, they were both frantic to leave the scene.

"The gun is clean, I've got Ronan's and Victor's tablets," Mei said. Li ran to the kitchen and rummaged in the cupboards until he found a plastic bag.

"We'll need to take a finger," he said, as he placed one of Victor's cut-off fingers into the bag.

"His tab is fingerprint-locked, right?"

"Good call," said Li. He glanced at his wrist; it was getting late. They both ran to the door, then turned back to look at the apartment. The once clean and tidy apartment was now a gruesome sight. Blood covered the carpet and most of the wall. Both Ronan and Victor lay motionless. The window at the end of the living room reflected the light of the shimmering stars in the black night sky. Li and Mei took one last look and then stepped into the hallway, closing the door firmly behind them.

***

The taxi ride to their hotel was quiet as both thought about what had just occurred. Li reached down and took Mei's hand in his own and she clung to him. Upon arriving at the hotel, they rushed to their room, locking the door behind them after entering.

Li made a grimace as he pulled out Victor's finger from the plastic bag in his pocket and dropped it onto the coffee table. The bag was full of blood. It was a gruesome necessity as he knew they would need the finger to unlock Victor's tablet. From her pocket, Mei took out Victor's tablet along with the tablet containing Ronan's Contraception profile. The two glass tablets lay on the table as Li and Mei stood side by side and looked at them.

"This is bigger than anyone could have ever anticipated. Can you imagine? What if this has been going on since it started? Ten years of corruption!" said Mei, running her hands through her hair in a nervous gesture. Li walked over to the mini fridge and took out a small bottle of whiskey. He opened it, poured some into a glass, and drank it in a gulp. His nerves were shot to bits.

"We've got to focus," said Mei. "We are the only people who have a chance to do anything about this and if Victor's suspicion that our government is behind this is correct, we'll have to keep our cards close to our chest until we are absolutely sure."

"Where do we even start?" asked Li. "We're in the same position as Ronan was, nothing more than a suspicion."

"We've got Victor on video, and we also have his tablet, which can access the list he was talking about. If we could find out who added the names to the list that would be enough."

"Even if we found out who was adding names to a free-market hitlist, it still wouldn't explain how Ronan's name ended up being given to us through Contraception. We need to figure out who has been falsifying applications. A hitlist is one thing, but corruption in an international program is a scandal."

Mei agreed, but both were at a loss how to proceed.

Li thought for a moment. "We know someone who could help us out," he whispered. "Lao Shu. He's worked in tech his whole life and still owns that electronic store."

"What would you have him do?" she asked, giving him a quizzical look.

"Maybe he could hack the tablet?"

"Hack it?"

"Well I don't know the technical term for it, but technology always leaves a trace. Perhaps he could look into our questions, first finding out who submitted the names to the list and trying to figure out if there is something not standard about Ronan's inclusion compared to the other two."

Mei thought for a moment. Lao Shu was over 70 and her expression conveyed her doubt.

"What other choice do we have?" Li tried to persuade her. "This is too sensitive to take to anyone else."

"Lao Shu it is then," she said.

Mei sat down at the table while Li walked back to the fridge, took out the other tiny bottles of alcohol and placed them, along with another glass, on the table. He poured each of them a drink, and they clinked glasses.

"To the truth," said Li. Mei nodded, and they both took a sip. After their drink, they took a shower together and got into bed. Li wrapped his arms around Mei, knowing everything they had been through was just the beginning. He thought about what lay ahead of them, knowing they were headed into dangerous territory. His friend had died and finding out who was responsible for his death, he thought, was the right thing to do. Perhaps this was a way to balance out the "wrong" he had done to have a child. He knew that wasn't how morality worked, but in his heart, he felt that doing this, despite the danger, was something he had to do.

The next morning, while they were getting ready to head back to Beijing, Li's band lit up, signaling a phone call. He looked at Mei and gave her a look before accepting the call.

"Mr. Hu! This is Xi from Contra. How are you today?"

"Fine, thank you. What is this call regarding?"

"I wanted to be the first to congratulate you on completing your three kills! Such a big accomplishment. I'm sure both of you feel not only immensely proud but somewhat relieved as well."

"Yes," Li said tiredly. "It was quite the process."

"At this point, all you have to do is have a baby, and once it is born, your name will be removed from the Contraception database and whoever has your profile will be given a new one. However, you're not out of the woods until that baby is born."

"Understood."

"Fantastic. Are there are any questions Mr. Hu?"

Li looked at the table with Ronan's profile and thought what could happen if he brought it up. However, last night Mei had said that Xi might be involved somehow, since he was the one who had provided them with the tablet. They had no idea how far the corruption went.

"All clear."

"Well in that case, again, congratulations and thank you for choosing Contraception! On behalf of everyone here at Contra, we wish you and your wife a truly exceptional life, assuming you make it until the baby is born. Last I heard, Mr. Zhuang was still in a coma, so I believe you shouldn't have any trouble. Goodbye!"

As he hung up, Li asked Mei, "How is he so upbeat all the time?"

"His cheerfulness makes me sick," she said as she walked over to the table, picked up the tablets and put them in her bag. After they had finished packing, they took a taxi to the airport and began their flight back to Beijing.

On the plane, Li turned to Mei and said, "Is this how you thought your first trip to Sweden would be?"

"Two dead men, one of whom we knew, plus the knowledge that Contraception has been compromised and finding out that my husband is on a hitlist. Well, at least I can say there were never any dull moments."

Li smiled. They had been through more than either of them had expected and he knew there was yet more to come. After landing in Beijing, they went straight to their apartment and once inside, collapsed on the bed. Despite the many advances in technology, there still wasn't a better way to deal with jet lag.

The next morning, they woke up and while eating breakfast, stared at the two tablets that lay on the table, almost taunting them with the unsolved mystery they contained. Li walked over to his study and from the drawer, took out both Sophie's and Chen's tablets and put them next to the other two.

"Do you think he'll be able to find anything?" he asked. The Hus had decided they would talk with Lau Shu and see if his years of experience in tech would prove useful in finding any information on what Victor had explained.

"It's better than us just staring at them," Mei said.

20. THE REVELATION

Beijing, China

Contraception has its own production facility that makes the tablets on which target profiles are stored and then given out to applicants. It also hosts and manages its own internal mainframe, which chooses applicants at random from its database.

▪ After breakfast, Li picked up all four tablets, put them in his pocket, and the couple took the elevator down until they had arrived at Lao Shu's apartment. They hesitated for a moment before knocking on the door. They heard the click of a lock, and Lao Shu appeared in front of them, wearing a loose-fitting blue shirt and gray pants, his black spectacles on his head.

"Li, Mei, good to see you alive and well. How are things?"

"Fine, thank you," said Li. "Sorry to trouble you, but we were hoping you could do us a favor."

Lao Shu gave them a look, intuitively realizing it would not be a simple favor and stepped aside to let them in. The apartment was well lit and packed with gadgets. There were microchips and motherboards strewn on a large coffee table while glass screens on the walls displayed information foreign to Li. Various tools lay on shelves on the far side of the apartment, organized in such a way that only the person who had put them there could figure out what was where. Lao Shu led them into the living room and sat in a black chair opposite to the couch where he motioned them to sit.

"What can I do for you?" he asked.

Li looked at Mei before leaning forward.

"We believe Contraception has been compromised and we're looking for answers."

Lao Shu was expressionless as he said, "And what brings you to this conclusion?"

Li shook his wrist toward the large screen on the wall and showed the old man the video he had taken of Victor. He also explained what had happened in Sweden before pulling out all the tablets and placing them on the table.

Moving one off to the side he said, "This is Victor's tablet, the guy from the video," and gesturing at the other three, added, "And these are the three that were given to us when we applied at the Contra building."

"What do you want me to do?" asked Lao Shu, his curiosity piqued.

"We are hoping you could hack into the tablets and figure out who added my name to the list on Victor's tablet; then see if you can find any differences between Ronan's tablet and the other two. We're trying to find out who put Ronan's name into the Contraception database though he didn't apply to have a child."

Lao Shu sat back in his chair and stroked his beard. Li knew what he was asking was dangerous, and involving Lao Shu carried with it a considerable amount of risk, for both parties.

Lao Shu thought silently to himself for some time before saying, "When you've lived as long as I have, you start to understand the world around you. People come and go, places change, but one thing has remained constant – man's desire for self-preservation. No matter what happens, humans and organizations will always look for ways to survive."

He paused for a moment before continuing. "Whatever we find, I guarantee it is just the tip of the iceberg concerning man's capacity to sustain his existence."

"So, you'll help us?" asked Mei.

"Give me a few days, and I'll see what I can come up with."

Li extended his hand, and Lao Shu shook it. The Hus stood up and went toward the door but before they had stepped over the threshold, Lao Shu grabbed Li's arm.

"Sometimes, when you go looking, you might not like what you find."

He let go of Li's arm. A subdued Li reached into his jacket and pulled out the bundle containing Victor's severed finger.

"You'll need this to get into Victor's tablet," he said in a low voice.

Without saying a word, Lao Shu took the bag. The Hus stepped out and the door shut behind them.

***

Alone in his apartment finally, Lao Shu walked back to the coffee table and picked up the four glass tablets. He took them into his office at the end of the hallway and put them on a glass table facing three large, curved screens. He sat down in the big black chair in front of the table and carefully put Victor's tablet on the table. Then with a moue of distaste he quickly pulled out the cold, bloody finger out of the bag and pressed it on the blank screen of the tablet.

As if from nowhere, small silver cables from the edges of the table inserted themselves into the tablet, as if a giant squid had wrapped its tentacles around its prey. The screens in front of Lao Shu sprang to life. The console at the center displayed the screen of the tablet while the ones on the left and right showed lines of code. With a swipe of his wrist, a hologram appeared in front of him, emanating from the table. The blue and white light displayed a cube, and as soon as Lao Shu moved his hands, the cube expanded into hundreds of pieces, each revealing a section of data from the tablet.

Lao Shu examined each section of hovering light in front of him until he found what he was looking for. He seemed to pick it up with his fingers and tossed it at the center console. The hologram faded away, and the giant screen now displayed a list of names accompanied by a price. He had found "the list."

"Eureka," he whispered, with a triumphant smile on his face.

Lao Shu scrolled through the names, each with a varying sum of money displayed next to it, along with the target's name, age, occupation and picture. He swiped left on the center console and a display marked "Open Contracts" appeared where he was confronted with a picture of Li Hu as well as the price for Li's death. Lao Shu knew diving further into this might bring repercussions, but as he sat there, staring at the kill list, he felt there was no other option than to go forward. He couldn't change his past, but maybe he could change the future.

Looking at the glass screen to the left, he went through the code, looking for anything that might provide a clue to where this contract originated. His fingers hovered above the glass screen on his desk, moving methodically to scan the lines of code.

After about an hour, finding no useful information, he automated the process. Lao Shu knew the code would be long and tedious, so he wrote a script to search for specific keywords, particular lines of code, and to alert him when there were any hits. Once finished, his swiped his hand toward the left screen and the script started to work, skimming through the code, looking for the information he had instructed it to search for.

The old man got up from his chair and walked to the kitchen, where he brought a kettle of water to a boil to make tea. Despite the abundance of technology, he still enjoyed the old-fashioned way of boiling water instead of using the instant-boil kettles that had been in the market for years. Lao Shu felt those few minutes that the water took to heat up gave him precious time to think, a rarity in a world flooded with inputs from all around. The world had got too noisy with constant information flooding all the senses.

As he waited for steam to erupt from the kettle, he thought about what he had just discovered. He wondered if the person he had helped his son kill was a legitimate applicant or had also been falsified like the Swede, as the Hus claimed. If it were true, he felt justified in his pursuit of the truth, despite what may come.

A small hum came from the kettle, and Lao Shu poured the hot water into a cup that contained a mix of dry plants and herbs. Despite the usefulness of a tea bag, Lao Shu was Chinese, and this was how they drank tea. He grabbed his cup and shuffled back into the living room, glancing at the three glass screens. He could see that the script was still running and decided he would work on the three Contra tablets in the meantime. He went to his desk and laid out the three glass tablets in front of him.

To the uninformed eye, each seemed identical. He picked each one up and examined the craftsmanship of the glass screen. He then put them down and tapped the glass desk. A blue light came on and measured the three tablets, displaying their height and width, and a number appeared above each one, showing the weight. The numbers were the same.

From the corner of the table, Lao Shu dragged out what looked like a big magnifying glass on hinges and positioned it in front of the three tablets. Once he put his eye on the circular glass screen in front of him, the tablets could be seen through a variety of spectrums. He tapped the thin metal edge of the circle and first looked at the electrical capacity of each. All three contained the same electrical components; thinly veiled wires could be seen running around the perimeter of each device. He then tapped the circle again, and this time, it was as if he was looking through an x-ray machine, examining the internal workings of the devices.

On the tablet on the far right, he spotted something that was absent from the other two. On the lower left corner, there was the outline of a small circle. He took his eye away from the magnifying glass machine and looked down at the table. Each tablet looked the same. Lao Shu looked through the device again, and the small circle once more appeared only on the tablet on the far right. He picked it up and pushed the circular device away. In his hand, he held Ronan's Contra tablet.

He sighed, knowing he was one step closer to confirming the suspicion the Hus had. A small beeping noise came from the console in front of him, and a message flashed on the main screen. "Parameter identified" the screen flashed in bright red letters. Lao Shu set down the tablet and looked at the left screen that had highlighted a section of code. He moved his fingers above the table, and the highlighted code moved to the center console.

Lao Shu moved his glasses further up the bridge of his nose to see better and found what he was looking for. A section of the code contained the appendage "gov.cn," indicating that whoever had placed Li Hu on the list as a target had done so using a Chinese government IP address. He drank his tea. His heart was racing as he realized what he had discovered.

With his right hand, he tapped the band on his left wrist and called Li.

"I found something; you better get over here."

Li and Mei arrived at his apartment within minutes, and as they sat together in the living room, he explained to them what he had found.

"What does this mean?"

"Well, from what the code says, whoever added your name to the list works for the Chinese government. I'm still working on who, but I don't know if we'll get a name."

"And Ronan?" asked Mei.

"I found something inside his tablet, but thought I'd wait for you two before I went any further."

He motioned for them to join him in his workroom where Ronan's tablet lay flat on the table. The old man moved the circular screen in front of it and had both look through it to detect the outline of the small circle that he had spotted earlier. He then showed them the other two tablets that contained no circle.

"What is it?" asked Li.

"I've seen it before, but never in a Contra tablet, nor one this small. The circle is a tiny processor that hijacks the feed of whatever happens on this tablet. Not only can information from this tablet be sent to whoever put the processor there, but it's also able to feed information into the tablet. In my shop, I see these a lot with couples, jealous girlfriends who want to see who their boyfriend is talking to. But I have a feeling this processor is a little more advanced than what I usually encounter. I guess whoever is responsible was using this chip to force fake profiles onto Contra tablets."

"Can you get it out of there?" asked Li

"That's the plan," replied Lao Shu, as he picked Ronan's Contra tablet from the table. The Hus gathered around the table while Lao Shu went to the shelves, looking for the tool he needed. He brought what looked like a light camping stove and put it on the table.

"We have to be careful not to damage the chip or trigger the warning system that will alert them someone has removed it. If we are lucky, we might be able to figure out where this originated from, and if we're very, very lucky, then we may find out who was behind this."

As the Hus looked on in fascination, Lao Shu held the tablet over the stove-like machine. A blue light shot up from its base. The old man moved his hands away and let the light hold the tablet in midair. As it hovered there, the Hus looked on in wonder, never having seen this kind of tech before.

From the left side of the table, Lao Shu picked up two thin pieces of wire and touched the top and bottom part of the tablet with them. The two wires instantly became erect and stuck to the tablet, extending a few centimeters vertically from it.

Li wanted to ask several things but he stayed silent, not wanting to disturb Lao Shu. Instead, he watched the old man's gnarled fingers as they positioned the wires and grabbed the next tool off the desk with a fluidity that suggested he had done this before. With surgical precision, Lao Shu picked up a metal rod about the size of a pen. He double-tapped it with his forefinger and a white light emanated from its end. Lao Shu ran the light along the floating device until he had covered all around it.

He then motioned for Li to fetch him a new glass tablet from the shelf and when Li brought it to the table, said tersely, "Just hold it steady." Lao Shu then set down the white light tool and looked at Mei.

"As soon as I pull the tablet apart, you're going to use these to grab the circular processor and place it onto the tablet your husband is holding," he told her.

Then he handed her a pair of tweezers that emitted two red prongs of light in place of the traditional metal pincers. These were needed since a metal instrument would disrupt any electrical signal that the microchip might be emitting.

Lao Shu looked at Li and then at Mei. "On the count of three," he said slowly. "One, two, three."

Holding a wire in each hand, he pulled the glass tablet apart. For a brief second, the circular microchip remained suspended in the blue light between both parts of the tablet. Immediately, Mei inserted the tweezers into the space between the two sides, pried out the chip, and swiftly moved it on the blank glass tablet Li was holding. As soon as it touched the tablet, it seemed to sink between the layers of glass, and thin wires could be seen coming from the chip and moving through the device. Within seconds, all the wires had disappeared.

"We've got it," Lao Shu said triumphantly as he let go of the two wires that were still attached to the glass tablet suspended in the blue light. All three then turned to the tablet that now contained the microchip from Ronan's old tablet. Lao Shu put it on the small glass screen on his table, and the three screens in front of him lit up.

"What happens now? Are you going to hack it?" asked Li.

Lao Shu looked at him with a grin. "Yes, now, we hack it."

He placed his hands slightly above the table and typed as lines of code appeared on both the left and right screens. After a short while, Lao Shu tapped above the table, and a new profile appeared on the center console.

The old man smiled and said, "Here's the guy responsible."

A young man in a suit appeared with his name displayed above him, "Jun Diao." Underneath his picture, was his position: "Lead Programmer and Technician for the National Institute of Population Management and Control, the People's Republic of China."

Other information also appeared in the profile including his government clearance, previous time spent in the PLA, and his education and training.

"I knew it!" shouted Li. "I knew the government was behind this!"

His head throbbed and he walked away from the screen. The confirmation that this involved the Chinese government meant that any further steps would hold dire consequences. His mind was flooded with emotions – anxiety, anger, fear.

Lao Shu continued to type until new information appeared on the screen on the right.

"It looks like the IP address used to upload your name to 'the list' on Victor's tablet matches the IP address where the microchip on Ronan's tablet is transmitting information. The worst part is that the IP address comes from the government."

Mei sat down in a chair next to the table and tried to collect her thoughts. "So, let me get this straight. The Chinese government, or at least this guy," motioning at Diao, "has been using a microchip to add to the hitlist the names of people who didn't apply to Contraception?"

"That's what the information seems to say," said Lao Shu. The three sat in silence, reeling under the weight of what they had just discovered.

Li finally broke the silence. "What do we still not know?"

"Getting that microchip into the tablets is not an easy process, Lao Shu responded. "So, the question is, does the government have access to the Contraception tablet suppliers or is someone from within Contra sending the tablets to be compromised and receiving them once it is done?"

"We also don't know if this was an isolated incident or how long this has been going on," remarked Mei.

"There's more," said Lao Shu. "I dug deeper into the list of targets that were added using the same government IP address."

"And what did you find?" asked Li.

"Thousands of names," said Lao Shu, "And all of them have something in common. Most of them are political activists, Chinese dissidents, politicians disagreeing with China's political ideology – people who caused an issue for the ruling party."

"My god," said Mei. "They've been using Contraception to silence the rising voices against them. How can we not have caught on to this? Thousands of innocent people must have died."

"Millions have died under Contraception, and no one batted an eye," said Li. "It was the perfect plan. Falsify applications and get married couples to kill whoever they needed to instead of doing it themselves. What have we stumbled upon?"

"This is dangerous territory," said Lao Shu. "Are you sure we go ahead with this?"

Li took a seat next to the desk. "What's the next step?" he asked.

Lao Shu got up from his chair and walked to the other side of the desk. He tapped a section of the glass and a smaller piece of glass, about the size of a gum, emerged which he caught quickly.

He came back to the Hus and said, "This is everything that just occurred in this room. The screens, and everything that happened on this desk, were recorded. With the microchip, the names of the targets on 'the list' that originated from the government IP address, and Victor's confession, there's substantial evidence here for higher authorities to take action."

"Besides doing the right thing, we have to make sure this stays between us," interjected Mei. "I'm all for cutting down corruption, but I won't die for my country." Li nodded in agreement.

The three of them sat there in the room with only the lights from the glass screens emitting a faint glow over the workspace. They discussed what was to happen next, deciding that the evidence should be presented before Contraception's governing board. However, figuring out how to get it there remained an insurmountable problem. Not sure if a mole was working at Contra, they had decided against mentioning anything to Xi or stepping foot inside that building again. The board didn't accept walk-ins, and it was rare that they granted a civilian a meeting. They discussed their options and then Mei had an idea.

"Why didn't I think of this earlier? Isn't my friend Xiaoli's father Zhang Tao the China representative for Contraception and one of the permanent ten members of the board?"

"Sorry, who?" asked Lao Shu.

"You're right!" said Li. "And I remember she was very skeptical about the entire system at the Contrabation party. She might just be the key to stopping whatever is going on. But what are we going to do, just ask her to help?"

"We've got no other options," said Mei.

All of them agreed that it wasn't without its challenges, but it was still the best idea that had come out of their brainstorming session.

"I'll figure out just how we're going to go about this and call Xiaoli. In the meantime, we can't discuss this with anyone, including your son," said Mei, looking at Lao Shu.

"You have my word," he said.

All three of them were subdued, thinking of what had just occurred. They were in it now.

Lao Shu took the wires off Ronan's tablet and waved his hand in front of the camp stove-like machine and the light changed from blue to white. The two pieces of the tablet joined back as one, and when the light turned green, Lao Shu took the tablet suspended in mid-air, picked up the other two Contraception tablets from the table and the glass hard drive, and handed them all to Li.

"I feel like we just removed a cancer," said Li.

"That's a good analogy, except that in this case, the cancer has already spread. Look," he said, gesturing at Ronan's glass tablet. Even without the chip, Ronan's profile had already been embedded into the hardware and still appeared on the screen.

"What about Victor's tablet?" Li asked.

"Better it stays with me. I've made a clone for you to take with you to the board, but I'm sure whoever is responsible for 'managing' Victor, the hitman, will be tracking it. Same as the chip, it's too risky to let you take it to the Contraception board in Canada. The video proof and coding that I pulled from it should be sufficient. You've still got work to do. It's all up to you now."

Lao Shu paused for a moment, before saying, "Sometimes, the hardest thing and the right thing are the same."

No more words were said as Lao Shu led the Hus to the door. Li looked at the old man, making firm eye contact, and nodded, knowing his appreciation and gratitude had been communicated through the silence between them.

As the Hus made their way back to their apartment, they understood that they had opened a can of worms. Still, it was time to finish what they had started. When they were inside their apartment, Mei called her friend.

Xiaoli answered promptly. Mei said, "Xiaoli, I need a favor, and you're not going to like it."

She then explained everything that had happened, including the revelations Lao Shu had made concerning the microchip and the government IP address.

There was a long pause from Xiaoli before she shouted, "I knew it! I knew there was something going on. Oh man, finally! I knew it was too good to be true!"

"Xiaoli please, I need your help."

After taking a big breath, she replied, "What can I do?"

"Your father, we need to meet him."

There was another long pause on the other end of the line, "That's asking a lot."

"How long have we been friends, Xiaoli? I wouldn't be coming to you if this wasn't important. Innocent people don't deserve to die and I'm coming to you hoping we can end the corruption."

Xiaoli knew Mei was right. She had always stood for what she believed in, and now, she finally had the chance to prove it. "I mean, I can talk to him, but I can't make any promises. My father believes in the system, and if there's any corruption, he would be the first to condemn it. But it's going to take some convincing. He and I aren't on the best terms ever since my husband and I decided not to have a baby. Something about us not being contributing members of society and all that. I'll talk to him and let you know what he says, but again, it's a long shot."

"Just talk to him. That's all I ask. Thank you." Mei ended the call and looked at Li who was sitting on the couch. She walked over to him and curled up against him, laying her head on his chest. "Let's go make a baby," she said.

Li stroked her hair and bent down to kiss her. They got up and walked toward the bedroom. The living room light automatically turned off and the bedroom door closed softly behind them.

21. THE COLLECTIVE II

Beijing, China

One of the first proposals to deal with overpopulation was to randomly select one fourth of each country's male population and sterilize them.

■ Diao sat in his dark office. The lights were dim as he and the other members of his team waited at their desks. They were expecting a call from their superior, and they did not have good news to share. Diao undid his tie and unbuttoned the top of his white collared shirt.

A stout man from the corner of the room tried to add a positive note. "It's not all that bad," he said diplomatically.

Diao turned to look at him and said witheringly, "Oh, so you wouldn't mind being the one to give the Deputy Director of National Security our latest updates?"

The round man bit his lips, shook his head and said, "I've got work to do." He hid his head behind his glass screen and began to type with a show of industriousness that didn't fool anyone. No one wanted to be the messenger of bad news.

Diao knew as director of the National Institute of Population Management and Control, it was his responsibility to relay all information, both successes and failures. He glanced at the band on his wrist, 23:53. He was expecting the call any minute. He stood up and motioned to his team to head to the conference room. The five people in the office silently made their way to a bigger room, dominated by a large black table with black chairs around it. At the center of the table was a glass screen. The team sat around the table, fidgeting as they waited. Diao took the spot at the head of the table and looked at the people he worked with. These were some of the brightest minds in tech. The government had plucked them from all walks of life to work here as a team. As one disgruntled member put it, "We are fucking government hackers, man."

Taken from top universities, a prison, a startup, and the IT department of one of China's largest state-owned enterprises, this team stealthily incorporated the government's list of people they wanted dead into the Contraception tablets. They were also responsible for adding the names to the state's hitlist as a precautionary backup since complications could ensue in the Contraception process and the results they wanted were not guaranteed. Each member, including Diao, a former tech operative for the PLA, knew the consequences of what they were doing, but with the full support of the People's Republic of China, they forged ahead without hesitation.

In the past decade, there had been bumps in the road, but they had figured out a way to make the entire process smooth and most importantly, untraceable. This time, however, something had happened. According to protocol, even the smallest aberration had to be reported to higher authorities, which is what had brought the team together on this evening.

The edges of the glass screen dispelled a white light and a holographic image of a man in a black tuxedo appeared on the screen. This was a member of China's State Council, the chief administrative authority of the republic, and he looked grim. "What do you have for me?" he said without preamble, looking intently at Diao and ignoring the others.

"Sir, Victor is dead. We received confirmation from a Swedish Dispo unit a few hours ago. It appears someone murdered him."

"Is there anything that can trace him back to us?" the man asked, a frown on his face.

Diao hesitated before responding slowly, "The Dispo unit informed me that no tablet was found on his person, nor on the premises where he was found."

"How could this have happened?" yelled the man, looking murderous with rage. "Victor was one of the best we had!"

"There is another matter to attend to, sir," Diao said in a low voice.

The man in the tuxedo barked, "What is it?"

"We received a report that for a brief moment, one of the microchips in a Contraception target's tablet was, for lack of a better word, removed."

"How is that possible? The chip is embedded in the tablet. How can it be 'removed'?"

"That's the question, sir. The chip's monitoring device said it was removed only for a few seconds. Although we don't have reason to believe it was compromised, it's a possibility that can't be overlooked."

"How did this happen?" asked the man.

Men in expensive suits and women in couture dresses walked behind him in the background. Diao guessed the State Council minister was attending an official dinner and had little patience for bad news.

"It could just be a bug, sir. However, we're considering all possibilities. The chip is back in Beijing. We're working on getting a tactical force to investigate within the next 48 hours."

"Keep me informed of any progress on this situation. And make sure there are no further incidents, or you and your team are finished. You won't go back to where you came from."

With that, the hologram vanished, and the light around the glass plate dimmed until it was extinguished. Diao looked around the table. Though they had taken every precaution to make sure there was no trace back to them or the government, however, not everything these days was fool-proof and in his heart, he had always felt it was only a matter of time until someone caught on.

"You heard him," he told his team, "Let's get a fix on that chip and initiate protocol to handle this mess."

"I'm not dying for this government," said a tattooed girl with short black hair.

Diao turned to look at her and said, "I'll make sure none of us do."

With that, he double-tapped the band on his wrist and after a second said, "It's me. Get the strike team ready. I'll be sending over a location soon."

22. THE PURSUIT

Beijing, China

Contraception's board is composed of ten representatives from countries that best represent the diversity of the world. For example, China and Iceland have the largest and smallest population in the world, respectively. The board was chosen from all 197 countries through a voting process until there were ten finally.

▪ The next afternoon, Mei's phone rang while she and Li were eating lunch at their kitchen table.

"Xiaoli, hi."

"I've talked with my father, and if you have the proof you say you do, he's willing to meet with you and get you before the Contraception board. But Mei, this is no joke. What you're claiming could change Contraception forever."

"That's the idea," she said. They then discussed when they would meet her father, one of the men responsible for making sure that Contraception ran without hitches and corruption.

"Also, my father has booked a hotel for you, use the last name 'Fang.' Once you check in, he'll be in touch. I can't say anything more, but I wish you the best of luck. You're doing the right thing."

After the phone call, she turned to Li and said, "It's set. He'll meet with us."

Li set down his chopsticks. "This is it. Hopefully, this will be the end of it."

"Well, we've got to fly to Canada."

For some reason unknown to the public, the Contraception representatives from each country had agreed that Canada would serve as the headquarters that oversaw all of Contraception's affairs. It was here that the board met to discuss all issues related to Contraception and managed the operations of all the Contra offices around the world. It was also here that the Hus were to make their case to the board.

"And to think that earlier this year, I thought we would have an uneventful summer," he shook his head in disbelief. "When do we leave?"

"Tomorrow," said Mei. "Xiaoli mentioned that the board was meeting four days from now. If her father believes the evidence to be strong enough, we'll be able to make our case before it then."

"I think we're about to blow the lid off this thing and whatever happens, we've got to be prepared."

"We have each other," she said, reaching across the table to touch his hand. The sun shone bright, and for a moment, Li thought it was perhaps a sign that everything would be ok. The dark days were behind them, and the bright sun represented the success he hoped would come from their trip to Canada. In the back of his mind, he also hoped that the future would bring a brighter tomorrow for their child.

Mei got up from the table, remarking, "Time to pack, again."

Li flicked his wrist and a screen to purchase plane tickets appeared on the window in front of him.

"Afternoon flight okay?" he yelled.

"Perfect," she said from the bedroom. He held up his wrist and purchased two tickets for Montreal the following day. They would need to get over their jet lag and convince Xiaoli's father before presenting their case to the board.

"Bought," he yelled. Although there were still many steps ahead of them, Li felt a sense of elation on this bright afternoon. He and Mei had survived the turbulent past few weeks, had done what they needed to do to have a baby, and were now involved in something he considered morally right. He knew it was too soon to celebrate, but still he couldn't suppress a sense of euphoria.

"We're almost there!" he cried out.

"Almost, babe," she called out, in a mix of elation and warning.

The next morning, after the Hus had finished packing their bags and tidied up their apartment, Mei looked at her band and said, "Let's go." They grabbed their bags, pressed the glass tag to compress them, and took one last look at their apartment. They hoped this would not be their final look at the place they called home but they were keenly aware of the danger they would be facing in the next few days. They clung to each other and kissed feverishly before opening the door. Once in the elevator, Mei sought to go to the first floor, but Li forestalled her.

"We should say goodbye to Lao Shu. He's the one who made all of this possible."

He pressed the button for fifty-fourth floor so they could say goodbye to the old man who had taken an incalculable risk for them. As the elevator arrived at the fifth-fourth floor and the doors opened, to their indescribable shock, the Hus found they were not alone on the floor. Four men, all wearing black clothes and equipped with large assault rifles, were casing the area. They wore belts containing tactical gear, and Li noticed grenades like the ones Wang had given him. Two of them wore glass bands that ran across their eyes. Li had seen these before, a new type of "glasses" that the military and medical professionals used to see infra-red, x-ray, heat patterns, UV, and the organs inside a person's body.

It looked like they were stalking Lao Shu's door. Li stood there in shock, half in and half out of the elevator, not sure what to do. Finally, he moved back into the elevator and tersely explained to Mei what was happening.

"We can't just go over there," she said. "What are we supposed to do? Any intervention is a risk to our own lives."

"I might've died if it weren't for him," he argued back.

"We could also end up dead because of him."

Standing in the elevator, the Hus contemplated their next move. But before they could decide, a loud thud could be heard from the end of the hallway. Li poked his head out and saw two of the men holding an "enforcer," a battering ram used to break down doors. However, there was something unique about this one.

As the men in black swung the ram backward, it looked to be the size of a billy club, but as they swung it forward, it seemed to gain mass, hitting the door with greater force. On the third swing, Li heard a crack and knew the lock on the door had broken. As they heard the door breaking, something unexpected happened. Massive flames burst from the doorway, throwing the two attackers back against the hallway wall. The other two men fell to the ground, engulfed in fire.

"What happened?" Mei asked, looking pale.

"I don't know," Li said helplessly. "There's seems to have been an explosion from Lao Shu's door."

He gingerly looked out of the elevator again. This time he heard one of the cursing attackers saying in disbelief to the band on his wrist, "They've booby-trapped the door. Two men down, send backup."

"We have to help Lao Shu," Li told Mei.

"He seems to be doing pretty well by himself," she argued, not ready to let him go.

Then gunshots rang out. Li could see the two attackers who had survived fire a barrage of bullets through the blasted doorway.

"We have to go," Mei said urgently. "Or everything that Lao Shu did for us will be in vain."

A reluctant Li knew she was right and pressed the elevator button and it began to descend, cutting off the sounds of warfare on the fifty-fourth floor. In the lobby, they saw five more armed men in black charging in through the entrance and heading for the bank of elevators. Mei and Li kept their backs to them and left the building as soon as the men had gone past.

"Let's get to Canada and end this once and for all," said a shivering Mei as the two of them made it to the street and hailed a taxi to the nearest security transport station. As the railway whisked them through the city, Li and Mei sat silently, their hands tightly locked together.

"He'll be alright. He's a fighter, and even if he dies, we will honor his name," said Li.

The train continued to fly high over Beijing, away from the chaos and drama that was inevitably occurring in everyone's lives below. Once at the airport, and settled at their gate, Li wondered about the Contraception hearing.

"Do you think we've got a strong enough case?" he asked.

"We have a testimony, the profile of a government official who is responsible for adding names to 'the list,' and the evidence of a microchip embedded into a Contra target tablet which was traced back to a government IP address. I think we have enough evidence."

Li worried about things. Perhaps it was inevitable that a universal system would one day be corrupted, as had most entities in the world, businesses, organizations, governments. All systems had loopholes that attracted corruption. Contraception was no different.

Over the course of the eight-hour flight, the Hus slept, talked, drank wine, and wondered what was happening to Lao Shu. The old man haunted them even as they tried to focus on the daunting task of trying to expose the corruption in one of the most powerful and influential policies in the world.

When their flight landed in Montreal, they took a taxi to the hotel booked for them. They were expected and upon giving the receptionist the name they had been asked to give, Feng, they were quickly shown to their room without any of the usual formalities. In their room, on the table next to a blank glass pad, Mei saw a note that just said "Olympic Park, 22:00."

"We've got to be somewhere by ten tonight, let's sleep until then," she told Li, who was putting their luggage away.

Li flicked his wrist and the room turned dark. Both he and Mei crawled into bed and were asleep almost immediately.

Hours later, Li's band vibrated and woke him up. It was 21:00. He rubbed Mei's shoulder, and she woke up immediately. Li moved his hand, and the room lit up. The windows became transparent and the night lights of Montreal flooded in. Although this city too had been affected by Contraception and experienced a population drop, the spirit and zest for life remained. Many young people who had not applied had moved here to Montreal, which experienced frequent protests against the policy. This might also have been fueled by the fact that Contra had established its headquarters here, making it an accessible location for demonstrations.

As the Hus got dressed, they kept an eye on their band, making sure they would be in time to for the meeting. Once dressed, they left the hotel and flagged a taxi on the street. The autonomous car took them to the Olympic Park with ten minutes to spare. The massive stadium, though considered a relic by many, still stood as a testament to the city and the spirit of friendly competition that the Olympics promoted. As the Hus walked around the stadium, darkness enveloped them. The place seemed to be deserted. The stillness of the night made Li feel uncomfortable, used as he was to the bustling and noisy streets of Beijing.

From the shadows of the tree-lined park, a voice whispered, "Follow me."

Startled, they stood still and looked around them frantically. Ahead of them a shadow disengaged itself from the sheltering darkness of the hedges and moved ahead. Unsure of what to do, they began to follow the mysterious figure. As their eyes grew used to the dark, they could make out it was a man. But the darkness and his dark suit which merged into it made it impossible to find out more.

He took them to the Montreal Tower and a waiting elevator. The three of them went in and once inside, the man's face was finally visible. The Hus wondered if it was Xiaoli's father or one of his underlings, but no one said a word until they reached the top of the tower.

"Sorry for all this mystery, I'm Zhang Tao," the man finally said, looking at Mei. "I am told you are a good friend of my daughter."

"That's right, we've known each other for a long time."

"We are hoping you can help us," said Li.

"This is a very, very serious business," Zhang said as he led them into a small room. "Let's see first what you've got."

Li began to play the video he had made of Victor. The dead killer came alive, telling them what he knew about the goings-on at Contraception. "That man had been hired to kill me," Li explained. "But we managed to neutralize him and make him tell us what he knew."

He then took out Victor's tablet and showed Zhang "the list" as well as Diao's profile. "This is the man who added my Swedish friend Ronan Sorensen's name to the government's hitlist, as well as thousands of others,'" he told the incredulous Zhang.

Ronan's tablet was then handed over, with Li explaining how the dead Swede had never applied to Contraception. Finally, he played the video showing Lao Shu removing the microchip from inside the Contra tablet that was different from normal Contra microchips and the information that it came from a Chinese government IP address.

"We believe the Chinese government is targeting anyone who goes against China, both at home and abroad, by falsely including them into the Contraception database so that other bona fide applicants kill them without knowing the truth. In my case, I had already applied to Contraception. But because they want to ensure my death, they added my name to the state hitlist too as a backup to make sure I died, one way or another."

Zhang was still, trying to process the information the Hus had just presented him. He shook his head in disbelief and then sighed.

"This is impossible, there's no way our government could pull something like this off without someone finding out."

"I'm sorry, sir, but we did find out. The evidence speaks for itself, and you're aware of the reach and power of China. If they want something done, it gets done, at any cost."

"*Xié mén wāi dào,*"[10] he said quietly. "What you've shown me is overwhelming. This will need to be assessed further by an independent analyst as well as someone more familiar with this tech than I. However; I believe we can have a full report ready before the board convenes in a few days."

---

[10] The devil's gate, crooked path; corrupt practices; crooked methods

"What do we do now?" asked Li

"After we compile the report, we'll need you to testify. This isn't so much a trial as it is a hearing. The ten members of the official Contraception board will be presented with all the evidence and testimonies and will then make an official ruling. It's best you keep a low profile before the hearing; if what you say is true, the Chinese government is certain to come for you and you better not be there when they do."

On the verge of handing over the tablets and USB device to him, Mei hesitated. "Can we trust you?" she said, swinging between hope and fear.

"I think the fact that you're here right now proves you can. Besides, what other choice do you have?"

He looked at them with an inscrutable expression on his face and then continued, "For now, lie low, and I'll be in touch within forty-eight hours. I will tell you then when and where to show up for the hearing."

"Thank you," said Li.

He felt lighter in his heart now that they had done what they could and apparently someone else was taking this on. The past few weeks had been a nightmare, filled with bloodshed, fear, and incredible adrenaline surges.

"It's better if you two leave first," Zhang said. "I'll be in touch."

The Hus made their way back to the elevator. As Mei looked intently at Zhang, he nodded before the doors closed. Once back on the street, they flagged a taxi, and instead of entering their hotel address, Mei looked up the nearest bar.

"We're in Montreal, let's get a drink," she said.

They found a table in the back of the cozy, dimly lit bar and Mei ordered drinks.

"You think this will work?" said Li, his body stiff with tension.

"Like Mr. Zhang said, what other choice do we have? We either try this, or you live the rest of your life being on a hitlist."

"Well, when you put it that way…"

Their drinks arrived, and as they sat there, with the candle flickering on the table and the smooth jazz playing in the background, they felt a sense of peace they hadn't felt in a long time. Both knew that there was more to be done, and nothing was final, but at the table, staring across at each other, they felt they had done the right thing.

***

Montreal, Canada

Over the last 48 hours, the Hus had been waiting for Zhang to contact them in what Mei had described as "an anxiety-riddled vacation." They went to restaurants, the gym, and spent time in their hotel, all the while waiting for the phone to ring and checking over their shoulder to see if they were being followed. After what seemed like an eternity, the phone rang. It was the middle of the afternoon, two days after their encounter with Zhang. The man himself was on the line.

"We've finished our report. Your case will be brought up during our preliminary hearing this evening," he said, coming straight to the point. He then gave them the location and time and hung up.

Li set down the receiver and looked at Mei. "This is it, the last piece of the puzzle."

They spent the rest of the afternoon filled with tension and at times, even panic. Time seemed to stretch on with the thought of what could happen if the board refused to believe them gnawing at them. When it was finally time to go, they stood up thankfully. They were both dressed in black, in keeping with the somberness of the occasion, Li in his black suit and Mei wearing a long black dress. Outside the hotel, a car with a chauffeur was waiting for them. The door opened automatically as they approached and once they were inside, it took off.

When it reached a large white building, it stopped. They had arrived at their destination. The Contraception logo, the focal point of the twisting tower, could be seen from at least a mile away. Its design was based on the DNA double helix, which Li found ironic since the purpose of Contraception was to end life.

A wall of light stood between them and the building. It looked beautiful but was deadly. Anyone trying to cross it without authorization would instantly disintegrate. Around 2030, people found barbed wire and thick walls to be too obtrusive and space-consuming, so a high-intensity light wall was created to act as a more effective barrier.

A guard approached the car, scanned the wrist of the driver, and the walls of light in front of the car disappeared, allowing them to pass through. It drove slowly along a path with two green scanners on each side, scanning every part of the car for weapons, biochemical agents, or anything else that the system had been programmed to pick up. Once cleared, a solid metal wall lifted and allowed the car to enter the main facilities.

It parked on top of a black square in front of the main building, and once everyone had got out, the black square swept underground with the car.

The driver escorted the Hus into the main building through a corridor of white hallways until they reached a room with a single elevator. It rushed them to the top floor. After walking down a long hallway, they entered a hall where a panel of ten men and women stood waiting for them, like a United State Senate hearing.

Each board member had a nameplate and their national flag in front of them. They were from China, the U.S., England, Brazil, Russia, Japan, Germany, India, Iceland, and Nigeria. Behind them was a large world map showing the fluctuations in the world's population in real time and to the left and the right, instead of walls, were giant windows with bullet-proof glass.

The Hus were hustled to a table in front of the panel. Their driver, a large man in a suit, stayed by the door. The view from the room was spectacular, as one could see the entire city of Montreal spread below like a galaxy of lights. But the Hus had no eyes for that. They stared ahead at the ten official representatives that formed the Contraception board.

"Ladies and gentleman, this is Li Hu and Mei Hu, who brought the allegations of corruption to me. Their evidence, along with an independent analysis, will be shown, and their testimonies. Afterwards, we will make our own judgment," said Zhang.

The representative from Iceland read from a screen in front of him, "The accusation is as stands: China has deliberately and maliciously been falsifying Contraception profiles and a member of their government, under orders from the Politburo, has been adding these names to a state hitlist. China is also accused of tampering with Contra property, abuse of power, and cyber-crimes against humanity. Let's begin."

With a flick of his wrist, the video of Victor appeared on the screen where the map was and the ten chairs automatically turned around to face the screen. Victor's bloody face appeared and the conversation between him and the Hus unfolded. Then the second video that Lao Shu had shot of him taking apart Ronan's tablet and uncovering the tampering microchip was played.

Zhang addressed the committee, "In front of each of you is a copy of the transcript, a copy of the code the microchip uploaded to the Contraception tablet containing the profile of Mr. Sorenson, though he had not applied to have a child, and the profile of Diao, the agent responsible for the tampered microchip and adding names to 'the list.'"

The ten board members all picked up a square piece of glass about the size of a book and looked through the evidence.

The Nigerian inquired, "And this has all been verified by an external source?"

Zhang replied, "Correct, everything except the hijacker chip itself. For safety reasons, it remains in China. But the code from the tablet has been verified as authentic, along with the Chinese government IP address. Diao has also been verified as a director of the National Institute of Population Management and Control, his specialty being IT and technology."

None of the other representatives spoke, each taking in the information silently. This was the first time in ten years that any corruption allegation had been brought to their attention. Over the years, changes were made to the system, since a policy written on paper is not always functional in the real world. However, something of this scale was unprecedented.

Under the table, Li grabbed Mei's hand and squeezed it.

The Russian delegate was the first to set down his tablet. "I'd like to hear from the Hus. I think their personal account would be more illuminating than analyzing the information on this cold piece of glass."

All the delegates looked at the Chinese couple sitting in front of them.

Zhang said gently, "Please tell us how all this unfolded, from the very beginning. The floor is yours."

23. THE TESTIMONY

Montreal, Canada

If a Contraception target is only injured and not killed by an applicant, then the latter will be charged with assault. The purpose of the system is to alleviate the strain population has put on society, not send another patient to the hospital.

▪ "Our suspicions began when we received Ronan's profile from Contraception. We confirmed our doubts when we flew to Stockholm to kill him. Ronan told us he had never applied to have a child. He was unmarried and lived in an apartment designed for a single man. Our assumption was corroborated when Victor, the hitman, revealed to us that because we had not killed Ronan, it was his duty to do so, as he was the one who had accepted the contract from the state hitlist to kill Ronan."

Li took a deep breath, trying to control his nerves.

The Indian representative asked, "And during your encounter with Victor, how did he lose a hand?"

Li looking right at him, replied, "My wife cut it off while Victor had a gun pointed at my head. She saved my life."

He explained how Victor had died, with Mei helping him along when he fumbled.

"I'm curious about your relationship with Lao Shu," the Brazilian said. "Also, how he came to be the one to discover this 'hijacker' chip in one of our tablets."

It was Mei who answered him. "Lao Shu is our neighbor. He lives in our building in Beijing. He had run a tech store for over 20 years, fixing damaged devices. Knowing this, we approached him and asked him to look at the three Contraception tablets along with Victor's."

"But you were not authorized to kill Victor," said the British delegate.

"Formally, no. But fearing a credible threat to our lives, I believe it was warranted," Mei said resolutely.

"How did Ronan die?" asked the German

Mei looked at Li. Before the hearing, they had decided it was best to tell the truth regarding Ronan.

"Victor shot him in the head."

"But our records show that Mrs. Hu used a Contraception tablet to scan his finger approximately seven minutes after his death."

"That is also correct," said Mei. "As far as I'm aware, there is nothing in the bylaws of Contraception that says I need to be the one to kill the target, as long as I am authorized to scan him. You already have a precedence of people hiring hitmen to kill their targets."

While some of the Contraception board members nodded their heads, others made disgruntled noises. As Mei had pointed out, these days, many people hired others to kill their targets, and after the killing, as the authorized party, scanned the body, just as Mei had done. Some Contraception representatives were "purists," feeling applicants should kill their own targets; however, they had to concede that Mei had done nothing illegal.

Mei addressed all ten members. "As we said, we were in Stockholm to kill Ronan. Did he die by my hand? No. But if Victor hadn't intervened, I guarantee you he would have."

The Hus continued with their story, telling the board about the attack they had witnessed on Lao Shu's apartment before leaving for Canada, and how they still had no news regarding Lao Shu and what had occurred after they had left the building.

When their testimony was over and they had answered all the questions from the board to the best of their ability, Zhang looked at them and said, "Thank you for your time. We will now review all the information that has been presented and reach a decision. If you'll excuse us for a moment while we deliberate."

He nodded to the driver at the back of the room who opened the door to the hallway as Li and Mei got up from their table, bowed to the board, and walked towards the open door.

Once it was firmly shut, the panel where the board members sat moved till both ends connected, forming a perfect circle. All ten members now sat facing each other. Zhang was the first to address the group.

"Tonight, we have been presented with a rare, yet urgent, matter concerning the fate of Contraception. It is up to us to determine a course of action based not on us as individuals or the countries we represent, but as custodians of this world and civilization. Although the allegations are against my government, I can assure you I will remain unbiased and rule in favor of what best serves humanity, as I have done since the beginning. Where should we start?"

The Japanese man spoke. "At this point, we cannot say for sure if Diao acted alone or received his orders from a higher authority. Is it fair to rule against China as the sole mastermind?"

The member from Britain jumped in. "You think something like this has been going on in China for who knows how long and the higher-ups aren't behind it or even don't know about it?"

Nods around the table followed this comment. China's ruling party had long since wiped out individual corruption from within its membership. However, if the entire bloc was corrupt, there was no way for them to be outed.

The German spoke up. "The question is, do we have enough evidence that provides, beyond a shadow of a doubt, substantial reason to condemn China, as a country, for their actions? And if so, what will those condemnations be?"

Zhang took the floor. "Based on what we have seen, I think none of us can deny that China has manipulated the system. While we can't say for certain if the Chinese president is behind this, it is still the responsibility of the Politburo to manage all branches of their government, and I still hold them accountable for what has occurred. Furthermore, not to shift attention, but we need to include the possibility that China may not be the only country involved in manipulating the system."

"How could this have happened?" asked the Indian board member. "Contraception was designed as a perfect system, although without morality. And yet, here we are."

"In Iceland, we say have a saying, 'If you build a five-foot wall, a thief will buy a six-foot ladder.'"

The American nodded. "Perhaps Contraception is still perfect, but our flaw was in trusting people. Greed, power, money, personal desires, these are all things that throughout history, have flawed human reasoning and impacted our decisions. To be honest, I'm surprised that we're hearing about something like this only now."

"Let's vote and see where we are," said the Nigerian. "All in favor of condemning China for their recent actions?" All hands went up, except for the Russian, Nigerian and Brazilian members.'

"Before you ask," said the Russian. "I'll explain. We've all done questionable things. All China has done is facilitate the termination of people who haven't applied to Contraception. Some might argue that their death was inevitable, anyway. Besides, isn't the point of Contraception decreasing the population? Why should we care if a non-applicant died?"

The other members began talking all at once in response.

A voice louder than the others spoke with authority. "Contraception brings order, and there are rules. That's what separates us from animals. Without a system, there is chaos. China violated these rules and did so in a targeted and intentional manner. The independent analyst verified that thousands of names, mostly of political activists who weren't supportive of the government, were added to what has come to be known as 'the list.' Most of these names were illegally added to the Contraception database. This is a crime against humanity that must be dealt with swiftly and with an equal measure to the crime that was committed."

The Japanese delegate had a stern look in his eyes after he finished speaking. He felt strongly about the strict observance of rules.

"I agree," said the British member. "Contraception was and still is a universal policy. We are all held to the same rules and expectations. If a country violates those rules, especially for personal gain or interest, they must face the consequences."

More heads around the table nodded. The Contraception board did not need a unanimous vote, but instead adopted majority rulings.

"Are there any more comments?" asked the German.

Zhang looked at each of the board members intently. "What my country has done brings me great shame. However, tonight we need to stand strong in the face of adversity. What we do tonight will set a precedent and a standard for what we come to expect from the world regarding this global policy. Though we will make the ruling, it's the world that will experience the impact of it. Together, we represent the best interests of Contraception, and as China has failed to adhere to the principles we have established, it's time they come to understand the severity of their actions. I call this board to another vote. All those who vote in favor of sanctioning China for their illegal actions concerning Contraception, say aye."

Nine voices around the table resoundingly echoed, 'Aye.'

"All those opposed?"

The Nigerian alone replied, "Nay."

Zhang's voice boomed, "The ayes have it, nine to one. China will be sanctioned."

Outside in the hallway, the Hus sat on a bench between the chamber and the elevator with their driver standing close to the elevator.

Mei held onto Li's hand tightly. He was stiff with tension. "We did the right thing, no matter what happens now," she tried to reassure him.

"Sure, we did the right thing, but at what cost? Do you think the Chinese government will simply let us walk away from this?"

"Look at all we've overcome. We'll deal with anything else that comes our way."

They stopped as door to the hearing room opened, got up from the bench and made their way back inside. They resumed their seat at the table in front of the panel that was no longer a circle, having gone back to its original form.

"Thank you for your patience," said the representative from Iceland. "We have reached a verdict and would like to invite you to the United Nations Summit meeting where the sanctions will be officially ruled and implemented."

Mei looked puzzled. "Why do we have to attend?"

"We believe you deserve to see justice served. You were instrumental in forming the case against China, and if any further testimony needs to be given at the UN Summit, it's better to have you there. In the worst-case scenario, you enjoy a free trip to Paris."

Li stood up, overcome. "It would be an honor. We had been trying hard to do the right thing, and now, at this moment, I begin to feel we have accomplished that."

He sat down and under the table, Mei put her hand on his leg. She was proud of him. The challenges they had faced over the past few weeks were enough for a few lifetimes. They had overcome so much, and most importantly, had survived.

The American spoke, "If that's everything, a flight is waiting for you at the Montreal airport. The Summit will begin in two days. Thank you for everything you have done. We can only imagine what it took to bring you before us today."

Mei looked at the population map behind the board and wondered briefly how many innocent people had died at the hands of a corrupt government. At this moment, she felt justified. Standing before this committee, and everything they had gone through, she now thought it was all worth it.

Li had asked her earlier if she felt they were betraying their country. She had responded that it was their country that had betrayed them.

"Thank you," said Li, struggling to find words. With that, he and Mei stood up and walked towards the back of the room. The driver opened the door, and they walked out, leaving behind them a situation that had the potential to change the course of history.

24. THE VERDICT

Paris, France

One reason the population exploded so much was due to many governments incentivizing childbirth. The rapid development of many countries required a labor force, so governments offered tax breaks, bonuses and other benefits to those having more than one child.

▪ The flight to Paris on a private plane was much more relaxing than the one the Hus had taken to Montreal. Their driver had helped them board the plane that had flown them without a human pilot through the night to arrive in Paris by early next morning. There were banners all over the city announcing the UN Summit that was focused on Contraception's effects on mankind's most important issue: overpopulation. A decade after the policy was implemented, many things had changed, and this UN Summit was meant to discuss those changes, among other global issues. Items on the agenda included implementing education programs to help children deal with the knowledge that their parents were murderers, addressing the possibility of "exemptions" for certain applicants, and as usual, deal with complaints from state leaders.

After arriving at their hotel, the Hus slept like the dead, worn out from their constant travel and not having enough time to adapt to the local hours. The Summit was due to start around 16:00, with dinner at 18:00, and then a continuation of discussions that, as usual, ran late into the night.

Li was the first to wake up, with the afternoon sun shining in from the open window and the breeze ruffling the thin, white curtain. His band showed it was 14:00. He turned over and kissed Mei, letting her know it was time to get up.

"Can we just lie here while the politicians do their thing?"

"How often does one get invited to a UN Summit?"

"Ugh," she groaned, turning over and pulling the blanket over her head. Li grabbed the blanket, pulled it down, and kissed her again, this time hard. She opened her eyes and smiled at him, showing her bright white teeth.

The Hus began to get ready for the Summit, not knowing what role they would play there, if any at all. It was unlikely they would get called to testify but there was still the faintest possibility. Li knotted his black tie that matched his black suit and, in the mirror, saw Mei emerging from the bathroom in a severe dark blue dress with her hair braided.

"You look amazing," he said.

"We look amazing. We should get involved in high-profile political corruption scandals more often. I think I've worn a nice dress more this summer than I have in the past five years."

Li laughed. He couldn't remember the last time he had laughed or felt this calm. All they wanted was to have a child and live out the rest of their lives in peace. It was not an overreaching ambition once. Yet in their world, to achieve that they had been forced to watch people die, kill people, and have multiple people attempt to murder them. It was difficult to deal with, both physically and mentally, especially as deep in his mind, he still felt that no matter what happened at this Summit, things would not be over. He knew the power and reach of the Chinese government, which remained a constant dread.

"Mr. Zhang has sent a message that our bands have been authorized to let us in. Also, if anyone asks us who we are, we're to tell them we're special attachés to the Chinese ambassador to France. Or that we don't speak English. He's warned us that under no circumstance are we to reveal the real reason we are at the Summit."

"And our testimony?" Li asked.

"It's still a possibility, so we must be ready for it."

"After what we've gone through, testifying in front of hundreds of world leaders doesn't seem like such a scary idea anymore."

Mei glanced at her band. "Let's get going."

Li held out his arm, and she locked hers with his. He opened the door and they left their room. Once through the lobby and in front of the hotel, a black car pulled up to meet them.

A man with a friendly face said in a French accent, "Good afternoon, I am Alexandre. You are headed to the Summit, correct?"

"We are," said Li.

"Off we go!"

The black car weaved through the traffic. On the way to the Summit, they saw churches, cathedrals, small coffee shops, and couples in love, all part of the Parisian scenery. The city, like many others around the world, had been affected by Contraception. Dispo units patrolled the city, corporate buildings were reinforced with metal sheeting, and signs on public buildings like banks and restaurants read, "Please, this is a Contraception kill-free zone."

This sign contained a stick figure pointing a gun at another stick figure, whose brains could be seen flying out the back of his or her head, all surrounded by a red circle and a red line through the image.

These signs began to be put up soon after an overwhelming number of killings took place in public places. People were murdered while queuing at fast-food restaurants, or waiting to mail a package. Legally, it was allowed, but private business and public places like schools and libraries did their best to discourage it to avoid having their premises littered with bloody bodies. These signs became as ubiquitous as the "No Smoking" signs, similar to traffic signs so that everyone could understand them universally.

The Hus realized they were getting close to the Summit venue as increasingly more black cars with diplomatic flags made their appearance on the road. Their car turned a corner, and they saw the massive Palais Garnier and electronic banners that seemed to flow vertically from the top of the building, reading, "2070 UN Summit."

Walking up the red-carpeted steps were dignitaries, presidents, ambassadors, prominent businessmen, and finally, the Hus themselves, an ordinary couple whose story was about to lead to punishment for one of the most influential countries in the world.

"Have a lovely time," said Alexandre, who had come around the car to open their door.

"Thank you," said Mei, who was now standing on the red carpet along with Li. They looked at the large building, impressed that it had stood the test of time. They were both excited, but unsure of what was in store for them. Mei took Li's arm and they walked toward the entrance.

Photographers, journalists and TV crews swarmed the leaders, hoping for a quote on the Summit agenda. The UN was one of the world's largest organizations that had been preserved down the decades. It witnessed and dealt with the fall of North Korea and the rise of China and had been a prominent player in dealing with overpopulation long before Contraception came along. Today was a historic day for the UN, proving that an intersubjective idea could be kept alive as long as the belief in the system or idea remained strong. Here, among all the world's elites, that belief prevailed.

Li and Mei passed through security – just two beams of light, only a few centimeters thick that could detect weapons, chemicals, and drugs, both on or inside a person. It could also discern between objects like a knife and a key, so it was no longer necessary to empty one's pockets. Once through security, the Hus scanned their bands and entered the venue.

It was an enormous hall with a high ceiling, from which huge sparking chandeliers ran the entire length of the room. The Summit wasn't set to start for another hour and the guests were in a relaxed mood, talking animatedly and helping themselves to the variety of drinks and appetizers served by waiters in black tuxedos. The Hus walked around, politely declining cocktails from a nearby server and taking stock of their surroundings. All around them were dignitaries and politicians from all over the world, talking, making deals, and fundamentally shaping the future of their country and the world.

A middle-aged man with graying hair and a tan approached them. He was wearing a gray suit and round black glasses.

"How do you do?" he said, in an accent that neither Mei nor Li could place. "My name's Rodrigo Pérez, Argentinian ambassador to China. Very pleased to make your acquaintance."

Li gave Mei a quick look before looking back to Rodrigo.

"*Bù hǎo yì si,*[11] no English," he said.

Rodrigo smiled and in Chinese, continued. "No worries, I've managed to pick up your language through my time as ambassador. Who are you?"

"We're special attachés to the Chinese ambassador to France," Mei said guardedly in Chinese.

"Ah," said Rodrigo. "How is Monsieur Zhao?"

---

[11] To apologize, feel sorry for something

"He's well," said Li, hoping the conversation wouldn't continue further as his knowledge of Monsieur Zhao was limited to what he had read online about the Chinese ambassador whose attachés they were supposed to be.

Rodrigo looked pleased as he delicately bit the quiche in his left hand.

"If there's one good thing about the UN, it's the food," he chuckled, amused by his own witticism, and then, to the Hu's indescribable relief, said, "If you'll excuse me, I'm off to find more tasty morsels. A pleasure to meet both of you."

With that, the man walked off, soon lost in the sea of people that had now flooded the hall.

Li looked at Mei, "When did so many people start to speak Chinese?"

Mei was opening her mouth to say something when she was interrupted by a loud voice over an intercom system.

"Ladies and gentleman, thank you so much for attending this year's UN Summit. The opening address will begin in 30 minutes. In the meantime, we welcome all of you to please enter the assembly room and make yourselves comfortable."

The message was then broadcast in a variety of languages as people began to make their way towards a pair of huge French doors that led into a vast circular room with hundreds of seats. Ambassadors and politicians found their places marked with a flag and a nameplate, while other guests, such as Mei and Li, sat on the upper balcony. The room was buzzing. There was much to be discussed. Finally, the UN Secretary-General, a scholar from Finland, made his way to the central podium.

"Ladies and gentleman, welcome to the 2070 UN Summit. Over the last few decades, we have overcome many challenges, both domestically and internationally. Here, together, we have the opportunity to unite against the global challenges of today. It is in that spirit that I would like to invite the board members of Contraception to begin the Summit."

The crowd clapped as the ten ambassadors made their way to the podium.

Once on stage, the American spoke first. "Over the last ten years, Contraception has changed the world. Global pollution has dropped significantly, global public transportation is no longer what many were calling a nightmare, and overall, people are living happier, healthier lives. It is with your continued support that Contraception continues to positively impact the world today."

Then the Russian spoke. "However, Contraception works because we abide by the rules and accept the nature of the system. As a universal, but also a third-party entity embedded within each of your countries, Contraception relies on your adherence to suit the needs of mankind. It is with deep regret that I have to inform you that over the past few days, our committee has uncovered information regarding corruption within Contraception."

There was pin-drop silence at this followed by the crowd breaking into a feverish buzz as nothing like this had ever happened in the past ten years.

Mei looked at Li, who said with admiration, "Getting right into it." They looked over to where the Chinese delegation, headed by the president, was sitting, looking utterly inscrutable.

"It has been brought to our attention, along with substantial and verifiable evidence, that China has been creating false profiles and clandestinely putting these names in the Contraception system. Unsuspecting couples are receiving these names as their target and killing innocent people for China's gain," the Japanese representative said. "These names were also added to a hitlist drawn up by the government and given out to contract killers to ensure the targets died. We have uncovered thousands of names, mostly political activists against China's current government, who never applied to Contraception, but were killed using our system. This was achieved through methods of hacking and manipulation of the tablets our applicants receive; uploading a false profile of someone that China wanted dead."

The room was silent, shocked by the allegations against the world's largest economy.

Then it was Zhang's turn. "As a Chinese citizen, it is with great shame that I confirm that this elaborate scheme came from the Chinese government and the ruling Chinese Communist Party."

The hall gasped audibly. For centuries, China had proclaimed corruption was the number one enemy and had done everything they could to eliminate it from within their borders. The accusation reverberated through the room.

The Chinese president stood up to address the assembly and his accusers. The hall focused their attention on him, waiting to see what he would say.

"Your accusations are simply that, accusations. With no evidence, your claims are a tactic to divert attention from the real issues our world faces," he said sternly.

The crowd murmured at his confidence. However, the Chinese president's challenge was soon met with a response from the Contraception board. The delegate from India moved his wrist, and a video began to play on multiple screens on the walls so that everyone could see it. It showed the testimony of Victor, the removal of the hijacker chip, and the profile of Diao, connecting him to the crimes.

"The record of a phone call between Mr. Diao and a State Council member was obtained yesterday which, along with the other evidence, implicates the Chinese government," the Indian delegate said.

The great hall was in an uproar now. Wrists were held up, taking pictures of this historic moment while people around the world either sat in shock or expressed their outrage at this blatant display of corruption.

"Furthermore," continued the Indian delegate, "the very people who brought this issue to our attention are here today."

He gestured over to where Mei and Li were sitting. Both froze as all eyes in the hall turned towards them. They did their best to keep their faces expressionless, hoping the attention would soon be diverted to something else.

"They noticed something was not right when they first received a Contraception target featuring someone they knew. Upon further investigation, which included them speaking to him as a fellow human being, and not simply a target, they discovered that he had never applied to Contra. Their resilience and bravery to not only further investigate but bring this before our board is unprecedented."

The room clapped thunderously, but to Li, who was as wound up as a clockwork about to snap, they seemed like volleys of gunshot. He shivered.

The Chinese president looked unflustered as if he had a trump card. He waited for the babble to die down and the hall to grow quiet before speaking. A member of his delegation whisper something in his ear. The president nodded and smiled. It sent a chill down Li's spine.

"It is true," he finally said in measured tones. "Have we been manipulating the system for our benefit? Absolutely."

The hall went berserk as hundreds of people expressed their agitation and outrage at the confession they had just heard. Never, in decades of international relations, had China ever confessed to something before putting up a long, drawn-out fight. However, today, at the UN Summit, the president had admitted to one of the most significant corruption and murderous scandals of all time.

He continued, "Did we add names to the system because, for whatever reason, we wanted them dead? Yes. Did we install microchips to hijack tablets? Also, true. Did we use hitmen to finish the job when Contraception couldn't? We did. But that's the name of the game. What country hasn't manipulated a system? America's banks failed in 2008 due to their greed and manipulation of the credit rating system and none of them did jail time. Brazil forged crime rates and poverty records to receive more funding in 2020. India murdered its untouchables in 2035 to clean up its society. And perhaps above all, the European Union knowingly financed terrorists in the Middle East in exchange of cheaper oil in 2050. Did we manipulate the Contraception system for our benefit? Yes. But we were acting in our self-interests, as every state has done for thousands of years and will continue to do so. You accuse China of corruption? Well, I assure you, we are not alone."

The hall was too stunned to speak. The confidence with which the Chinese president spoke resonated throughout it. Everyone remembered the global incidents of which the president spoke, and some acknowledged the truth in what he said.

At length the German Contraception board member spoke. "What you have done is illegal. Your speech does not absolve you of the thousands of deaths that were perpetrated by your administration. Nor does it exclude you from cyber-crime, hacking a universal organization, or engaging with hitmen to kill non-applicants."

"With that said," the Russian added, "This board finds you guilty of crimes against Contraception, and the world. What we have discovered is sickening; the thought that your country's survival is more important than human life."

"We did what we had to do to survive. We overcame," replied the Chinese president.

"Yes, but at what cost, Mr. President?" said the British board member.

Mei and Li sat frozen in shock. They had never dreamt that China would admit to such a horrendous crime. But at this moment, it was all out on the table. The truth they had discovered and brought to light. Like everyone else, they sat still, unsure of what would happen next.

"China is prepared to accept the consequences of our actions. However, so too must everyone else involved," the Chinese president said. There was menace in his tone.

"Excuse me, Mr. President, but what do you mean?" asked the Brazilian. As people watched the Chinese leader, trying to anticipate what he would say next, Li thought perhaps there was apprehension as well.

"For far too long, China has been condemned due to our growth and development. We have always been an easy target. However, today, China will not fall alone."

The president extended a hand and one of the ministers in the delegation handed him a tablet. The president placed it in front of him and continued to speak.

"This tablet contains information, or as you might like to think of it, evidence, of five other countries being involved in manipulating Contraception."

The hall gasped again, "This is going out of control!" someone exclaimed.

The tension in the hall could be cut with a knife.

"There will be order!" the Japanese board member said sternly. The room grew quiet, surprised at the booming voice coming from such a small man. A thin, young man took the tablet from the president and carried it up to the committee members on the podium.

"As we did with the evidence against China, this information will be verified before any actions are taken. This board cannot overlook further allegations of corruption. This meeting will reconvene in 24 hours to address the accusation made by the Chinese delegation. There will be no further discussion on this matter for now."

With that, the Contraception board stood up and left the podium. The Summit tried to continue with the other agenda as well as it could, but with the news about Contraception being on everyone's mind, it was a lackluster meeting. Several hours later, a tired and still shocked group of politicians, policymakers, and world leaders left the great hall to rest for tomorrow's proceedings. Mei and Li were among them, weary from listening to politicians making empty promises to resolve global issues.

Mei respected Contraception, in the sense that it had defined rules, objectives and parameters. Many other policies could be considered fluff, serving no real purpose but Contraception, despite its arguable mission and methods, didn't pretend to be anything it wasn't.

Outside the hall, black sedans lined up, waiting to pick up their respective guests. Mei and Li made their way around the block where their French driver was waiting.

"A good Summit?" he asked in his accented English.

"Interesting," said Li briefly. The car sped through the streets, arriving at their hotel faster than they had arrived at the Palais

Garnier. Li thanked Alexandre and he and Mei headed into their room.

A little while later, as she and Li sat cross-legged on the bed across from each other to discuss the day's events Li's band lit up to indicate a phone call.

Wondering who it could be, he double-tapped his wrist and said, "Hello?"

"This is Zhang. Thank you both for coming today, it showed great strength and courage."

"Yes, it was a little intimidating, but we were honored to be there."

"What I'm calling about now might alarm you, but I want to ensure you that we're taking every precaution necessary."

"About what, exactly?"

"The board believes that although you were instrumental in showing up the corruption, your lives are in danger due to that. We've seen the measures our government can take to neutralize a threat. So tomorrow, after the meeting, special arrangements will be made for you. Please bring your bags with you and leave them in the car with Alexandre. He will oversee your transport."

"I suppose it would be foolish of me to ask for more details over the phone."

"It would be," Zhang agreed somberly. "I will see you tomorrow, and again, thank you."

After ending the phone call, he turned to Mei and said, "Pack your bags, we're leaving tomorrow. I don't know where we're going, or what will happen."

He leaned over and kissed her. Mei took the development in her stride. She was a fighter and would always fight to protect what she held most dear. She wanted a change. She was ready to be a mother and bring a child into this world, despite the cruelty she had seen, especially in the past few weeks. She was not going to buckle under after all that they had gone through and achieved.

The Hus had another 24 hours until this was all over, and for them, it couldn't come soon enough.

25. THE OUTCOME

Paris, France

Although the Contraception board functions as the sole authority over Contraception, the United Nations plays a large role in how the system is implemented worldwide.

- "Ready for round two?" asked Li.

"Let's get it over with," said Mei.

Again, the atrium full of people in suits walked into the hall and found their seats. The UN Secretary-General gave his opening remarks and thanked everyone for returning.

"Contraception prides itself on not having a central leader or sole individual in charge, so the German representative was chosen to reveal our findings," he said, welcoming the German to the stage. The board member adjusted his tie and addressed the audience.

"In itself, Contraception is a perfect system. Throughout the course of history, humans, through personal greed and the impulse to achieve their self-interests, have destroyed perfectly functioning systems. That is also the case here today. After thoroughly looking into the allegations by the Chinese President about other countries' involvement in the corruption in Contraception, we are afraid the accusation is true."

It was time for the hall to gasp again. A loud hum arose as people began to speculate which other countries could be involved. The Chinese President sat there, the cynosure of all eyes again, with a hint of a smile on his face. As the Chinese government often warned the world, any challenges, confrontations, or leaks about China's involvement with Contraception – or indeed anything else of global importance – would bring consequences, and now, they were coming to life.

The German continued onstage, "Along with our investigation, the tablet provided by the Chinese delegation afforded us with accurate information, photo evidence, and IP addresses linking back to several other governments. This evidence was concurrent with that used to convict China and leaves us no choice but to condemn five other countries. Along with China, the following countries have been found guilty of digitally manipulating Contraception, which has resulted in the bloodshed of tens of thousands of innocent people."

He took a breath as the tension became palpable in the hall with the audience holding their breath. Then he began to enunciate the names, "Australia, Malaysia, Belarus, Mexico and Nigeria."

The room exploded. There were shouts, wild gesticulations and loud denials from the delegates of the countries named. As the Chinese Contraception representative Zhang walked onto the stage and took the microphone.

With a booming voice, he said, "Ladies and gentleman, there will be order!"

The hall seemed to freeze as they all looked towards the man who had issued the command.

"Please take your seats; there is still much to be dealt with."

Everyone sat down, and the hall once again grew quiet as they waited for the representative to continue.

"We do not take these criminal offenses lightly, especially while hundreds of other countries and regions have and continue to abide by the same laws and regulations that these six countries have chosen to flout. The gravity of this situation is unprecedented, as the public will no doubt have lost trust in the very thing that is at the center of our society and life. We feel that the punishment must fit the crime."

"Each country's list of actual applicants compared to confirmed Contraception deaths was analyzed, and thousands of deaths turned out to be illegal without official sanction. These names were intentionally and systematically submitted to applicants so they could be murdered, just like China did. So far, the confirmed deaths for these countries are still being analyzed to look for patterns or commonalities between the chosen targets, but as things stand now, according to the UN Charter which you have all signed, along with this board, and the International Court of Justice, who convened last night to deliberate, find you guilty. If you six countries think you are above the law, that the regulations of a universal system don't apply to you, then perhaps it's best if you are shut out from our global society. After this summit ends and we return to our respective countries, within 72 hours, all six nations will be subjected to a digital iron curtain for the duration of one year. Dr. Hans Freidrich, the lead engineer behind the iron curtain, will now explain what it means."

Everyone in the audience was on the edge of their seat as a tall man in a dark blue suit and black glasses walked on the stage.

"The digital iron curtain is a digital wall that will surround the borders of your respective countries. Nothing can pass through this barrier, either physically, or digitally. That means any information from the outside world will be blocked from entering and no data from inside shall exit. Trade will continue, but all ships, trucks, and planes that enter and leave your countries will need to be checked by

Contraception authorities to ensure that all cargo is what it claims it to be. The passes of all these countries' citizens will also be restricted for the period, prohibiting all travel outside of your countries. Any person currently residing in another country that does not have a visa will be returned to their home country. A full list of restrictions and other things that the digital wall will stop will be given to your State leaders. And now, I'm open to answering any questions you might have."

The calm and relaxed way the man spoke did little to palliate the severity of the measures he spoke about.

The Australian President was the first to comment. "I take full responsibility for my actions. But why must our entire country be punished? Millions of our citizens had no idea of what was going on within our government."

The Icelandic representative responded, "That is the very problem with how modern governments operate. You say you act in the best interest of your people, yet they are lied to and deceived while those in power make executive decisions that suit their interests and not those of the state. The digital curtain is a reminder you represent your country, and the choices you make as a leader, whether good or bad, affect an entire nation."

A hand in the audience shot up. The woman who raised her hand introduced herself as part of the African Alliance. "With Nigeria and China both listed as countries involved in this horrific scandal, and with both having representatives serving on the Contraception board, how can we be sure about the integrity of this board?"

Zhang looked at her and said, "Both the Nigerian representative and I will return to our countries and step down from the Contraception board. The remaining eight members will hold a meeting and vote to elect two new representatives. I can only speak for myself when I say I had nothing to do with what was happening concerning my government's involvement nor knew anything about it. It brings me deep shame that innocent people lost their lives, sacrificed for a cause that only a few believe in. I hope that one day, China will once again be able to stand in the world as a respected nation and rid itself of leaders who continue to hold us back from social progress."

Another hand went up and Zhang nodded, letting the man say what he wanted to.

"With six countries involved in corrupting Contraception, what will happen to the system? Will it be refined? Or kept the way it is? Or will it be abolished?"

All eyes swiveled back to Zhang, who stood in front of the microphone, looking at the vast crowd impassively.

He paused before answering the question. "The ten of us have spoken and deliberated. This is a strenuous and challenging time for us all, but we believe Contraception will continue to serve the best interests of humanity and our world. Yes, this is an unprecedented occurrence, but we can't overlook the achievements Contraception has accomplished. Cleaner air, cleaner water, curbing global famine, better access to medicine and health care, our schools are no longer overcrowded, and as a whole, society has got smarter. The punishments for these six countries will hurt them, that's for sure. Globally, we need to send out a message that this kind of behavior will not be tolerated. Sanctions or trade restrictions are no longer enough. Any further questions will be answered by the directive that will be drafted in the following days. Thank you."

With that, Zhang left the stage along with the other nine members. The hall seemed frozen still, both shocked and drained by what they had just seen and heard. Never in history had the digital iron curtain been used. It was created as a security measure in case of a large-scale digital breach or hacking attempt but never had anyone thought it could be used as a punishment. They thought they had witnessed it all but there was more to follow. The Secretary-General made his way to the podium to sort out the remaining issues.

"Each of the six countries will have seventy-two hours for all of their government officials and citizens not on a current visa, both here and around the world, to return to their home country. Anyone found to be still abroad after those seventy-two hours will be put in jail for no less than one year. After the seventy-two hours, the iron curtain will be deployed over each of your countries. Any attempt to leave the country will be tracked through your pass and authorities in all surrounding states will be notified. This year is not so much a punishment as it is a time for reflection. What kind of country do you want to lead, and what sacrifices are you making to serve the people and not yourselves? I repeat again, that any questions you may have will be answered by the directive that will be issued in the next day or so. Thank you. This year's Summit has officially concluded."

For a moment, everyone sat in their seats. Then chaos erupted. Everyone was on their phone and there was the additional commotion of hundreds of people rushing out. Frantic calls were being made to media outlets, governments, and multi-billion-dollar conglomerates to explain this ground-breaking action the UN had just sanctioned.

Mei and Li were among the last to leave the room. They had accomplished what they had set out to do; justice had finally been served.

"We did it," Mei said, sounding both incredulous and triumphant. He squeezed her hand. Before he could say anything, they were intercepted by Zhang.

"We can't thank you enough for your bravery and commitment to the truth," he said in a rush. "The board discussed your return to

China, and as a precaution, and also, for lack of a better word, to compensate you for what you've been through, we would like to relocate both of you."

"Relocate us?" Mei exclaimed.

"If the Chinese government can kill thousands of innocent people, it will only be a matter of time before they find you. Also, we believe you deserve to live out the next year in peace, not under the digital iron curtain. Norway has offered to take you in, giving you both citizenship and a place to live. As for work, you're both well educated, I'm sure you can find something. The alternative is you go back to live in China and take your chances."

The Hus felt a sense of relief mixed with a feeling of pain at what the future would now hold for them. They would become aliens, cut off from their roots, family and friends.

"Can we ever go back to China?" asked Li.

"You certainly could after the year is over, but then I wouldn't be able to guarantee your safety. Think about it and let me know. We'll have a team fly you into China, gather your belongings, and you'll be out before the iron curtain comes down."

Zhang extended his hand and both Li and Mei shook it.

"I can't imagine what you've been through to make it here, but the world is a better place for it. We'll talk soon!" he said as he walked towards the exit. Li looked at Mei.

"What do you think?"

"Let's do it. Life is short."

Before Zhang had gone out, Li called out, "Sir, we'll do it."

Zhang turned around and with a smile on his face said, "I'll make the arrangements."

Outside, there was pandemonium with the din of the press and cameras flashing endlessly. The news had broken, and the world was preparing for what would be considered the most severe punishment in its history.

They heard a voice call out to them, "Let's go!" Mei and Li spun around. It was Alexandre.

"It's a madhouse out there. Let's get you back to your hotel. You've got a busy seventy-two hours ahead of you," he said.

The three of them walked through the back of the Palais and took a small door that opened to an alley where the black sedan was waiting. The ride back to the hotel was quiet, with their minds in a frenzy, wondering how the iron curtain would affect not only those six countries but also the world.

Once the car stopped outside their hotel, Alexandre turned around and said, "Tomorrow morning, 6:00, I'll be here. Mr. Zhang has informed me you'll fly back to China and have forty-eight hours there to pack. Then you'll be on a flight out before the iron curtain is deployed. I will see you tomorrow!"

Li and Mei walked up to the hotel and embraced each other. It was a dizzy feeling to think that they were safe now, finally. "It's finally over," Mei whispered as he stoked her soft black hair that fell over his shoulder. To his shame, he felt tears welling up in his eyes. As he sought to hide his tears from Mei, he felt a sense of relief. He could let go of his feeling of guilt, knowing what they had done had ultimately led to the right end. Despite the blood on their hand, they had prevented the slaughter of countless more innocent people.

A little unsteadily, he walked over to the mini bar. Wiping his eyes with his sleeve, he took out two bottles of tequila and held out one to Mei. They held them up and Li said, "For Ronan."

"For Ronan," she repeated.

Sleep came swiftly for the Hus that night as the events of the day had drained them of all energy and emotions. Though the anxiety that had been building hadn't entirely dissipated, – they would still have to return to China – exhaustion won the battle. The next morning, they were up by 5:00, packing their belongings. They then compressed their bags and made their way down to the lobby. The sky was still dark, with the sun just beginning to creep up on the horizon. At 6:00 on the dot, a black car pulled up in front of the hotel and they were greeted by the cheerful smile of Alexandre.

"To the airport," he said, handing them two cups of coffee.

"Thank you," said Mei.

"Pleasure," he said while he put his foot on the gas.

"You think we'll ever come back to Paris?" asked Mei.

For the first time, Li smiled. "Well, we'll be Europeans soon enough, I don't see why not."

The flight back to Beijing seemed endless as they were not sure what to expect upon landing. Alexandre had given them a tablet and instructed them to turn it on after landing. He wished them both good luck before driving off back into the city.

Once back in Beijing, Li turned on the tablet and it started to ring.

"Hello?" he said gingerly.

"Mr. Hu, I work for Mr. Zhang. Welcome back to Beijing."

"Thank you," said Li, wary of the voice on the other end even though the man identified himself as working for Zhang.

"Please return to your home and pack your things. In two days' time, we'll pick you up and fly you out of China. The iron curtain will be deployed in fifty-five hours, so please be ready to go in forty-eight hours."

"What about my job? Or our lease?"

"All that will be taken care of. Before you leave, a letter will be sent to Peking University explaining the situation so that your leave of absence is extended. Returning after a year is entirely up to you.

Any other questions will be answered in forty-eight hours. For now, please just get ready."

"Okay."

A long pause followed before the man said, "I regret to inform you that Lao Shu was killed during the raid on his apartment. His identity was confirmed at the morgue and his apartment has been sealed pending a further investigation. I'm sorry for your loss."

The man hung up. Li felt flooded by guilt, sorrow and a wish that things could have been different. Part of him had suspected the old man had died but hearing it out loud for the first time didn't make it easier.

Mei paused for a moment before asking, "What happened to Lao Shu?"

Li looked at her and said, "He died in the attack." Mei felt guilt and sadness, but her face remained stoic as she reached down and held Li's hand.

He looked at Mei and said, "We've got a lot to do in the next two days."

26. THE FINALE

Beijing, China

Although experts continue to speculate, Contraception has no defined endpoint. Some argue that once the world reaches a certain number, Contraception will be revoked, or at the very least, modified to better adapt to the decreased population.

▪ The door to their apartment opened, and Li and Mei stood in the doorway, looking inside.

"Two days," sighed Mei, who wasn't thrilled about the process of packing. They entered and set their bags near the door. Mei sat at the table while Li made a quick tour of the apartment, trying to satisfy himself that there had been no intruders when they were away and no one was lurking inside, waiting for them to return.

"Do you think coming back after the iron curtain is lifted is a smart idea?" he asked, after satisfying himself things were right as they had left them.

"We could have a conversation where we posit that our life is here, and all of our family and friends as well. We could even argue that our 'roots' are here. But for me, my life is with you, and the question is, do you think we'll be safe if we come back?"

Li poured himself some water and thought the question over. He had attempted to answer it while on the airplane but hadn't come to any firm conclusion.

"If I'm honest, no, I don't think we'll be safe. We exposed the Chinese government. We were, at the very least, the catalyst behind what will happen in two days. I don't think we can ever come back."

Mei nodded. She was relieved. Part of her felt attached to this city, as she had grown up here, worked here, and had a life with Li here. However, Beijing was not the same city she remembered from when she was a kid, and the issue of safety loomed over their heads.

"I agree with you."

"So, we'll just take the essentials, nothing that won't fit in two suitcases each. We'll be able to buy everything we need once we're in Norway."

"That's still the part that surprises me. Why would Norway volunteer to give us sanctuary?"

"A sense of doing what they think is right? Or maybe brownie points in the international community?"

"What about the stuff we are leaving behind?" she asked.

"I think we should have someone sell them and wire us the money after the curtain is lifted."

"I like it. A new life, a new adventure, a new start. Beijing these days isn't what it used to be."

"Agreed," she said.

They looked around their apartment once again, thinking of all the memories this place held for them.

"Let's get to it," said Li.

The Hus spent the next forty-eight hours sorting out their possessions. Mei stacked the chairs on top of the table and rolled up the rugs. All the plants were taken out and placed in the lobby with a 'Free' sign next to them. They emptied the fridge and unplugged all electrical appliances and made calls to get the electricity and water supply disconnected after their departure.

They had an argument about their dinner. Li wanted to order Peking duck, dumplings, and a buffet of other traditional Chinese foods as he regarded this as probably the last opportunity to have Chinese food in China again. But Mei put her foot down in no uncertain terms.

"Are you crazy?" she said, in angry disbelief. "This is still a deadly place for us. I am not going to take unnecessary risks at the last minute. They must know we are back and they must also know we would not be here for long. What if they poison the food? And have you forgotten what happened to poor Ronan when he opened the door to a stranger? I am sorry but it's going to be instant noodles for lunch. You can eat all the Peking duck you want in Norway."

In a way he admired her caution. Their life was about to change yet again. Although on the surface they were ready, deep down, both harbored apprehension about the move. For Mei, it was the logistics. Until she was in the air, beyond China's borders, she was fearful that something would happen.

Li was worried about starting a new life in Norway. Would he be able to teach? Be able to trust people and make friends again? Guilt hung heavily over him, nagging him about Lao Shu and Ronan's death as well as the murders of their two Contraception victims. He couldn't help wondering how their families would cope with the year-long punishment. They were the victims and now they would be punished as well. These feelings continued to haunt him but as he forced himself to pretend to pack, he also felt a deep sense of relief. They were making the right decision. Staying on would be a death sentence, no matter how much they would miss the city, and even if there were no more attempts on his life, his conscience would not let him rest in this city that had turned him into a murderer. No matter what they had achieved, he felt there would be no personal redemption for him because he still had blood on his hands.

The next day, they remained holed up in their apartment as well, finishing the packing.

Finally Li turned to Mei and motioned for her to come to the large living room window.

"Our last day here," he said.

Li opened the window and brought out his binoculars. "My last walk in Beijing," he said sorrowfully.

They saw the cars below whizzing past as clearly as if they were standing on the road. A salesman on the street advertised his cheap goods, while a mom beat her naughty child, and teenagers fought mock fights among themselves in their blue and white school uniforms. The buildings, in the afternoon light, looked almost beautiful, despite the thick metal panels that barricaded most of the windows. Bicycles flew by, and Beijing milled around the Hus as they took their last lingering look at the city.

"A part of me will miss this," Li said with a sigh. "But another part of me, a big part of me, is ready for something new."

"Change is good," responded Mei. "And I could think of a lot worse places to start a new life than Norway. We'll make the most of it, and we will move on from this chapter in our life. We did what we needed to do, and I think we saved more lives than we took."

No matter how he or she justified it, he had done things he had never thought himself capable of. However, much like the city they were leaving, people also changed and adapted to their circumstances.

The summer had been a whirlwind of events, with times when neither of them thought the finish line was in sight. However, by luck and their doggedness, they had overcome the barriers. Looking at the people walking in the street, Li wondered if this is how they felt all the time. Unbothered. Happy. Impervious to the surrounding corruption.

He shut the windows and put away his binoculars carefully. No sooner had he done so, than there was a phone call. It was the man who had called earlier. "5:00 tomorrow morning, a car will be at your apartment to pick you up," he said. "We'll fly out of Beijing Shahezhen Airbase to Seoul, and your flight to Norway will leave from there. Have you made all the necessary arrangements for your apartment?"

"We've done the best we could, given the circumstances."

"Good. The iron curtain will be deployed at 7:00 tomorrow. If everything goes according to the plan, we should be out of Chinese airspace by the time that happens. I'll see you tomorrow."

The phone call ended. Li looked at Mei and said, "Tomorrow morning." She understood. She put her arms around him and held him. As the stars illuminated the night sky, the two of them stood still, holding each other in a warm embrace.

"I love you more than you'll ever know," Li said, looking into Mei's big brown eyes.

She kissed him in answer. Then they walked into the bedroom, knowing now there was nothing more to be done. Li lay with his arm around Mei, his face buried into her neck, breathing in her smell and envying her ability to fall asleep immediately like a small child and then, he too had fallen asleep.

The alarm rang, signaling 4:30. In the haze of the early morning, the Hus got dressed, compressed all their luggage, and once again, stood in the doorway looking at their apartment.

"Are you going to miss it?" asked Li.

"It's just stuff; we'll get more."

Without another word, they turned their back on the apartment and left. Outside their complex, a black car waited, and a thin

Chinese man emerged and opened the doors for them without saying a word. The vehicle drove through the empty streets, as people still slept, or waited alone in their apartment, anticipating the fall of the iron curtain. News of its deployment had been broadcast around the world following the sanction at the UN Summit. Riots had broken out in the six sanctioned countries, with people calling for a change in government for illegally killing its citizens.

Other people had responded differently, apathetic to the whole situation, not surprised that this had happened. For many in China, life wouldn't change that much. The internet was already heavily censored, and many didn't have aspirations to travel abroad. Beyond that, the curtain wouldn't affect their daily life, and if it didn't, they had no reason to lose any sleep over it.

On a long strip of road, outside of the sprawl of the city, the car began to slow down and suddenly came to a stop. The driver came out and wrenched the passenger door open. There was a gun in his hand.

"Out, now," he barked. The disbelieving Hus got out of the car slowly and stood in the cold morning air, looking at the man who now held them at gunpoint.

"What is this?" asked Li.

The man held the gun at Li, his voice trembling with emotion as he spoke. "My father is dead and you are both to blame."

Comprehension dawned on them immediately. "You are the son of..."

"Yes, Lao Shu was my father," the man almost took the words out of Mei's mouth. "He told me he was helping you and now he is dead. His involvement with you led to his death and now you need to pay for that."

The man's face was taut with emotion, both anger and sadness. Li tried to reason with him.

"We are both terribly sorry for what happened to your father," he said slowly, choosing his words with care. "But he was a very wise man and though he must have foreseen what the consequences would be, he still did what he did to save the world from a catastrophe. He is not just your father but a savior for all of us and his sacrifice will never be forgotten. He would not have wanted it any other way. If he had, he would not have gone along with us. If you kill us, it's not going to bring your father back to life. If he were alive, he would not have supported you. Think of that. By killing us, you would dishonor your father's thoughts."

Lao Shu's son's face twitched. "How do you know what my father thought? He was my father, not yours. His thought was for us to complete our Contraception application and give him a grandchild to carry on the family name. Since I couldn't do it on my own, he had taken my assignments on his shoulders and now he is dead and he will never have a grandchild!"

His face twisted with grief. "Do you know what you have done?" he said savagely. "You have not only killed my father but you have killed my family. The government is holding my wife in a labor camp to ensure that I don't say or do anything to stir up more trouble. We have been branded as dissidents. People don't talk to me any more for fear, I have become an outcast. And now you, the people who ruined my life, are going to make a happy little new life for yourselves. Do you think I'll let that happen?"

"You have no option." The response came from Mei and there was steel in her voice. As Lao Shu's son turned to look at her, surprised by her reaction, in a quick continuous movement she brought her hands from behind the back where she had been secretly taking off the bracelet she wore around her wrist. In a trice she had double-tapped it and threw it at him in a burst of energy. It was the strangler.

He saw the movement, pivoted the gun at her and fired, but the impact made by the strangler as it landed on his leg made his aim falter and the bullet flew by, grazing Mei's arm. As she faltered, she saw their attacker falling to the ground with the strangler wrapped around his leg and tightening its coil. He shrieked in pain.

Li rushed to Mei and picked her up in his arms. "We have to go," he said urgently. He ran to the car with her and gently put her on the backseat. Then he quickly tossed off his jacket and unbuttoned his shirt, tightly bandaging her arm with it to stop the bleeding.

"You're going to be fine," he said reassuringly. He looked back towards the man writhing in pain on the ground as blood continued to pour over the road and then opened the driver's door. Once in, he turned on the car and slammed on the gas, soon leaving Lao Shu's son far behind.

"Honey, you're going to be okay!" he yelled, as the car flew down the road.

"Just get us out of here," she said determinedly.

When the Hus arrived at a private airstrip in the airbase containing a few small planes and a large black Apache helicopter, the man standing next to it was looking at his band in impatience.

Stopping the car, Li got out and ran towards him.

"Mr. Hu, if you could please scan your pass for authorization," the man said, looking relieved, and extending a portable scanner. As Li did so, the pilot said, "This will take you to Korea." "Flight time is a couple of hours, but you'll be out of China by the time the iron curtain is deployed."

"My wife, she's been shot. We got ambushed by our driver," Li said in a rush.

"Let's get her in the chopper, we'll take care of her in the air. Right now, we have to go." The two men rushed back to the car, got Mei and with their bags, clambered on board.

The helicopter's blades began to spin, making their hair fly about their face wildly. It was still dark, with just a hint of light illuminating the tops of the mountains that surrounded Beijing. The noise of the swirling blades drowned out every other sound around them. Then the black Apache lifted off the ground, rising higher and higher.

"There's a first aid kit on the wall," said the pilot over the headset. "We'll get your wife better medical treatment in Seoul, but for now, we just need to stop the bleeding. In the kit, there's something that looks like a small gun. Take it out, hold it a few centimeters away from the wound, and pull the trigger."

Li did as the pilot said and before squeezing the trigger, he looked into Mei's eyes and asked, "Ready?"

"Just do it."

He pulled the trigger and a clear gel shot out from the device, covering the wound and sealing off the bullet hole. The bleeding had stopped, but Li could tell from Mei's face that it still hurt. He held her hand, pressing his head against hers.

The helicopter flew towards the East, heading out of Beijing and towards Seoul, the stepping stone to their new life. Li and Mei continued to hold hands while gripping their bouncing seat with the other hand.

The pilot said, "We'll be arriving in Seoul in a few hours. Don't worry; we'll clear Chinese borders before the iron curtain."

He flashed them a smile and continued to guide the aircraft over a sleeping Beijing. The city below them looked tiny, then became a distant speck on the horizon. The Yellow Sea came into view, signaling they were almost out of China. Mei looked at Li, smiling, though there were tears in her eyes. Li clutched her hand tighter, understanding her feelings. He also felt the same way.

The pilot checked his band, it was almost 7:00.

He looked at the Hus and pointing out the cockpit window said, "Any time now."

They looked back at their home country, the green and brown of the landscape fading behind them. Then they saw it.

From high in the sky, a bluish green barrier started to descend on the ground. The iron curtain looked like a digital blanket, with green and blue electrical components tightly intertwined. Right where the land met the sea, it touched down, creating a barrier between China and the outside world. It was still possible to see through the iron curtain, but no digital information or person could pass through. The curtain shimmered, giving off a blue-green light that now extended across the entire coastline. Around the world, five other countries were also experiencing the same thing.

As Li continued to stare out the window in awe, Mei reached into her pocket and pulled out a thin white stick. She then handed it to him with an enigmatic smile. Confused, Li took the thin object and as he turned it over, he realized what it was. The digital screen held the symbol for what they had both hoped for: Pregnant.

He looked at her wide-eyed, "Is this..." he stuttered, not able to finish his sentence.

"This is everything we've worked so hard for," she said.

Tears fell down his face as a flood of emotions rushed over him. Mei smiled in satisfaction and then rested her head on his shoulder, closing her eyes contentedly in his embrace.

"Gōng dào zì rán chéng,"[12] she whispered.

---

[12] Effort will undoubtedly lead to success

The helicopter continued to fly over the sea as the iron curtain completed its descent across China's vast borders. Then it was behind them, and began to fade, appearing as nothing more than a distant blur in the rear. Li and Mei resolutely turned their eyes away, looking forward now, to the future that awaited them.

AUTHOR BIO

Degen has lived in Beijing, China since 2013, working as a writer, editor and travel enthusiast. He holds an MA degree in Chinese Politics & Foreign Policy from Tsinghua University. He enjoys working out, eating street food, and thinking about unconventional solutions to global problems. He's also a big fan of dystopian novels & film. This is his first novel.

www.ingramcontent.com/pod-product-compliance
Lightning Source LLC
Chambersburg PA
CBHW062110170626
46813CB00002B/394